LOVE, LOSS, AND LOST CAUSES

LOVE, LOSS, AND LOST CAUSES

SAHIL MEHTA

REBEL SATORI PRESS
New Orleans & New York

Published in the United States of America by
REBEL SATORI PRESS
www.rebelsatoripress.com

Cover design by Sven Davisson

ISBN: 978-1-60864-405-6

For my family, who made everything possible.

For my chosen family, with immense gratitude.

Lara and Alisha, you inspire me.
Milo, thank you.
Shahla and Kristen, thank you for being the first readers.

PROLOGUE

Elephants have always been familiar to me. The elephant-headed god, Ganesha. Remover of obstacles. Most popular in the tightly packed pantheon of the Hindu deities. Ubiquitous. Smiling benignly from behind many a shop counter, shrouded in fragrant plumes of incense. The voluminous body adorned with garlands of marigolds and jasmine. Dancing on the car dashboards, head wobbling to the rhythm of potholes and traffic. Stop. Go. Stop. There he is, on calendars and posters. Making a cameo on pencil boxes. Omnipresent. Familiar.

Lord Ganesha's worldly, non-celestial counterparts are not as numerous, but still common. Beasts of burden. Plying goods in cities and towns. Hulking forms heaving heavy loads on highways. The older specimens, relegated to temple duty. Begging for money and offerings from pilgrims and the pious.

And there are the circus elephants performing for packed audiences. Gemini Circus. Rajkamal Circus. Jumbo Circus. Others conscripted to provide rides for children and adults for a small fee. Elephants are familiar to me.

They are also exotic. The majestic wild creatures populating the pirated video cassettes of National Geographic specials. Staple childhood viewing from when we had only one part-time TV channel. Roaming the dusty plains of Africa. Foraging in the forests. Savannah and the Serengeti. Kilimanjaro and Kalahari. Matriarch leading her charges to food and water while fending off the dangers of lions and man. Loyal. Intelligent. Complex. I can still see them silhouetted against an orange, orbed African sun. Baritone voiceover conveying awe of these gentle giants. Exotic.

It'd be convenient to say this was why I got an elephant tattooed on my arm. Mostly hidden but the long trunk peeking past the edge of the short sleeve like a little tease. Ask me what it is. Have me show you the rest.

It'd be easy and not entirely untrue to say elephants have been with me from the very beginning. Familiar and exotic at the same time. That these are the reasons why I got the tattoo. Really though, I got the elephant tattoo because I liked the design. It was clean, elegant, and beautiful. I picked the design first, then searched for a justification for my choice.

Four decades without tattoos. Then two in a year. I'd always wanted a tattoo, you see. Back when I was young and madly in love, I'd drawn a design for Arun. A birthday present. Fish to represent Pisces. A dolphin, actually, since we had gone swimming with dolphins. On a gray morning. They told us to sing under the water. The dolphins, curious by nature, would come to us. They didn't. Not to me anyway.

The tattoo design was of a dubiously aboriginal style to mark our semester abroad in Australia. On the day of the appointment, the tattoo artist called out sick. Arun never ended up getting the tattoo.

I carried the original design with me. I still have it. That's the one I'll get, I thought. It's unique. Personal. Means something. I just had to pick a time, a place, and someone to tattoo it on me. Simple. The hardest part, the design, was already decided.

But I never did get it. The original design, drawn on a piece of tracing paper, now creased from being folded a dozen times over, traveled with me. Changed rental apartments. Stayed in a shoebox with old letters in my very first condo. Came with me to the next one. It's still there somewhere. But when I finally got a tattoo, it was an elephant. Not the dolphin. The dolphin did not make an appearance in the second tattoo either.

There's a metaphor for life somewhere in that story. You think life is going one way. Until it goes another way. I have always been a romantic. A believer in happy ever-afters. The one special someone. Princesses, I thought, in my childhood. Princes eventually, when I knew better. Not literal princes with crowns and palaces. My fantasies weren't limited. Anyone, within reason, could be the *one*. I just wanted to be loved. Arun happened to be the first in a string of great loves that were short-lived, or unrequited. Romantic love has thus far been elusive in my life. My yearning for love, perversely or consequently, that much keener. Is this a story about love then? Let's find out.

GOA

I must learn to be content with being happier than I deserve.

– Jane Austen

RAVI

The location of our first encounter: Goa. The land of glorious beaches, crumbling Portuguese buildings, and aging hippies. There are tourists everywhere: families, individuals, groups; Indians, Israelis, and so many Russians. Refugees from reality, all of us. There are the sunbathers and sand seekers, resort dwellers, rave dancers, eve teasers, and ecstasy lovers. A veritable Choose Your Own Adventure, Paradise edition. Press one for hangovers. Two for hashish. Think luxury resorts and lap pools. Palm trees and peacocks. Frangipani, bountiful.

For the duration of your visit, Goa plays along. Dances with you. Dazzles you. There's no poverty or pathos in paradise. All that earthly unpleasantness not quite banished but hidden. Out of sight and mind behind tall gates and tinted windows of fancy cars. Third-world opulence, afforded to a few and allowed by the prodigious poverty outside.

I'd been to Goa a number of times. On this particular occasion, I was on a family vacation. Parents, sister, and my lovely brother-in-law Ranbir, whom I fondly call Jiju. We had just flown into the Dabolim Airport. It was a short flight. An hour and fifteen minutes. From Bombay to Goa. Took almost as long to get to the airport in Bombay and even longer to check in for the flight. At the other end of the plane ride, there was a bumpy car ride from the airport to the resort. Two hours away. All of us were a little cranky from the early wake-up call and the travails of travel. But we made it.

The resort was perched on a high cliff overlooking the Arabian Sea. Down a steep path lay the crescent-shaped beach. Piled with sand the color of gold and honey. Kissed by a silvery sea in the merciless afternoon sun. A set of dramatic wrought-iron gates opened up to manicured lawns. The lawns punctuated here with patches of emerald vegetation, there by flower beds thriving in the limitless sunshine. Bamboo and breadfruit. Bougainvillea. Coconut palms and cashew trees. Jacaranda and jackfruit. And peeking through the lushness, flashes of shimmering blue, the swimming pool.

The soaring thatched roof made the reception desk feel tiny in comparison. There was a family ahead of us—alternately using charm and threats to score themselves a room with a view. A room with a better view, I should say. The parents at the desk, the kids running off vast reserves of pent-up energy. The woman behind the desk didn't seem fazed, parrying the persistent guests and their demands with grace and good humor. Cool as a cucumber in the noontime heat. We waited patiently to check in. Slumped on the wicker sofas. Serenaded by the sounds of distant waves. Soothed by the shade and salt-laden breeze.

A uniformed young man came by with a brass tray in hand and five frosty glasses. Welcome drinks. *Thank you for being patient* drinks. Coconut water with mint and jaggery. Mom and sister first, dad next. Brother-in-law. I appreciated the order of his offering. In a country where the *ladies first* maxim is often losing the battle to an entrenched, retrogressive patriarchy, this felt refreshing. Good manners. Training. A combination of the two. Small victories. I took the last glass.

"Thank you . . . Usman." I read the name off the name tag. He looked up. For a second. As if surprised to hear his name. Our eyes met. Briefly. For the length of a single heartbeat. His hazel eyes, extraordinary. Incandescent. Mesmerizing. I watched him walk away. Spellbound.

I'd like to believe there is a hardwired instinct common in homosexual men. In the Castro and in Calcutta. Untaught. Unlearned. An electric pulse carrying its message of naughts and ones down the meandering pathways of the nervous system. A message of mutual acknowledgment. Recognition.

Eyes lock. Look away (or not). One beat. Two. Three. Reestablish eye contact. Suspicion confirmed. Target acquired. Mating dance.

USMAN

Arre yaar, I am very used to the arrogance and entitlement of the resort guests, especially the domestic ones who all have a battalion of servants at home, ready to fulfill their every wish and command. The family my Ammi worked for had two drivers, a bawarchi to cook the food, Ammi and another ayah to look after the children, a safaiwala to sweep, mop, and dust the bungalow twice a day, a part-time maid to wash the dishes and another to wash the clothes, plus a mali for the garden. That's nine servants to run a household of four people. Even at the resort, some guests bring their own driver, or an ayah to look after the children but most of them are forced to leave behind their servants when they are on holiday. The servants' quarters at the resort are not large enough to fit more than a dozen people. Theek hai, no problem bhai. The guests just end up treating the resort staff as replacements for the help they left behind.

I am lucky because my English-speaking ability and uniform with its smart waistcoat and bow tie give me a higher status than many of the other staff members. I am generally spared of low-grade tasks but not always. Just yesterday, one of our guests, Mrs. Jhunjunwala, decided that her "precious babies" could not be trusted in the care of ordinary housekeeping staff. I was to take care of them personally while she and the family enjoyed their afternoon drinks at the clubhouse, where dogs are not allowed. I was left in charge of Fluffy and Pinky, two innocent-looking but very mean Pomeranians who kept on trying to bite my ankles only.

The foreigners are not so used to having servants, I suppose. They are more independent and not needing someone to do everything for them. But the thing about these foreign tourists is that even though they may not be making demands all of the time, they will ask anyone for anything. They don't understand that even the servant class has its own complicated status and caste system. To these foreigners, a manager in a waistcoat is just as good for fetching a beer as the waiter. The foreigners and some of the more broad-minded Indians may not treat me like a servant, but even for them, I'm not a unique person. As long as someone is there to fulfill their immediate needs, they are not concerned with who it is. *You need someone to make travel arrangements? Of course, Ma'am, consider it done. You want someone to take care of the frog that has gotten into your room? Sure Sir, we will get right to it.* I can be changed out and replaced with any other person in a uniform.

Where was I going with this story? Oof, sometimes I start and keep going on and on like a chatterbox, forgetting what my original point was only. Oh oh yes, I remember now. I was saying that I am used to being this nameless, faceless character doing this thankless job for anyone and everyone. So when someone is nice, I am always shocked. It happens very rarely na. This guy even used my good name while thanking me. The name thing is always interesting. People are used to calling their servants by their name, you know? *Raju, get me a glass of water. Ahmed, where are my shoes?* They act all close-close with you but you know you cannot call them by *their* name. It's always *yes sir* or *yes sahib* for you. It is a one-way road only. I suppose, in this case, this guest was actually trying to be nice. His whole family was also very nice only. And even if he was not trying to be nice, it is always better than the people who cannot even be bothered to learn your good name. They call everyone *hero* or *boss*. *Boss*, my foot! Like I would be doing this work if I was the boss! Everyone knows who the real boss is, so they are just pulling your leg, na?

The other reason I noticed this particular guest is a little more complicated and as you are starting to learn, I am not capable of making a long story short only. So here I go again, starting from the very beginning. When I was growing up, all the boys in my mohalla just wanted to be outside, playing cricket or football. Their mothers had to threaten and scold them to bring them inside to do their homework or when it got dark. I was the opposite only, Ammi had to force me to go outside to play with the other boys. I wanted to be inside reading or playing with my younger sister, Sharmeen. I just was not interested in all the things that the boys got up to. What is the fun in destroying things or torturing the street dogs and cats, na? I was happier filling my drawing book with designs or working on crafts projects instead of roaming the streets with these idiot boys.

I also had no friends. I mean I was friendly with two-three boys but I had no real friends, not until I was in the eighth standard and I became friends with two of the neighbor girls. With them, I could be a chatterbox, with Ammi and Sharmeen also, but with the boys and strangers, I was quiet. Basically, I knew I was different and that I was not like the other boys. No one had to tell me that. It was just something I knew, and I also knew that it was not a good thing. I learned early on to hide many things about myself. I was quiet like a mouse because I did not want to attract attention to myself, even though my nature is to be very talkative. I studied hard, got good marks, and was always a topper in my batch so that everyone would like me. I was the teacher's pet. The whole time I was praying to Allah to make me into a normal boy, like the other boys around me.

I did not understand what was different about me at first but I figured it out as I got older. The more I learned about myself the more I also figured out that I was screwed, royally screwed, yaar. I come from a Muslim family, ok? We are not very strict type Muslims if you know what I mean. Abba drank a lot, like it was his main business. Feni, beer, Old Monk when he had money, and anything else he could get his hands on. I drink sometimes also, but not like him. Ammi is a little more religious but even she skips the masjid when she is tired. But at the end of it all, we are still Muslims only. Sharab-daru is one thing, many Muslims will look the other way but my type of problem is cent percent haram. Tauba tauba, it gets you thrown out of the house. Your own family will drop you, making you an orphan overnight. People will beat you black and blue, or even kill you if they are in the right mood.

Despite all my prayers to be cured and promises to myself that I would never stray from the path of righteousness, I had, in moments of weakness and poor judgment, lost control of myself. I had fooled around a few times with other guys: in the park, on the beach, on a dark side street, different-different locations but always in the dark only. These times when my self-control and willpower failed me, the whole thing was short and so scary that I didn't know why I did it only. I was too afraid of being seen by someone, of being caught, of being beaten or killed, and even when I got away in one piece, I would feel so much guilt and shame that I would vow not to do it again. I would go for months, days, and years without straying, and then it would happen again, like a bad dream that kept coming back only, and the cycle would start again.

This was the other reason I noticed this guest, the nice guy with the nice family. When he thanked me, I looked up and I just felt this very same, dangerous connection with him. It was the same type of look that I had gotten before when guys were checking me out. Sometimes the look was very low key and you could almost miss it, or you questioned yourself if it even happened. Other times it was very bindaas, the hungry eyes looking you up and down, inspecting you like you were a bloody brinjal at the sabziwala. This guy was not trying to be cheap or vulgar, but it was still the same coded connection that tied all of us shady characters together like we were in the same bloody secret society. Maybe I was wrong only but I thought this guy was also a fellow musafir on the highway to hell.

It scared the shit out of me, oof! I lowered my eyes to avoid looking at him and carried on like I did not notice anything. This has happened a few times with guests at the resort, and each time it caught me without warning, like the person was looking deep inside me, discovering all of my dirty-dirty secrets. If I am found out, I will be dismissed from the job quite fast only and that is not a hassle people like me can afford. I like my job, man, but more importantly, I need it. I am the only one with a job in my family and I have to support Ammi and Sharmeen, na?

You see I have been supporting my family since seven-eight years back, when Abba walked out one evening and never returned. Yes-yes, he disappeared only. But it was probably for the best. Abba was always in a bad mood when he was around, getting angry and threatening to beat someone. Ammi was his main target but also us children. Black eyes and beatings were common when he was drunk or hungover, which was always. He'd disappear for two-three days at a time but he would come back, with black and blue marks to match the ones he gave us. When he did not come back of his own will, someone from the mohalla would bring us news of his location and condition, and Ammi and I would have to drag the drunk home.

The final time he disappeared, we thought he would be back to terrorize us again but days turned to weeks and months and years. Ammi reported him missing but the police could hardly be bothered to look for a man of such little importance: poor, alcoholic, and a Muslim. Scars healed and broken parts got mended in the peace and quiet that was left behind after his disappearance, and I feel very guilty for saying this but I think we were all relieved to have lost him for good.

Anyway, this is why my job is so important to me and my family. My pay is not like amazing or anything but it is more than we've ever had before. We have a roof over our heads and food on the table. This type of job you have to protect at all costs, especially in a country like ours that churns out lakhs and crores of people, people who are employment-aged and those who are underaged but desperate for work. There are people who have passed out of college and those who are angutha-chaap, people who passed the twelfth standard and those who bunked school way before then, all chasing after jobs and competing with each other for work. We desperately dream of good employment or any employment at all.

But back to the guest, the nice guy, who called me by my name, I wasn't going to let this guy make problems for me. I had a lifetime of practice hiding my true nature and tendencies. I waited for the family to finish their drinks and check in. I had their bags loaded on the luggage cart and took them to their rooms. My eyes stayed focused on the footpath in front of me and there was no turning back to look at him. I had to avoid temptation at all costs. Maybe this was all in my imagination and did not actually happen, like a bad dream that I would wake up from. I find it helpful to think that these crazy thoughts and abnormal feelings were all in my head only. There was no other normal person in this world feeling these unnatural feelings, only me. My hope and my prayers were that the feelings would just disappear one day since they were not real, like the scary shaitan I thought was hiding in the dark when I was little. Then my life would be sorted out properly. InshaAllah!

For the next few days, I tried my best to avoid him only but it was not easy. He was at the swimming pool quite a lot and the whole resort is built around the swimming pool. Anywhere you go, you have to pass by it. The swimming pool and the lounge chairs around it are normally filled with goras only, all trying to get a complexion like the color of cooked prawns. The Indians are too busy applying Fair and Lovely cream to be in the swimming pool for very long. They come early and leave before the sun gets too high and hot. God forbid they get too dark. But there he was, laying out in the sun, wearing a bright orange swimming costume, all alone, reading his book. His skin was always shining from sunlight and sweat, or from being wet from swimming, like mahogany furniture that has been polished a hundred times. He was fit and trim with proper muscles, not like the Salman Khan types where it looks like he lived in a gym. His legs were hairy and damn hot, man. It is hard not to stare at him, just saying.

Every now and then someone from his family would come by to talk to him. I stayed in the shadows, without being seen; inspecting, supervising, and fixing made-up problems, finding excuses to do time waste even though I should know better. I had a hard time keeping my eyes away from the orange swimming costume, like a bloody mad parvana going round and round the flame only.

I do not think he noticed me. I was very careful only. He would be reading, slowly-slowly sipping on his beer. Every hour or so he got into the swimming pool. He did not swim in a straight line, always moving a little to the left, but he was a good swimmer. His body would be shining when he left the pool, muscles all tight and outlined like they were carved in stone. Oof I really needed to stop doing all this time pass stuff and start working.

When he wasn't at the swimming pool or sightseeing with his family, he liked going to the beach. I saw him coming back from the beach one time, a towel in one hand and a book in the other hand. He was graceful like a tiger, or a blackbuck, as he climbed up the steep slope, not aware of his own beauty only, or of being watched. His parrot green shorts and pink, sleeveless T-shirt were shining, looking like jewels against his dark skin. There was a tattoo on one arm, which I made out was an elephant, once he got closer. Unfortunately, I misjudged my timing and ran into him just as he entered the resort grounds. Oof! There was that look again, a little longer this time, before I stopped looking at him, pretending I was interested in my shoes only.

"Good evening," he said, trying to catch his breath from the sharp climb.

"Good evening," I replied. I smiled because I couldn't help myself.

"I am Ravi," he put his hand out.

I shook his hand, feeling an electric current rushing up and down my body, the hairs on my neck standing at attention only.

"Myself, Usman. Hope you are enjoying your stay, Sir."

I walked away before any more chit-chat could continue, which was a small relief, I suppose, but also mixed with a little bit of regret.

RAVI

Vacation life follows its own rhythm. Languid. Predictable. To start the day, a morning walk. The preferred exercise of India's sedentary class. Ten laps around the resort grounds for Dad. Speed: mild to moderate. Five for Mom. Speed: indeterminate. I prefer sleeping in but will join them occasionally. Sis and Jiju practice and preach abstinence from any and all avoidable early morning activities. The walk is followed by a family breakfast. Long and leisurely. And conducted in stages. My parents are usually done eating by the time we get there but they sit with us, pretending to be patient and supportive of our late wake-up times. And chronic tardiness. My nutritional and caloric intake is of great interest to my parents. They are perpetually worried about the availability of adequate amounts of vegetarian food in Boston, where I live. Alone and bereft of the services of two cooks and a doting mother. Quelle horreur!

Unless there is a sightseeing trip or excursion planned, the family seeks refuge in the great air-conditioned indoors after breakfast. To play cards or board games. The sun is already too strong and the heat is not novel enough to tempt them outdoors. I beg to be excused from the games. Opting to stay at the pool for a few hours instead. Soon I'll be heading back to Boston. Where winter reigns. Dark. Dreary. Damp. I'm hoarding the heat. Savoring the sun. Building reserves for the frigid months ahead. A squirrel stashing away sunny acorns.

"Do you sunbathe because you like it? Or because you've been in America for so long?" asked my mother one day.

My behavior is puzzling to my parents. The idea of lying in the hot sun, literally foreign to them. Something only foreigners do. No one in their right mind would want to get so dark! My choice seems practically seditious in light of India's collective national obsession with fair skin. Right up there with cricket, this obsession.

I suspect my parents have largely made peace with my sun-worshiping ways. The true cause of their vexation most likely stems from my being able to pursue these sun-worshiping ways alone. Away from them. My annual visits to India are usually about two weeks long, sometimes three. My parents leave no doubt of their displeasure at my living in Boston. An abandonment of loving parents. A betrayal of filial duty. A tragedy. And until they can reverse this transgression, they'll settle for the next best solution: unabashedly lay claim to all of my time while I'm in India. Every minute. To make up for a year's worth of deprivation.

I'm happy to oblige. Pay the truancy tax. And yet, the abrupt transition to constant companionship and togetherness is tough. I try not to protest. I try to be generous with my attention and affection. A week or so into this routine, though, I'm ready for a break. A tiny break. A couple of hours here. A few there. Opportunities to carve out some time for myself. By myself. Essential. Sanity savers. Conveniently, this falls right around the time of our customary family trip. Like this one to Goa.

So, I plead for some more time in the sun. Trade board games for a lounge chair. A book in one hand. A frosty beer in the other. Like a lizard in the sun. Basking. Luxuriating. Every so often I remember to look up. Wonder if Usman's around. If he's seen me. If he's interested. If the attraction is mutual. If it's imagined. So many ifs. All of this is a fool's errand, I realize. Yet it's a delightful fantasy. A fateful encounter with a mysterious stranger. Dark and handsome. Chemistry. Fireworks. Love. I'm a romantic at heart. Predisposed to believing these things can happen.

I did see him. Often when he thought I wasn't paying attention. Sometimes our paths crossed. By design or by chance. Cursory interactions. Polite. Tension taut between us. No solution in sight. My family. Their constant company. His job. The brief duration of my vacation. Unspoken but acknowledged, even in my fantasies, the many differences that made our worlds so far apart. Worlds that are far, far apart. Intersecting purely by coincidence and circumstance here. A temporary overlap. Unrealistic. A vivid flight of fancy destined for an introduction to reality. So we continued the age-old dance of star crossed lovers. Touch. And go. Pull. And push.

◆

We had two more nights in paradise. The vacation flew by, predictable routines and languid pace notwithstanding. My parents retired early, tired from a packed day of sightseeing. The rest of us took over the hammocks by the pool. Cold beers in hand. It was a chance to catch up with my sister and her husband. We have an interesting relationship, my sister and I. Six younger than me, she was twelve when I left for college. I saw her over the summers but mostly I was absent for her growing years. Post-college, it was brief phone calls and hurried visits. I don't think either of us doubted that we loved each other. But we weren't close. Not for a long time.

Adulthood and all its accompanying adventures brought us closer. She's grown up to be an outstanding human being. I say that without bias. We still don't talk often. The connection feels authentic though. Mature. Meaningful. Based on mutual respect. So it was nice to reconnect. Sans parents. The wine at dinner had made us more effusive. The beer kept the momentum going. A gentle breeze and the sounds of crickets lulled us into a sociable trance. We chatted for a while. About my life. Their lives. Our parents. The extended family. We traded funny stories. Discussed serious matters. Gossiped. A couple of hours passed. My brother-in-law threw in the towel. It was just the two of us. Sis and I.

I told her about Usman. "Who?" She had no idea who I was talking about.

"He is the young man who brought us drinks when we were waiting to check in on our first day here. My height, maybe a little shorter. Dark hair. Handsome." She feigned a vague recollection. "He brought us towels yesterday when we were at the pool. Helped us find a taxi this morning," I pressed.

"The guy with amber eyes. I remember his eyes!" She finally figured out who I was talking about. "Has anything happened between you two? Where was I?"

"Calm down, yaar. Nothing's happened. It's probably just a silly fantasy. For all I know, he's straight."

"He is certainly very good looking. A total babe. And those eyes! How do you know if he's gay or straight? Have you talked to him at least?"

"Ok, chill with the million questions. Agreed, he's beautiful. And those eyes, the first thing I noticed about him. So luminous. So unusual." I hesitated for a minute. Thinking about how to answer the rest. "I don't know if he's gay or not. It's just a feeling. I think I'm right about him playing for my team but there's no way to be sure. I've talked to him briefly. But it's hard. He's working. You guys are always around."

"Man, I don't want to throw cold water over your fantasy but maybe it's for the best. Mom and Dad ... Well, you know what that'd be like. And if he is straight, maybe he won't react well to being hit on. Plus what do you think can come of it even if something were to happen? We are leaving the day after tomorrow."

"Listen, I agree with you and nothing's happening anyway. For the record though, Mom and Dad know I'm gay so they can't be all upset about that."

"Yeah baba, but they've only ever dealt with your being gay in a theoretical sense. Knowing them, they've blocked it all out mentally. Mom probably prays that she never has to hear the word *gay*."

"I'd like to think they've come around but you're probably right. It's too bad that I haven't been in a relationship serious enough for me to introduce a guy to them."

"Oof, I can totally imagine them flipping out. But they'll blame it on something else, not on their distaste of the whole gay thing. If your guy was American, they'd be opposed to it because he wasn't Indian. If he was black or Muslim, forget about it. Speaking of which, Usman is a Muslim, right? I mean, it's a very Muslim name."

"Probably, but I don't know for sure if he is. Nor do I care. Doesn't all this blatant bigotry bother you?"

"Of course it bothers me. But that's just how it is here, dude. Especially with our parents' generation. Look at how much they freaked out when I told them I wanted to marry Ranbir. It took them two years to come around and that was all because Ranbir was Punjabi, and not Gujarati like us. The veg/non-veg thing is also huge for them, you know that. Luckily, Ranbir and his family were already veg. They are our parents, yaar and we have to accept them as they are. They are good people in the end."

"I don't know." I thought about the time when she told our parents about Jiju. They had been dating for a couple of years by that point. My parents didn't speak to her for weeks. Now they love Jiju. Of course. They're always bragging about him. *Our Ranbir is so successful. Our Ranbir this and our Ranbir that.* Sis and I are convinced they like him more than us.

"*Everyone says it* is not an excuse, Sis. People here will casually throw around stereotypes about Biharis. Some *observations* about Marwaris. Some bullshit about Punjabis. All South Indians are, of course, lumped into one giant group. Tamil is indistinguishable from Telugu. Or not worth distinguishing between. Trafficking in stereotypes. Disguised as facts. The implication, always, is that we are perfect. Everyone else is flawed."

"Unfortunately you are right, Ravi. For all this talk about India and the pride we feel as Indians, we tend to be quite open in our contempt for every other group of Indians except our own. But that's not new, yaar. We've been hearing that stuff since we were kids."

"Fine, but the religion thing is new. Okay, so not *completely* new. But newer. More vehement. More fanatic. Don't you remember when we were in school, the prayers in our morning assembly couldn't even mention the god of any particular religion? Just a generic god. The idea of unity in diversity was drilled into us. We took pride in being a nation of many religions. Secular. Unlike our neighbors. To the east and west. This doesn't feel like the country I grew up in. We weren't so open about our hatred."

USMAN

The change in tempo is very shocking only. The resort goes from a very happening scene to basically a sleepy village as soon as the two restaurants on the resort grounds shut down. It is like night and day, haha. We are a little too far from the party scene in North Goa and there isn't a lot to do here after nine. Some guests go out to North Goa to go to nightclubs but most of them return to their rooms, being tired from the sun and the boozing. The resort feels very chill by this point.

Mind you, I like the peace and quiet at the end of the day. The air is cooler with night breezes coming off the water. The smells of wood fire and smoke, of naan and tandoori chicken start fading as the tandoor cools down. They are replaced by the magical perfume of the raat ki rani. It is amazing to me how these little-little flowers send out such a strong smell.

Once the hallaa gulla of the day is gone, you can hear the night orchestra. Do one thing, listen carefully and you will hear the hoo-hoo of the owls and the chorus of mendhaks and sikadas. The sound of the waves crashing on the beach below, the swish-swish of the palm leaves dancing in the wind, nature puts on such a great show, no? I am a big fan of film music but even A. R. Rehman can't compete with mother nature, just saying.

Anyways I was thinking of all this as I changed out of my uniform, deep thoughts you know? Haha.

I walked towards the back gate, very much enjoying the sounds and the smells of the night, but also wanting to go home and rest before I have to do this all over again tomorrow. I almost made it to the gate but just as I was about to make my bloody escape, I saw him. He looked so damn beautiful in the moonlight, hanging out on the hammock, one foot on the ground, pushing himself back and forth, and back and forth, like he was a bloody hypnotist, trying to cast a spell on some clueless victim. Except I was the bloody fool who was the victim, about to walk straight into his trap. You hit the jackpot, Bro!

I smiled at him. I was going to continue walking towards the gate but something made me stop, and I turned around. Oh shit! I don't know what I was thinking in that moment.

"Good evening, Sir. How was everything tonight?" I asked.

"Good evening, Usman. Thanks for taking such good care of us tonight. We had a lovely dinner. How are you? I'm assuming you're done for the day."

"Yes Sir, I just finished my shift. Did you need anything?"

"No! Not at all. I was… I was wondering if you'd like to join me for a beer. If you drink alcohol, that is. Sorry, I shouldn't just assume you do."

"No need to say sorry, Sir. I drink a little bit here and there. Not all the time but I do. Ammi doesn't like it but she doesn't say anything. She knows I work hard and that I won't do anything stupid." I am not sure why I gave him such a long story. I was nervous talking to him.

"Would you like to join me for a drink then? I have plenty of beer here. Also, please call me Ravi."

"That's very nice of you but I am not allowed. They do not like us mixing with the guests when we are not working. You enjoy your evening, I won't bother you anymore."

[25]

"You are not bothering me at all but I just realized that you must be tired after a long day or have other plans. Please don't feel any pressure to say yes, but if you wanted to, is there a bar or some place nearby where we can get a drink? Or we can take the beer to the beach, right?"

"Oh no-no, I don't have plans but all the bars will be closing down only," I looked at my watch. "I can give you company to the beach. It will be quiet now so the police will not hassle us for bringing alcohol there."

We started walking down to the beach. I offered to carry the beers but he would not allow it. My heart was beating so loudly, dhak dhak dhak, I was afraid he could hear it and that I would wake up half the resort from the sound.

I must have looked back a thousand times, checking and checking that no one saw me leaving with a guest. I cursed the full moon for making it so bright that everyone could see every-thing, but thank god for the light because the path from the resort to the beach is very steep and slippery.

We took our sweet time getting down and at the end of the path the beach was mostly empty. I could hear the clinking and the clanging of empty bottles being collected and tables and chairs being put up as the beach shacks closed for the night.

Ahead, I noticed some people walking, most likely the last customers from the beach shacks, kicked out at closing time. They were probably heading back to their homes and hotels, alone or in small groups, many of them swaying and staggering from too many pegs of booze. Their loud conversations and arguments, the drunken singing, all faded as they walked farther away from us.

There were a few couples here and there, taking advantage of the privacy offered by the mostly empty beach. Privacy being a rare thing in most Indian homes, na.

Other than these last few people, the beach was very quiet.

The moon was huge, so bright, almost making you forget it was nighttime. The moonlight danced on the water and colored everything shiny and silver. The waves were breaking softly on the beach, the white foam looking like a delicate lace on the sand. Oof, it almost looked like dosa batter being spread out on the tava. I dipped my foot in the water, it was so nice and refreshing. I rolled up my pants so I could walk at the edge of the waves without getting them wet.

Pukka, it could have been a scene from a hit picture, the hero and heroine starting a song as they romanced each other in the moonlight. I could not believe we were alone, just the two of us, but I had no idea only what would happen next.

We walked for ten-fifteen minutes, quietly enjoying the beautiful night before he picked a place for us to sit down.

"Is this okay, Usman? Do you want to walk some more?"

"This is fine. But I can also walk more if that is something you want."

"No, this is fine." He sat down in the sand, making a soft thud noise. I sat down also, not quite touching him but near enough to feel his warmth.

He smelled sexy, his smell being clean like a mixture of soap and sandalwood.

He opened up two bottles of beer, one for me and one for him. The bottle was still cold, sweating with dew drops that trickled down my arm, making me shiver each time. I played with the label, *Kingfisher Ultra*, peeling it off piece by piece, gold, red, gold pieces, trying to focus on something other than my fears. I had gotten myself to this point by little bursts of courage or maybe it was stupidity, with no plan only, but now that I was here, meri phat gayi: I was scared, yaar and totally doubting myself. Poor chap, he probably thought that I was dumb or something.

He tried to break the silence, asking me questions about my day and all. These sort of small talk questions I could answer. I told him about my normal routine at the resort, trying to make sure I was not boring him, you know. But how much can someone talk about a typical job, na?

Then he said, "Tell me something about yourself, Usman."

I was quiet for a few minutes, trying to think of something interesting to say. "Sorry, I don't know what to say. Ask me something and I will answer." I don't usually talk about myself, na? And even if I was more confident, what would I say that was interesting to someone like him? My life was so small and boring.

"Say anything you want. I don't really have an agenda, I just want to get to know you." He looked at me but I was tongue-tied only. "Okay fine, I'll ask you a question. Did you grow up around here, in Goa? Family yahan hai or do you live by yourself?"

"I belong to Goa. I grew up here in a town about a hundred kilometers away. I have a small family, Ammi and a younger sister, Sharmeen. We moved closer to the resort when I got a job there. It takes me about 20 minutes to walk to my home from the resort."

I stared at the beauty of the cloudless sky. There were some stars towards the west, where the light of the moon didn't blot them out.

"How about you? Are you from Mumbai?" I asked him.

"My family lives in Bombay… err Mumbai. Sorry, I just can't get used to calling it Mumbai." he smiled. His smile was so sweet, it made me want to keep staring at him only. "I live in the U.S. now. In Boston."

"Wow. Are you staying there by yourself? Your family doesn't live with you?"

"My parents think it's too cold for about eight months of the year. And for the other four they complain that they wouldn't know anyone else there. They would rather I move back to India."

"They must miss you, no? America's so far away. I have a cousin brother who is working in America, in Pittsburgh. I don't know if that's near to you, but he's there for a year on assignment. He works in IT."

"Pittsburgh is great. I went to college there! Does he like it there?"

"He was shocked by the cold when he first got there but I think he likes it. He wants to stay there but it's hard to get a green card. Even if he doesn't get the green card and he has to come back, he'll be all set-up here. Foreign-return people are getting very good jobs now. How do you like living in a foreign country? You don't get lonely so far from your family?"

"I miss my family. Of course. But I love living in Boston. Ever since I was young I wanted to escape. You know how it is here. Everyone is in everyone's business. *Why aren't you married yet? When will you get married?* Every uncle and aunty. And their thousand questions. Living away from my family, from India, it is easier to have a lot more freedom. Freedom I couldn't have here."

Ravi was quiet for a few minutes, looking at the waves before he turned back to me. "Freedom to live my own life. Rather than listening to everyone and doing what made them happy... But enough about me. Back to you, tell me more about yourself."

"Okay, my age is twenty-six running, twenty-five complete. I work a lot but in my free time, I like to do drawing and painting. I also like movies. Shahrukh Khan and Shahid Khan are my favorite film stars. One time I saw Shahrukh Khan on this beach, not far from here. What else…"

The conversation went on, awkwardly at first but more smoothly as I felt less afraid. He was nice and damn sweet and he kept on trying to make me feel comfortable. And after a while I could feel the nervousness leaving my body, not all at the same time like a flock of birds frightened by a sudden sound, but slowly-slowly. I didn't notice it at first but suddenly I was not as scared, my hands were less sweaty and my heart was beating at its normal speed.

I wasn't completely out of the danger zone but I was feeling a lot better.

This was so different. Ravi was so different. He was actually getting to know me, asking me questions about myself and my family and my life. When I tried to cut my answers short because I felt like I was boring him, he asked me about the details. He was actually interested in learning things about me, not just doing it as a formality.

And he hadn't even tried to force me to do anything. Pukka gentleman, he was behaving like, na?

It was also not a one way road. When I asked him questions, he was very frank and open and not trying to hide anything.

I felt like I could talk to him all night and I still wouldn't get tired. He was so sorted, sensible, and the mature type, no? It felt like I had known him my entire life only. I just wanted to reach out and touch him, to make sure he was real and that this was not a dream.

Oof.

RAVI

"I'm so damn hungover today. Why did you let me drink so much man?" My sister looks a bit worse for wear in the morning.

"I'm a little tired myself but feeling fine otherwise. You just need to practice. So you can keep up with me." I joke.

"No, thank you! I'm never drinking again," she grimaces.

I smile. A knowing smile. She'll probably be ready for a beer in a couple of hours. I have heard such declarations too many times before to take her seriously. We are walking to get breakfast. Our parents walking a few steps ahead of us. Impatient. Hoping we would hurry up so that we can eat something before they clear the buffet. My brother-in-law is taking the morning off. Also, hungover. Like my sister.

"I have a story for you. I finally talked to Usman." I tell my sister, quietly.

"How? Did it happen after I left you last night?" She closes her eyes and massages her temples. "I want all the details." The eyes are open again, squinting. "I really do but right now I am dying. I need something greasy to settle my stomach. I need alu paratha. Or potato chips."

We catch up with our parents. Sit down for breakfast. I can't really focus on the conversation though.

Mom and Dad alternate between chiding and coaxing us.

Something about how my sister shouldn't drink so much. Something else about how I should eat more. Or eat the right things. Or eat more of the right things? I don't know. My mind's elsewhere.

I am thinking about Usman. Our night on the beach. Trying to remember the details. The little details. Commit them to memory.

It is an old habit. Every time I meet someone I like. Or someone in whom I am remotely interested. No matter how unrealistic or improbable my prospects. I try to remember all the details. The time and date of our initial meeting. The circumstances. Our conversation. All the details. In case he is the *one*. Because I am always hoping this is the *one*. The details of our first encounter will be priceless. Details that will determine anniversaries. Celebrations. Commemorations. Details that will feature in love letters. In wedding vows. Details. Repeated again and again. In the *how I met your grandfather* stories.

I don't need due cause or any specific reason for such optimism. I may have mentioned this before but it bears repeating. I'm a romantic at heart. Predisposed to believing in such possibilities and probabilities.

So I relive the night. Reenact its twists and turns. Remember the details. Record it in my mind's eye with the fidelity and devotion of an amateur historian. Usman and I had talked for a while last night. The beginning, awkward. Fits and starts. Banal at times. I needed the conversation, though. The *getting to know you* part. The familiarity. I consider myself somewhat of a sapiosexual. But I am even more of a demisexual. Beauty. Brains. Bonding. All essential. Bonding, most of all.

He was curious about my life in the U.S. Couldn't imagine being that far from his family. He mentioned how he had thought about going to college in Pune. It was too expensive though. And he'd have to leave his mother and sister by themselves. He went to a local college instead. Studied art.

Art is his true love and passion, he told me sheepishly. One that has survived the capriciousness of his childhood. The chaos of college. And persisted into adulthood. He still paints. In every spare moment. Even when those are rare. During peak tourist season, for instance. When the resort is typically full. When he works seven days a week. It balances out, he explained. Things slow down during the summer. And in the rainy season. Beaches aren't exactly popular in the sizzling hot Goan summers. Nor when monsoon threatens to unleash its fury, leaving man and beast drenched in downpours and deluges. Those are productive painting periods for him, especially the monsoon season.

He described the monsoons as a time of abundance. The rain-washed landscape, sparkling. Festooned with brilliant colors. A testament to nature's exuberance and her extravagance. Nature, beautiful as it is, features only tangentially in his work though. He described his work as abstract. Referential but not realistic. He isn't interested in realism. Or replication. It is the light he chases. And the shadows.

The light is quite special during the monsoon months, he elaborated. Whether sieved and softened by the brooding rain clouds. Or made dramatic by storm clouds. And lightning storms. A beautiful contrast from the blinding sunlight that prevails during the rest of the year.

He waxed poetic about his idols. Ram Kumar. S. H. Raza. Tyeb Mehta. Pausing at one point. Unsure if he'd carried on for too long. I am rapt, I assured him. Hanging on to every detail. Every ebb and flow and winding curve of his story. Fascinated by his enthusiasm. Intrigued by the possibility and extent of his talent. By him. Spellbound.

He came alive when he talked about painting.

He was electric. Magnetic. Mesmerizing.

Prodded on by my interest and curiosity, he continued on. About the inspiration that comes from deep within. A creative compulsion that takes over his mind and body, leaving both restless until it finds a release. On canvas. Cardboard. In sketchbooks. Doodles. Drawings. Dreams. And nightmares.

As he led me on this magical journey through the kingdom of art, I realized that our differences were irrelevant. They were dwarfed by his knowledge. Obscured by his passion. Neither wealth nor class were of much importance. Nor religion. Neither society. Nor its barriers. This was a remarkable young man in the thrall of his art. And me, enthralled by this young man and his devotion.

We talked for hours. Watched the night sky grow wan. Night herons returning to their perches. Soon to be replaced by roosters and other denizens of daylight. Light emerging around the corners of the sky. Hopeful fishermen heading to the sea. Nets in tow. The spell about to be broken, we retreated to a place of silence. Both hesitant about the next step. If there was to be one.

We were timid. Tired. Cautious.

Then he reached out for my hand. Seemingly out of the blue. The touch, tentative at first. Tender. Insistent later, encouraged by a desirable reception. My heart, so full. Reveling in his touch. A simple act of intimacy, long in the making.

Desired. Dreamed about.

Dreaded. Dismissed.

Desired some more.

My heart and mind, a fast-spinning carousel of joy.

At the breakfast table, the recollection of his touch fills my being with such immense ecstasy, it's tinged with grief. A sorrow that originates from the awareness of the rarity of such affection.

I think back to a coming of age shaded with guilt and shame. The arrival of adulthood and all the associated longings tainted by terror and trauma. A lifetime of diffidence and doubts of my own desirability. So many fundamental acts of intimacy and love that come so naturally to others. Fluently. Frequently. These feel so out of reach for me.

Neither fluid nor frequent.

Tinged with sorrow or otherwise, I can barely suppress the joy I feel. Elation and exuberance are my resolute companions today. Prevailing over my natural propensity towards melancholy. My feet feel lighter. Clouds beneath them. A smile that refuses to leave. My mood sunnier than the Goan sky. My mother, noticing my demeanor, inquires about the cause for such glee. I conveniently attribute it to the seductive charms of our beachside destination. The lure of the sun, sand, and sea, I say.

My sister's face reflects a mixture of amusement and apprehension.

But I, a master of deflection, give her no cause for further apprehension. I change the topic to our plans for the day.

The daily plan provides a topic of inexhaustible discussion for my family.

Five people with completely different and conflicting interests trying to land on a common itinerary and plan of action, a recipe that devours vast amounts of time. A perfect distraction from prying questions about my suddenly sunnier-than-normal disposition, and a tactic I frequently employ to escape discussions trending in an uncomfortable direction.

My father wants to watch TV in his airconditioned room.

My mother admonishes him for wasting time doing something he could've done at home. She proposes a visit to a site of doubtful historic distinction.

My sister, feeling a little better now, proposes a trip to the flea market.

I'd rather not leave the resort grounds at all.

For obvious reasons.

However, staying put at the resort is vetoed, so I agree to the trip that takes the least amount of time. As a compromise.

USMAN

was so confused, yaar. He brought me to the beach and was being damn nice to me, giving me all the attention like I was someone special. But he had not made any moves on me. Maybe he just wanted to be friends? Maybe I was imagining there was something else between us. This was all so new to me, na?

A part of me thought I should not make a fuss and let him sort it out. But as the night started changing into day, the water getting rosy from the morning light, I felt like I was so close to hitting the jackpot and then very quickly I could see it slipping out of my hands. (No, I don't mean jackpot like I was going to get money. I don't care about that.) Guys like Ravi, who were decent, from educated backgrounds and nice families, didn't slum it with people like me. I usually got the mean, asshole types. This was my one chance to experience something, anything, with someone high class like him, and I was so desperate not to let it go.

So, I said fuck it, and I reached out for his hand. I mean I didn't know what to do and touching his hand felt like it was the safest move I could make. He didn't shoo me away which was a very big relief. Actually he took my hand in both of his hands, holding my hand so sweetly. Then he leaned in and kissed me.

I swear his lips were so soft, like makkhan, and smooth like malai. He tasted a little bit like beer and saunf mixed together. I had no idea a kiss could light your body on fire, that it could feel like Diwali firecrackers were setting off all over my body. Dhoom, dhoom, dhadaka left and right, all over. I felt warm and tingly, my whole body exploding with feelings that I still don't have the words to describe only. I mean I had been kissed one time before this but that happened against my wishes, forcibly only. This was new and different. I could hear my heart thumping and thumping, and I could feel his heartbeat, fast like mine, racing-racing. The sound of our heartbeats, it felt like a Zakir Hussain tabla jugalbandi, that only he and myself could hear. I could not breathe, I was so on fire. Finally now, I can understand the big deal they make in the movies, when the hero and heroine kiss, oof.

We kept on kissing only, for a long time, as if we were scared to stop, because we wouldn't know how to breathe on our own again if we separated. He started slowly, kissing me softly, waiting for my response, and then kissed me hard, and then soft again. His beard and mustache were tickling and tickling me until I almost lost control. Every time I thought I couldn't take it anymore, he would take it easy, driving me crazy with little bites, biting me on my ears and neck, lips, and then he went back to kissing me. His hands were touching me, feeling me, holding me, as he kissed me. Wow yaar!

Before I knew it, it was quite bright and the beach had started coming to life. The water and sky were now the color of ripe mangoes and then amber and gold. I straightened my shirt, brushing off the sand that was everywhere, feeling very conscious of being seen and maybe recognized by somebody. The daylight was pushing all of my courage back into whatever dark corner I had brought it out from. He didn't pressure me to continue or anything, and we watched the sun come up, quietly, hands slightly touching, before we said bye. He walked back to the resort and myself, the other way, towards home.

I replayed the night in my head, rewinding and replaying, rewinding and replaying every scene, like the four video cassettes of movies Ammi plays again and again on our ancient VCR. When we first walked down to the beach, I had no idea where the night would go only. My imagination and my expectations were limited, shaped by the very few previous experiences I had had. I thought that maybe it would be the same like before, hush-hush, like a dirty secret, fast, and filled with shame. I thought that maybe he would treat me like a bloody vernac, like a cheap toy to play with and throw away when he was done. I thought he might use his status and money to pressure me into doing whatever he wanted, taking for granted that I would do what he asked. Maybe he would be aggressive, abusive, and violent. People of my caliber are used to being treated like we don't have control of our own lives and decisions, no? What I did not expect was a night full of interesting conversation and holding hands. I did not imagine in my wildest dreams, watching the sunrise like the hero and heroine in my favorite films, or the kissing.

I don't remember the walk home because I was in shock only. So many thoughts and emotions to process, no? Ammi is used to me working night shifts when someone is out sick or something, so she did not say anything when I got home, which was good because I don't like lying to her. I was so tired only, my eyes were fuzzy and my brain so jumbled up that I thought I was going to fall into a very deep sleep. I tried but I couldn't fall asleep even though I was so exhausted. Like a giant wheel at a funfair, my feelings went up and down, round and round, from happiness to shock, to doubting the happenings of last night, and from excitement to fear. I finally gave up on sleep and got ready for work.

I was so obsessed with him, yaar, I could not stop thinking about him only. For some strange reason, I was reminded of a tattered, old book, *Man-Eaters of Kumaon*, that I had borrowed many years ago from the pathetic library in my school. It's about man-eating tigers in British India. Some of these tigers were injured and were forced to attack people because human beings couldn't run as fast as the deers and other animals. Other times the tigers got a taste for human flesh by accident, but mind you, it did not matter how they got started. Once the tigers tasted human flesh there was no going back only. They were addicted to it. Maybe I should not compare my obsession with Ravi to a man-eating tiger's thirst for human flesh, but I kept thinking about last night's encounter. For the first time, I could even imagine the possibilities of romance and love, and all the other things I had never let myself dream about. I got a little taste of it and I was hooked only. I wanted more, more kisses, more holding hands, and more of everything, yaar.

I was screwed, no? Because I could want all I wanted but there was no bloody chance of me getting any of it, not for long.

I mean I would have to pretend I didn't even know him when I saw him next time, at least not more than any other guest.

His family might be okay with him doing whatever he does, all bindaas, but I was quite sure even they wouldn't like him hanging out with my type. We weren't even allowed to use the same toilets as the guests. You think these society people were going to be fine with their American son hanging out with a low life like me?

And the resort management? They would basically kick me out on my bum if they found out any of the nonsense I'd gotten myself into. Plus, Ravi was here only for a short time. I did not get to ask him exactly how long he was staying here, but it wasn't going to be permanently, right? Suddenly I started feeling all down. I should at least enjoy last night's memories for a little while, before I got all down and depressed, na?

And so I walked to work, trying to control the emotional cyclone inside me. I thought seeing Ravi again would put a smile on my face, hopefully. At work I did my daily rounds, looking out for Ravi and his family in all their regular places. I felt like I was on a treasure hunt, my pulse speeding up, faster and faster, as I was looking around the swimming pool, hoping to see him and his orange swimming costume. Alas, there was no Ravi and no orange swimming costume only. I carried on with my rounds and duties, thinking I would see him at the restaurant for lunch. That also did not happen.

I was panicking a little, and looked up their reservation and guest notes on the office computer. They were out on a trip with one of the resort cars. The notes said the car was booked to take them to the flea market in Anjuna. Oof, what a relief! I looked through the rest of the reservation details. Their check-out was scheduled for tomorrow. I knew this was going to happen sooner or later, but seeing it made it final. I could see the end of our story, na? Our story was going to have a sad ending, guaranteed, a tragedy instead of the love story I had started to imagine. Suddenly I could not keep up the show of this fake happiness only. My mood was off, man. What was the point of all this na? Why would I risk everything for nothing?

Life hasn't always been easy for me but this was India, man. We believe our destiny is predetermined: our successes and our failures are decided by the wishes of a higher power and therefore beyond our control. Khuda ki marzi or bhagwan ki, depending on which god you believed in. We might go to the palm reader to get an advance look at our future or we go to the dargah and tie colorful strings to the tombs of great saints, hoping to change this predetermined future, but we all accepted that our fates were decided by someone else.

We accept life, fair or unfair, because koi option nahin hai, yaar. You don't have a choice only. And anyways there is so much suffering in this country, you can always find a poor bugger worse off than you. So, you accepted your life. You even learned to appreciate the few good things you had, unlike that poor bugger whose suffering was worse than yours. I, myself, had learned to live my life, to love it for what it was, and for the small pleasures it had provided for me. Then just as I had learned to accept it all, life was giving me a taste of something I couldn't have, like it was pulling some cruel joke on me. Here, have a taste of this or that, but don't enjoy it too much, because you were going to be kicked back into your world, back to your reality, very fast and very soon.

This taste of happiness and the guarantee of it being taken away, it was too much for me to handle only. I was disappointed that Ravi wasn't there and irritated that if he was there, I would have to pretend I didn't really know him. I was sad that in the most optimistic scenario I could imagine, this crazy affair of ours could only last one more night. I was upset that until last night I didn't know that love was an option for someone like me. I was angry because even though I could see the possibility now, I didn't actually get to have it. I hated that I could lose my job if someone found out about me. Even worse, I was afraid I would break my mother's heart and I was damn scared that she would kick me out of the family.

The cyclone was back, tearing me apart from the inside and I was drowning in wave after wave of sadness and disappointment, anger and pity, and a thousand other feelings. The waves were pushing and pushing, this way and that way, but wherever I looked I saw the same conclusion. This cursed adventure was the beginning of a very slippery slope to nowhere only. There were many risks and the rewards seemed very-very few. I wanted to return to my old life, on my own terms, before it was too late to do it. Ravi came into my life, which was like a Xiaomi flip phone, and suddenly changed it into a fancy iPhone. It was wonderful and amazing but I forgot for a few minutes that I could not afford an iPhone. Aukaat, you had to remember to live within your means and not dream about things you could not have.

So what if my life was lonely before Ravi, I would get used to the loneliness again. It was better to be alone than to be afraid, so very afraid of losing it all if anyone found out about your dirty, little secret.

I switched with a colleague so that I would work the second part of my shift at the resort's seafood restaurant. She must have felt quite lucky only, because I gave her my office shift. The hours were the same but you could chill on the computer when you were on office duty. Sometimes you could even get some sleep, and you did not have to deal with guests and their constant demands all the time. The restaurant was ten times more work, specially when you had to wear heels like all the women staff did. But it was the only place where I wouldn't run into Ravi or his family. Pukka guarantee! They were strictly veg and would never come there.

I had made up my mind. I was going to avoid him today so I wouldn't be tempted to repeat last night's mistakes. I could not risk my life and livelihood for one night of fun, no matter how much I wanted it. It was not worth the risk only.

I let down my guard last night, but today I needed to use all the courage and discipline I had to keep myself in line. I had dared to dream dreams that I couldn't afford. My punishment was to surrender those impossible dreams and vow to stay away from such forbidden luxuries in the future.

RAVI

We had a late start. Hangover recovery. Arguments about the destination choice. A complete absence of urgency. Or timeliness. All very usual and par for the course. Time moved slowly in the tropics. Or maybe it was just my family. I'd heard the same argument between my parents. For as long as I could remember. Dad dawdled. Mom was always early. Prepunctual. You'd think a lifetime of knowing each other's habits would force one or the other to change. Or compromise. That hadn't happened, not yet.

We finally made it out of the resort but not very far. It was already midafternoon by then. The sun was merciless and the flea market completely devoid of shade. A change of plans. We decided to go for a leisurely lunch first. To avoid the peak afternoon heat. So much for the flea market option being the quickest one.

Picking a restaurant for lunch presented yet another challenge. The Venn diagram of our individual food preferences was scarce on overlapping areas. Another example of familial disagreement that was familiar on account of frequent repetition. A disagreement that had evaded a reasonable solution thus far.

Goa is crammed with eateries but we could rule out the beachside shacks selling fresh seafood. Vegetarian-friendly options only, please and thank you. There were Italian and continental restaurants of varied caliber. All designed to attract the foreign tourists craving a familiar taste and a break from curry. For the domestic vacationers they presented an exotic alternative. And a break from the familiar. Sis and Jiju argued in favor of an Italian joint. They were "sick of eating Punjabi food all the time." Mom and Dad preferred an Indian eatery, voting for one advertising SHAHI MUGHLAI cuisine. In capital letters. Or the one next door that served south Indian food.

I got to be the tiebreaker. Again. This privilege was sponsored by the imagined (and imaginary) dearth of decent (vegetarian) food options in Boston. I would have had us go back to our trusty resort restaurant. So I could see Usman. But we were an hour away. And a visit to the flea market was still in the cards once the sun calmed down.

I chose a completely different option from the ones advocated by the family. My choice was a rare commodity in Goa, and in India generally. A mostly authentic interpretation of Greek food. Opened by an expat Greek couple who came to Goa on vacation three decades ago. And never left. The restaurant's popularity had weathered the decades and the changing clientele gracefully. A beautiful patio shaded with grapevine covered trellises buzzed with contented guests and busy staff. The water views were expansive, the music lively without being obtrusive, and the food smelled wonderful. There were plenty of vegetarian options.

I was keenly aware of my parents' limited range of food preferences. Vigilant about the presence of stray egg or meat and fish products in menu items. And very eager to avoid a marathon study of the menu with countless questions to match. So, I tried to speed things along. Suggesting that I order for the table. My sister, now feeling much more like her old self, decided there was no need to rush. She was enjoying herself. Immensely. As she tortured me in a manner that is second nature for one's siblings.

Teasing me by dragging things along. Enjoying my growing impatience. And inability to do anything about it. I decided to surrender to the inevitable. Tucked into the delectable spread. Sipping on chilled bubbly. A couple of glasses of wine and I was feeling pretty fine. I was happy we left the confines of the resort. And its sanitized, Disney-esque recreation of Goa. Replete with native dancers and other cultural activities of a puerile sort. Usman would have to wait. Just a little bit longer.

I was excited to see him. Hoping to plan another clandestine, late-night trip to the beach. Last night, blinded by infatuation and with the optimism of new lovers, we assumed the night was endless. That time was infinite. The eternal night of our optimistic imagination did in fact end. Like the last of the sand in an hourglass, it even sped up towards its grand finale. Neither he nor I had the sense to discuss the logistics of our next rendezvous. I wasn't even sure if he was working today. I assumed he would have mentioned it if he wasn't. I didn't think to inform him that I was leaving tomorrow either. Something I planned on doing today.

We ventured over to the flea market after an elongated lunch break. The sun was past its zenith now and the heat felt less oppressive. The cool breeze, pleasant. The stalls at the market were squashed together. Arranged in serpentine rows. Weaving in and out. Interminable. Bulging with merchandise of all kinds and sorts. Sarees and sarongs. T-shirts and tchotchkes. Incense. Bronze statuettes of various gods and goddesses. Brass dinner sets. Gemstones. Jewelry. I stopped at a stall selling Tibetan goods. Robes, thangka paintings, and turquoise jewelry, displayed in gleaming arrays. A veritable explosion of colors. I picked out a couple of pendants to bring back as gifts for friends in Boston. And one for Usman. Turquoise and silver with some red accents. Vaguely

Tibetan motifs. But no religious connotations, I made sure.

It was a quiet ride back to the resort. Worn out from the expedition, the heat and the sun, everyone retired to their rooms. For a pre-dinner interlude. I feigned a need for some exercise and set off for a stroll. Walked around the resort a couple of times. No sign of Usman, so I walked over to the beach. To catch one last sunset in Goa. The sun magnanimous in its final act of the day. Painting everything in sight pretty. Pink. Fuchsia. Purple. Magic. I headed back to the resort as the light faded. Did another lap around the grounds in an unsuccessful attempt at conjuring up Usman.

Dinner with the family. Usman was still nowhere to be seen. I debated asking the staff if he was working but I didn't. He was adamant that neither he nor I should do anything to compromise his employment at the resort. Fraternizing with the guests was strictly forbidden to begin with. Add a whiff of gay scandal to the mix and all bets were off. India had changed a lot since I was growing up here, but I understood his concerns.

Unlike the sort of rabid opposition that was based on religion, and there was quite a bit of that, the generalized hostility towards sexual minorities in India, was based more on the idea of the violation of established social norms. Here we relied on forced social cohesion to prevent dissent and disharmony.

I, with my relative privilege and the ability to escape the country entirely, was ill-suited to argue with his fear of discovery. My now-Americanized notion of individuality and rights based on personhood did not align with a more expansive definition of personhood here. In India, your wellbeing wasn't based on your happiness alone, but on that of your family members, immediate and extended. And the larger community. Your sexual realization and freedom might result in personal happiness but if the larger community was unhappy, threatened, then the price for your liberty was too high. This expanded definition of the self was conducive to developing deep social bonds but it could also be devastatingly rigid for those whose needs and wants didn't coincide with those of the majority.

I waited on the hammocks after dinner. For a while. Pretending to read. Hoping that Usman would find me. Like he did last night. Hope often defied reality and expectations, to survive in the most barren places. And against severe odds. Unfortunately, tonight, hope reaped no benefits for its perseverance. I returned to my room. Desolate. Turned in for a night of tortured sleep.

A midmorning flight meant a very early departure from the resort. Tired and groggy, we waited for assistance with our luggage. I sat on the steps outside the bungalow. Hoping for one last chance to catch Usman. A hopeless mission. Suitable for a hopelessly romantic heart. Imagine my surprise, disbelief, and exhilaration when I saw him walking over with a porter and the luggage cart. There was so much I wanted to say. So many questions I had. Unfortunately, I wasn't the only one who had spotted him. My dad started bringing out the bags from the room. Assisted by my brother-in-law. I wasn't going to be able to talk to Usman. Not alone.

I helped with the bags. We started walking towards the waiting car. Usman leading. The family following behind. I struggled to find a way to get him alone. Desperate to say something. Anything. So, I pretended I had forgotten something in my room. Raced back with the key. There I hastily scribbled down my email and phone number. On a paper napkin. I raced back to the reception to drop off the key. Everyone was in the car. Waiting for me. I extended my hand to shake Usman's. To thank him. And to slip the napkin in his hand.

BOSTON

I get hard, I said. Just don't get hard with anyone.
Shy, Fiona said.
Social terror, I said.

-In the City of Shy Hunters, Tom Spanbauer

RAVI

Springtime in Boston. Soggy. Sodden. Sooty patches of stubborn, slow-melting snow. Skies, a gunmetal gray. Bare boughs and brown earth. A long, slow farewell to another winter past. Old man winter, though, is loath to go. Threats of snow and temperature tantrums. Lingering traces of death and decay. Then suddenly from showers to flowers. Leaves of grass. Fifty shades of green. Buds. Blooms. Bursts of color. Pink and purple. Pansies. Peonies. Mauve and magenta. Magnolia branches weighed down by profuse sprays of fragrant flowers. Dogwood. Daffodils. Tulips, omnipresent. A season of endings. And new beginnings.

In my life too, endings and new beginnings. Strictly speaking though, both were a long time in the making. The seasonal metaphor is a convenient coincidence. I've decided to give up on love. The romantic kind. It's not just that things didn't work out with Usman. Before him, there was at least a decade of looking for love. Of desire and longing. Searching. Aching and craving. A few blips of fulfillment, of hopefulness. Temporary blips. Few and far between. Mostly a long, uninterrupted line of disappointment and heartbreak. Love prospects: flatlining. Do not resuscitate.

A decade at least, of longing and aching. Desire and craving. But also of primping and prepping. Self-improvement plans and projects. Reminiscent of Soviet-style five year plans. Mine were designed to better my dating prospects. Through the development, modification, and improvement of physical infrastructure. Obviously deficient physical infrastructure, or so I believed.

There were surface improvements. Wardrobe upgrades. Winter whites. Wooly delights. Copious clothing purchases. Ecru. Eggshell. Beige. Monochromatic. Plum. Pink. Paisley. Multicolored. Egyptian cotton. Belgian linen. Nylon and neoprene. Leather. Lace. Lycra. Tight clothes. Oversized ones. Deep Vs and turtlenecks. Short shorts. Shorter shorts. Prints. Patterns. Cosmetic enhancements. Potions and lotions. Cleansers. Creams. Surface improvements.

There were attempts at structural improvements. Gym routines. My body segmented. Workouts grouped by designated areas of improvement. Chest. Shoulders. Back and biceps. Legs. Weight lifting. Muscle building. Protein shakes. Vanity muscles. Coaxing the reluctant ectomorph into a muscled Adonis. The one you thought *they* thought was more attractive. Slow progress. Suboptimal results. Weight and muscle didn't follow directions well. Meandering in the double chins scenic region. Lingering on the fleshy belly tour. Missing the bicep exit completely. Boondoggle. White elephant.

Then there was the revised five year plan. To reverse the previous boondoggle. Attain more equitable distribution. Of muscle and mass. Work with my body type. Running. Swimming. Cardio. Calorie counting. Salad bars. Lean protein. Muscle definition. Six-pack chasing. Mirror gazing. Weight watching. Slow progress. Suboptimal results. Invisible abs and an endless chase of an impossible ideal. The ripped body, a pink elephant.

Speaking of pink elephants. Too many drinks. Beer and wine. Manhattans and martinis. Too many nights at different bars. Chasing boys. Or the dream of one: a suitable boy. Hoping to be seen in my colorful clothes. Or the somber ones. Wanting to be noticed. For the newly bulked-up frame. Or the leaner me. For wit and charm. Anything really. I was there, ready and available. Find me. Please.

It may sound depressing but this is the life's work of an eternally optimistic mind. A mind that can ignore the meager returns on its tireless toil. To return again and again to the scene of the crime. Today will be different. Tomorrow can be different. The day after will surely bring with it Lady Luck. And Mr. Right.

But it takes a toll, all this wishing and hoping, all the chasing. All the planning. Primping. Prepping. Even for the eternally optimistic mind. The supplies of optimism may be vast. But they are finite. The daily dose of hope is harder to procure. Stocks of positivity dwindle. Consumed by the cycle of projection. Rejection. And Dejection. I woke up one day. Tired. Unable to conjure up a day that could be different. Too tired to believe that today is the day I will be noticed. That tomorrow is when I will finally be seen. Looking for love started to feel like an exercise in futility. After so many fruitless runs.

So, I've decided to give up. Temporarily. Or permanently. Abandoning the five year plans. I'm telling myself that today, tomorrow, and the day-after likely won't be different from all the yesterdays and the day-befores. That love isn't for me. Cancel out the possibility of love from the left hand side and the deleterious side effects of its pursuit from the right side: balance the equation. Emancipation from the exhausting circle of hope and dejection. Twenty-first century nirvana.

My unsuccessful pursuit of love was most likely a result of a combination of garden-variety errors and self-inflicted wounds. Looking for love in all the wrong places, for instance. Oblivion to signs of interest. Self-doubt. Self-pity. Dangerously low self-esteem levels. And many other, yet to be identified speed bumps that made the road to love so treacherous. But I didn't know that. Not yet. Not at this point in my story. It felt easier to believe myself unlucky or unlovable. Or both. So, giving up on love seemed appropriate. A season of endings.

The relief is discernible. Immediate. Expansive. I am freed from the all-consuming hunt for the happily-ever-after. And consequently, the constant reminders of my obvious inadequacies. Life feels easier. Less complicated. More forgiving. I have more time to savor love and companionship. Of family and friends. I spend less time primping. And prepping. I give up the reflexive scanning of the crowd for a potential mate. The suitable boy. Focusing instead on the company of friends and family. I seek solace elsewhere. In success and stability. In good health. In life after love, which is fair and fine on all other fronts.

I chide myself for not being grateful enough for all the other blessings life has showered on me. For my myopic focus on love. As if I am only allowed one or the other. But I do believe that I only deserve one. Or the other. My obvious defects have disqualified me from having it all. Self-criticism, a fecund and familiar terrain. Comfortable territory. So here's a new self-improvement project: be more grateful.

Yoga. Meditation. Morning prayers. Mindfulness. All with the intention of maximizing gratefulness. Different approach. More focused on improvement of the inner self. Still based on the same foundation of self-identified personal deficiency. Old habits die hard.

Still, the relief is evident. I proclaim my newfound independence. Shout it from the rooftops. Say I've never been happier. I am sorry that it has taken this long to realize how liberating life without love can be. I am sorry that I didn't see this as an option before. I don't need love. Not the romantic kind. I'm happy. Happier than ever before. I even believe it. Really. A season of new beginnings. Personal perestroika.

For the skeptics, who don't believe I am actually giving up. Or that I am happy. And there are a few. For those concerned about my premature surrender. And there are many. I explain that my self-imposed exile from the land of love is temporary. I argue that I am not closing myself to the possibility of love. I'm just not actively chasing it. Even if the banishment is permanent—and I don't know that it is—I am happy. Happier than I have ever been. Even I believe it.

And boy did I enjoy my newfound freedom. Dancing and laughing. Ball change. Box Step. Dos-i-do. Not a care in the world. No one to impress. No one to entice. Dancing and laughing. Cackle and a chortle. Guffaw and a hee-haw. Belly laughs. Dancing and laughing. In the moonlight and in the sunshine. On starry nights and stormy days. With spring flowers and through sodden showers. A season of endings. And new beginnings. I am starting to believe. In life after love.

ADAM

I t's my last day at work and dude, it sucks! Our program ran out of funding, probably as a result of some Republican hack's wet dream: slashing public services. A group of over-priced, Ivy League-educated pendejos, I mean, management consultants, probably circle jerked in a conference room, plotting a PowerPoint offensive to make government more efficient. I can just imagine this group of guys, literally, because it's still the good old boys club, all of them clothed from head to toe in matching Brooks Brothers outfits, planning to achieve said efficiency by canceling programs and services they didn't think the poor needed or deserved. Bloody hell, as if the unwashed masses didn't have enough problems already. The whole system is rigged.

We need to demolish the corrupt nexus of capitalism, corpo-rations, and the two-party system via a people-powered revolu-tion. Bernie or bust! But better yet, I say put some fucking drag queens in charge. Can you imagine RuPaul and the Drag Race crew taking a hammer to the status quo? Goodbye patriarchy. Fuck you corporate greed. Adios, my racist amigo! The future is queer and a Stonewall-style riot is just what the doctor prescribed to flush out the garbage infecting our society.

But I digress, the program closure is not a surprise. We've had a few months to wind down the operations, to hand over our clients and their fat files to their new, more "efficient" and overburdened advocates. Despite the advance warning and preparation, I still tear up when I do the final rounds of the empty office. Dude, it's like a dystopian diorama of a once vibrant civilization that is now barren post-apocalypse, with just some litter and debris remaining as clues of its former glory. The cubes look particularly depressing under the bright fluorescent lights, shorn of their various decorations and other signs of inhabitation. I find a couple of plants, abandoned by their humans, which I add to the already overflowing box of things I am bringing home. I may be romanticising this drab gray-walled maze of randomly arranged cubicles but these walls, this space, they have stories to tell, stories that are way more fucking precious than the faded decor suggests. Comprendes?

This was my first cube. I had come here fresh out of college, bright-eyed and bushy-tailed, brimming with idealism and a thirst to cure the world of its ills. I still remember meeting C, my first client, like it was yesterday. We sat at that desk, sipping on two large iced Dunkin Donuts coffees.

C's previous case worker had told me that she always got C an iced coffee when she came in for her appointments, cream and four sugars, and I decided to keep the tradition going. By the by, what is it with these fucking crazy New Englanders and their iced coffees in the middle of winter?

Anyway, I've had C as a client since that first serendipitous meeting six years ago. She stayed with me, from that tiny cube to a larger one, and then to an office with a door. She is fabulous, feisty, and funny as hell. She's made me laugh so hard I've cried, snorted, and totes lost my shit. We have spilled the tea and thrown shade. We've bawled our eyes out as we navigated one crisis after another. I love her so much, it fucking broke my heart seeing her for our last appointment yesterday.

C belonged to that first wave of survivors of the HIV/AIDS epidemic. She's had a full, adventure-filled life and you can still see that incredible spirit in her, but she was barely hanging in there when I first met her. She was struggling with all kinds of health issues, which were compounded by homelessness and addiction. She's better now, not completely out of the woods but she has housing. She's on methadone. Her viral load is undetectable. I'm keeping my fingers crossed for her.

She is one of the thousands of people we served through our now-closed program. We did some important work here, with and for people that are underserved, marginalized, and generally falling through the cracks. These people have HIV and AIDS but more often than not that was just the tip of the proverbial iceberg. Our clients suffered from all sorts of problems ranging from isolation to incarceration and everything in between. Poverty, hunger, homelessness, mental health and addiction issues, domestic violence, you name it, guy, and we've dealt with it.

I am as happy as anyone about PREP and other advancements in prevention and treatment but I feel like it is making people believe and act like the epidemic is over, especially the fucking rich, white, gay men. Yes, I am a white man but I am definitely not rich and I'm not some fucking CIS-het wannabe, pink pants-boat shoe-wearing quasi-Republican asshole. Okay fine, so maybe that's a little harsh but it's just so fucking hard to see the funding dry up, government funding and private money from events like the AIDS Walk. I really wish everyone would stop pretending that this shit is all over. Blargh!

I turn the office lights off, wiping away a stray tear with the back of my hand. I can't get emotional now, I still have to say my goodbyes to my coworkers! Those goodbyes will come later, at the gathering we've planned tonight at Giovanni's, our favorite local restaurant and bar. It's going to be current and former coworkers, many of whom I feel closer to than I do to my own family. There are some I don't particularly care for, but tonight even they seem precious. Their rough edges and sharp elbows have been magically smoothed over by the impending parting of ways. Tonight we will hug and kiss, reminisce, and fucking cry like babies. We will promise to keep in touch, always and forever. We will drink more than we should. Spend money on drinks and food to augment the bare-bones spread the department could afford, money we should probably conserve, what with this being our last day of work. Oh well.

I bring the box of office stuff home and make my way back to Giovanni's, where the party is already in full swing. The room is packed to the rafters, so many people that quite a few have spilled out onto the patio. Luckily, it is one of those perfect late spring evenings that is so rare in New England, warm with the promise of summer but cool enough to need a sweater. I stay out on the patio for a while, catching up with my old boss, Nancy, but I go inside after she leaves. Boy is it loud, the room reverberating with sounds of so many conversations and so much laughter and joy. I make my way around, taking it all in, stopping to chat with folks every few steps. I am not easily prone to sentimentality, having learned at a very young age about the impermanence of things, but I am feeling pretty emotional today. With these friends and coworkers, our bonds were formed through some pretty intense, shared experiences; forged in the trenches, you could say. My predictions are on the nose too. It's a goddamn love fest. I've lost count of the hugs I've received, the number of times I have teared up, or flat out cried. Heyo, shit's getting real. This is rough.

Fast forward a few hours of a whirlwind of conversations, catching up, and goodbyes, and the crowd has dwindled, with only the core crew and the hardcore drinkers remaining. Mind you, these two groups aren't necessarily mutually exclusive. I'm not a big drinker myself, which is not to say I'm a lightweight. I just don't like drinking that much. But tonight I'm determined to stay as long as I can, maybe even drink a little more than I normally would, so I can spend time with these lovely peeps. I do realize though that it is past the time we'd reserved the room for and we may be overstaying our welcome. I figure I should check.

I walk out of the private space that the restaurant has reserved for our party and into the main dining area. The restaurant is quiet, the moody pink light from the lamps, the flickering candles, and the soft Italian music, lending it an ethereal air, like a classy bordello and *Roman Holiday* had a baby. (*Roman Holiday* is Mama's favorite movie.) It is late on a Monday night and not everyone is out lamenting their last day of work. We are probably keeping the staff here. I check in with Tim, our waiter, on my way back from the restroom. I want to make sure it's fine if we stay for a bit longer. He insists it's not a problem.

I've known Tim for a while, we all have. His wife used to work with us. I ask about her, how she's doing, and the kids of course. You know, taking a few minutes to catch up with the guy, now that the party is waning and we both have a few minutes to spare. I also happen to have an ulterior motive for being out here in the main dining room. There's a coworker of Tim's I've noticed a few times tonight, who I have never seen here before. He is dark and handsome, Latinx or perhaps Middle Eastern, and very much my type. I'm intrigued by him, have been all night, and I am determined to talk to him before the night is over.

Aha! There he is, sitting at the end of the bar, polishing glasses as I shoot the shit with Tim. He's close enough to hear our conversation, and I think he is half paying attention to us, or pretending not to be paying attention, or actually *uninterested* in me and the damn conversation. I can't tell which it is. When Tim excuses himself to attend to some of the folks in the party, I use the opportunity to say hello and introduce myself to the guapo. I'm no shrinking violet to begin with but it doesn't hurt to have had a few drinks. Liquid courage, ya know?

His name is Ravi, which I am pretty sure is an Indian name, and that, I would not have guessed. I was so convinced he was Latinx! We don't get to chat much before Tim returns and then I get pulled away, back to the party. There's a round of shots to be had. Probably not a good idea, but tonight's not the night for quibbles and qualms. Shots, it is.

As the party gets progressively smaller and sloppier, I make my way back to the main dining room. Tim and Ravi are both at the end of the bar this time, the service area. I plop myself on the bar seat closest to them, declaring myself a refugee from the drunken shenanigans in the other room. Tim introduces us officially and explains to Ravi how he and I know each other. The three of us chat about Tim's wife, Ines, and their kids, establishing some commonalities and connections. Tim is busy enough with the drunks in my party that Ravi and I get to talk to each other alone.

We end up talking for more than an hour, with parts where Tim joins in, or the few times when I have to excuse myself to say goodbye to someone leaving the party. We talk about my year in Colombia, about his childhood in India, about his other job as a kindergarten teacher, and my work in the social-work arena. We talk about my plans for the summer, I have three months off before I start grad school in fall, about books and movies, and languages. I love that the conversation isn't one-sided. He's smart and witty and can carry on a conversation about a wide range of subjects but he is also attentive, interested in my stories, asking me questions and following up on my responses.

The back and forth between us is easy. It doesn't feel forced or like small talk, which I absolutely detest. I may be slightly prone to hyperbole, but I rank small talk somewhere between hangnails and Hitler on the list of things I can't stand. I'd rather fucking talk about real things, things that matter, and not some bullshit conversation about how the weather is too hot or too cold. Guess what? The weather's always up to something in New England! This conversation with Ravi is so damn refreshing, an adult conversation that is intellectually stimulating and emotionally mature. It is the exact opposite of all the shallow bullshit that passes for conversation when you meet people at clubs. I don't care about what designer you're wearing nor do I want to fall down some Kardashian K-hole.

Don't even get me started on online dating apps. I'm more than happy to hook up with people. In fact that's pretty much all I want, but it's such a turn off when people have no fucking manners. Would it kill you to say hello before demanding dick pics? I've tried the whole dating/hookup apps routine a few times but I haven't had much luck with them. I've had even less success at gay bars and clubs. This, on the other hand, feels more legit, more interesting. Hallelujah!

I could have chatted with him for another hour or four, but unfortunately, all good things must come to an end. It is getting late and I realize we are keeping the staff here. They are all polite and patient with the borrachos in the party but I'm sure they want to go home too. I go back to the party, encourage the last of my crew to settle their tabs, collect their belongings, and make sure everyone has a safe way to get home.

Before I escort the last folks out, I run over to Ravi and ask him if I can have his number.

RAVI

had noticed him earlier. He was out on the patio. Hanging out. With another guest from the party. A guest with severe mobility restrictions. She was probably avoiding the crush of people inside. I happened to have a few tables on the patio around the same time. And I happened to observe their inter-action. He was sitting on the edge of the raised flower-bed. She, on her motorized scooter. Next to each other. Both deeply engaged in their conversation. Gesturing and laughing. Crying and chatting. While the rest partied inside. Their connection was obvious. Even to a casual observer.

In a world where everything feels transactional. Give and take. Take and give. In a world where time is a scarce commodity. Where kindness is in even shorter supply. Watching them and their interaction, their connection stood out to me. It didn't seem perfunctory. Or born out of pity. Or duty. He wasn't just biding his time until someone relieved him of his post. He was genuinely engaged and happy to be in her company. While the rest partied inside.

It stood out to me. He stood out to me. Adam. Not because he was cute, although he was. But for his obvious empathy. Kind-ness. That sort of thing does more for me than cute. He stood out to me enough that I asked Tim about him. Tim didn't know if Adam was gay or straight, not with any degree of certainty. It didn't matter, I told Tim. I wasn't looking anyway. I wasn't. I had

[63]

given up on love. The romantic kind.

This was all before Adam introduced himself. Before we talked. Before Tim introduced us again. Before Adam asked me for my number.

You know those plotlines? In a novel or on your favorite show. Where you didn't see the twist coming. Or the turn. Where the progression of events left you surprised. Completely surprised. Shocked. It was like that. Except I wasn't the unsuspecting reader. Or viewer. I was the protagonist. In my own story. Caught unaware by the turn of events. Did Adam just ask me for my number? Was I dreaming? Pinch me. We had a nice chat. Yes. We did. But he was talking to me because Tim was busy, or so I assumed. He was just being friendly, I thought. Our conversation wasn't flirtatious. Not particularly so. Or amorous. Maybe I'd turned off my gaydar once I decided to give up on love.

I certainly had no idea he was interested in me. Me! Maybe. More likely, it was because I happened to be terrible at recognizing the signs when someone was interested in me. Me? It came from a lifetime of finding myself unattractive. Or marginally attractive, on a good day. And the miserable track record on the love and romance front. Which reinforced the not-attractive thing. The self-loathing and the spotty track record were related. I knew. Intertwined. I didn't know which came first. The lack of confidence. Or the sparsity of success. My very own chicken or egg conundrum.

It was also such a rare event. This overt expression of interest in me. That I had to find a reason for it. A vector or a catalyst to hold responsible. I was convinced that Tim had put Adam up to it. Tim must have mentioned it to Adam that I had inquired about him. No, he did not. Tim was adamant that he had not mentioned my queries. Nor had he encouraged Adam to ask me out. I was just going to have to believe that Adam was *actually* interested in me, he said. Without being coerced or cajoled.

I still had my doubts. Old friends, these doubts. Childhood friends. Hard to let go. If Tim was not responsible for encouraging Adam, perhaps Adam had acted impulsively. I blamed it on the alcohol. Beer goggles. Adam would come to his senses. Tomorrow. And regret his actions. I probably wouldn't hear from him. Once he reconsidered this proposition more carefully. Soberly.

But Adam texted me about an hour later, interrupting my train of doubts. Thanked me for a lovely conversation. Asked if we could hang out. The two of us. I liked that he wrote back to me as soon as he got home. That he didn't wait for some arbitrary amount of time. The three day rule, for example. As if waiting three days could somehow make you appear less desperate. As if three days for no reason didn't just make you an idiot. I liked his style. It showed confidence.

I responded a few minutes later. Even though *I* had the urge to wait for an arbitrary amount of time. To disguise my desperation. And elation. Not quite three days, but a reasonable amount of time. I ended up ignoring that urge. In my swift response I offered up a few potential dates as options. For us to go out. The two of us. He had family in town so we settled on an evening two weeks later.

Adam's decision to push back our date, it worked for me. I like the chase. You see, I'm inherently suspicious of people who like me. Of people who like me too soon. Of people who like me too much. I am most definitely leery of people who like me too much *and* too soon. My version of Groucho Marx and the Friars Club. I'm not willing to trust that which comes easily. Easy come, easy go. This application of brakes worked for me. Worked very well.

It wasn't that I thought I was completely worthless. Or devoid of loveable qualities. I just thought you needed to dig deeper to see mine. More Miss Congeniality. Less contender for the crown. I had redeeming qualities. Many of them. I just needed you to probe and pry. Get to know me. Sift for those nuggets. Spend more time. All that glitters is not gold.

I was happy that Adam contacted me so quickly. Glad that he pushed back our date. Slightly bothered that he couldn't find a suitable time earlier. I'd like to have seen him sooner. Or maybe not. So much thinking about a simple date. Overthinking. But allow me this indulgence. I didn't have much experience being in this position.

As I waited for the day of our date, afflicted with equal parts of apprehension and anticipation, his image gradually became fuzzy. I couldn't picture him. The details blurring into a vague outline. With a few broad details. Blond hair. Or was it light brown? Maybe dirty blond. Glasses, I remembered. Beard. Cambridge-Somerville hipster chic. It is amazing how time erases the actual, specific details. Substitutes it with imagined or inaccurate interpretations and stand-ins. In the age of social media, there is an easy way out of this problem. Except that he had very few pictures online. Which I respected. There is nothing more obnoxious than someone with a thousand selfies, a modern-day Narcissus, dexterously capable of capturing his own image. Adam just happened to be on the other end of the spectrum. A handful of pictures. None of them recent. Or flattering. I guess I'd just have to see him in person to refresh my memory. Anticipation. Apprehension. Equal parts.

ADAM

've been working a fucking boring temp job this week and dude, today has been especially brutal. I spent most of the morning filing away boxes and boxes of financial records and just when I thought it couldn't get worse, the office manager had me switch to transcribing seminars on retirement accounts. IRA and Roth IRA, blah, blah, blah...I couldn't give a shit about any of it. My mind keeps drifting off, daydreaming about my rendezvous with Ravi tonight. Five o'clock can't get here fast enough.

I can be pretty indecisive and Ravi is too deferential to my wishes, so we went through some complicated text-message gymnastics to figure out a place to meet. I finally suggested meeting at the Eagle and he agreed. I figured we could support a queer space and it conveniently happens to be close to his place and just a few blocks from my new gig. Now that I'm here though, I'm thinking it probably wasn't the best choice. For starters, the place smells like stale beer and BO, which is ironic considering that there are barely any *bodies* in here. The Eagle at 5 PM is not the same as the Eagle at late night, it's eerily empty. The air conditioning is cranking and my shirt, a little sweaty from biking here, feels like it is fucking freezing where it clings to my back. Once my eyes adjust to the darkness, I scan the space to see if Ravi's here and to scout for an appropriate spot to park ourselves. There are a couple of old drag queens yukking it up in one corner, their laughter way too loud and obnoxious, so I move away from them, heading towards the pool table in the back, when I spot him. He is sitting on one of the stools, just outside the circle of unflattering light that surrounds the pool table like a cheap halo.

He looks up from his phone just then and on seeing me he walks over and gives me a big hug, his warmth a lovely contrast to the Arctic air. I catch a tantalizing whiff of his cologne, light but earthy, maybe eucalyptus or some wood of some sort. He looks sharp too, the simple white T-shirt, brilliant against his skin, and a pair of red shorts revealing long, muscled legs. Sweet baby J, the man should not wear long pants because those legs are too fabulous to keep 'em covered. We head to the bar where the cranky bartender shakes himself out of a bored stupor to ask us what we want. We both get beers, a safe choice here, and head back to the stools by the pool table. Unlike the room, the beers are not very cold and taste like lukewarm piss. Blargh.

I was afraid that this would be a little awkward, at least initially. Dude, I mean I've met the guy once. He was working and I wasn't exactly sober that one time. But on a scale of tedious to ten, this isn't even remotely close to the bad end of the scale. I'm actually surprised by how effortless talking to him feels. Of course, it's easy to get caught up in the moment and feel like two giddy teenagers out on a date, each determined to put their shiniest, brightest foot forward, but it also feels real. I love that he can talk knowledgeably about Colombian politics but confess sheepishly that he knows next to nothing about music, any kind of music. I appreciate the eclectic nature of our free-flowing conversation and his candor.

There's one piece of information that sticks out to me and it came pretty early on in our conversation, while we were still on our first drink. Somehow the topic of age came up. He asked me how old I was and I told him, twenty-eight. He luckily didn't do the whole guess-how-old-I-am shtick, and volunteered his age readily, but his answer floored me. The cabrón is forty years old! I would have guessed a little older than I am but not *that* old. Mamma mia, he certainly had me fucking fooled. I don't feel strongly about age one way or the other and I am also not looking for something serious, so this revelation doesn't bother me. Still, it was shocking.

After the first round of drinks, we decide to walk for a bit since it is a beautiful evening and it seems shameful to waste it inside a dark bar. I am more of a Camberville guy but it's hard to deny the South End's historic charm. We walk down the tree-lined streets, stopping here and there to admire the colorful window boxes decorating the curved brick facades of the row houses. (Ravi's quite the plant aficionado, pointing out this specimen or that as we walk. I, on the other hand, can't tell a pansy from a peony. Okay, I'm exaggerating but you get the picture.) It's cool to see people gathered on their stoops, drinking wine, mingling with their neighbors. There are cute dogs all over the place, more dogs than children for sure. We walk and we talk some more. We sit on a bench watching children jump in and out of the fountain in Franklin Square Park, a stone's throw away from my old office. It's a lovely summer evening and I'm glad we ditched the Eagle.

Once the sun goes down, we figure we should get a bite to eat. I was starving. Ravi chooses the restaurant this time. I've never been to it and I'm pleasantly surprised when we get there. It's a cool place, tiny, all wood paneling and record covers on walls, mismatched vinyl chairs and an Elvis lamp. The best part is that it all looks like it's been there for a while, the patina real, and the kitsch not some fake attempt at creating *character*. Extra snaps for the Sufjan Stevens tracks. I'm glad he chose this place. I was worried he'd pick some froufrou place with precious food and fancy cocktails that cost a fortune.

They all know him at this place even though he claims he doesn't come here that often. We are treated like long lost friends, even me. We get drinks. His choice, Miller High Life and a shot of tequila, neat. The shot, he sips over the course of the dinner, no lime and salt bullshit for him, nor some frat-boy initiation ritual of downing booze to get wasted. Again I'm surprised. I don't know what I expected, maybe someone who was a little more pretentious, sipping on dirty vodka martinis, pinky out, or a heavy drinker like most of the people I know in the restaurant industry. Ooh, The Smiths! I like this place even more.

He's vegetarian and I am ambiguously, flexibly vegan. (I mean I'm vegan about 90% of the time but I cheat occasionally when it comes to a sexy slice of Bessie or Babe.) There are plenty of promising options on the menu, almost too many. He chooses the cashew stir-fry, and I, the tempeh BLT. He offers me a taste of his chow and I offer him a bite of mine. We end up sharing and swapping our meals. It just felt so comfortable, ya know what I mean? The dinner is perfect, casual but not in a boring, chain-restaurant, soul-sucking way. I'm enjoying myself even more than I thought I would. It's nice every once in a while to be surprised like this. It keeps my inner cynic at bay.

At the end of the meal, our charmingly salty and incredibly hot server, Jenny, brings us shots of fernet, that disgustingly bitter liqueur that all my restaurant friends seem to love, or at least pretend to love. Jenny is doing a shot with us so I try to hide my grimace and down that vile stuff as fast as I can. It's like your mouthwash punched you in your fucking face. Fuck. Ravi pays for dinner which is very sweet. I don't fight him on it, because Jenny tells me (at Ravi's instigation, no doubt) that my money is no good there. I let it go. I figure it is the price Ravi pays for making me do a shot of fernet. Yuck! Although to be fair, he didn't order the shots.

The night is still young enough when we leave the restaurant and Ravi suggests one more stop. He picks another neighborhood joint, this one is even more vintage than the last spot and just as charming. It is cave-like, in a good way, with dark wood paneling and dim lights. There are some funky knick-knacks and other random-ass paraphernalia on the walls, on the shelves, and even on the ceiling. (How the hell did those stilettos get on the ceiling?) The bar is packed and there are plenty more folks crammed into old school booths. The patrons are young and old, there are blue hairs and the blue-haired, and all kinds and sorts of peeps mixed in. This is totes my kind of place, I think, admiring Ravi's picks.

Again, everyone knows him at this place. How often does this guy go out? I'm not sure I can keep up with him or afford his lifestyle! The bartender has his drink ready before we can even order. She hands him a High Life. He introduces me to her and I am instantly obsessed/in love with her. She's so fucking badass, running the jam-packed bar like a well-oiled machine, totally rad in her head-to-toe black outfit, tats for days. Dayum! I get a High Life as well. We look for a couple of bar seats, in vain, and end up finding a couple of vacant spots at the drink rail instead. Our knees touch as we sit, perched on bar stools, accidentally at first and then on purpose. I'm feeling pretty good, not drunk, but in a happy place.

After we finish our beers, he asks if I'd like another drink. I decline because, you know, I'm not a big drinker. Plus I have my damn bike with me and I really shouldn't have more to drink. He insists on paying again. I try but the bartender won't accept money from me. So I have no choice but to let him pay. I swear I'm going to get him back. We head out of the bar. He starts to say good night, giving me a quick peck on the cheek and a big hug.

"Chill homie," I say to him, "I want to walk you home." He argues that there's no need for that and that he's perfectly fine walking home by himself.

"I'm not trying to walk you home because I'm playing some macho, bodyguard man. I want to walk you home because I want to make out with you. Maybe on your stoop?" I tell him, "I don't need to come up to your place or stay over." I am not *that* presumptuous.

He stops protesting. We head back towards his place, me walking my bike, and us walking side by side, holding hands. There's this tension in the air as we walk towards his place, deliciously charged anticipation. This night is going splendidly well, I think, as we turn the corner on his block, only to be greeted by the sight of a construction crew tearing apart the road outside his building. We look at each other and start laughing. The prospects of a makeout session on his stoop suddenly don't look so great. He invites me up to his place instead, apologizing in advance for the state of his room.

His roommates are asleep so we take a quick little tour of the common areas, quietly. His place is nice, with lots of books and plants. He's apologetic and a little self-conscious about the state of his room. The bed's stripped and ready for fresh sheets, strewn with clean laundry that needs to be folded and put away. Hardly the pig sty I thought he was apologizing for.

I tell him it's really not a big deal and I mean it. I help him put on the new sheets. Clearly, he wasn't expecting company tonight and I feel slightly guilty that I may have pressured him into inviting me over. It doesn't matter though because he pushes the clean clothes into the empty hamper, turns off the lights, and lights a candle. We make out for an hour, more or less. Yes, you got that right sugar plum, an hour. He's a good kisser, passionate and ferocious, voracious. I am happy to go further and faster than the kissing, but I want to respect his boundaries and wishes. I don't push him when he stops.

RAVI

Adam gets to the Eagle, a little sweaty from his bike ride, a little out of breath. And my first thought is that he's better looking than I remembered. More handsome than the blurry outline from my memory. It's an auspicious start. A good omen, if you believe in those things. Given my history of self-doubt and -deprecation, you would expect first dates to be treacherous territory for me. Surprisingly, that isn't the case. I can talk to just about anyone. I've got the gift of gab. I also have a wide range of interests and am curious by nature. First dates are easy. Getting one is hard, the actual date not so much. Easy, breezy, Cover-Girl beautiful. On the surface. With Adam, too, the conversation is easy, entertaining, engaging. And it's not just because of *my* conversational skills. He's charming. Smart. Interesting. Considerate. And more. The conversation is flirty and fun. It's fluid. On the surface.

Underneath the surface, complex calibrations. And recalibrations. I've gone for so long thinking and believing there was something about me that wasn't attractive. Now here's a person who finds me attractive. Attractive enough to ask me out. Attractive enough for one date. At least. That requires a modification of internalized assumptions. Not a full scale reassessment. Not yet. A temporary reprieve. For a trial period only. Not valid with other offers or discounts.

The problems of self-doubt. Of low self-esteem. These are not new. They didn't just show up one day. They are the sum of a lifetime's worth of subtle and not so subtle messaging. Internal and external. Intentional and unintentional. A growing and thriving organism within. Symbiotically parasitic by nature. It feeds on doubts and insecurities. Reinforcing them in return. I may temporarily be forced to rethink my lack of attractiveness. Based on Adam's interest. But it's a lot easier for me to believe that that is an aberration. That he is an aberration. I'm still half convinced he's made a mistake. That he'll come to his senses. Anytime now. And run for the hills.

Time is of essence then. I have been given a chance to prove that I am worthy. Of the one date. Of a second one. And maybe more. A chance to prove that I have redeeming qualities. Undetectable at a cursory glance. Inner beauty. Invisible to the naked eye. The burden of proof lies solely on me. He is perfect and has nothing to apologize for. Nothing to compensate for. It's akin to looking in one of those funhouse mirrors. It magnifies all my shortcomings. Makes his disappear. If, however, I can convince him that I am worthy of his time and attention, in spite of my numerous flaws, then I have a chance here. A slight chance.

Calibration. Recalibration. No detail is too frivolous, no effort too great. The choice of the restaurant for our first date, for instance. Something with character. Not too fancy. Or expensive, in case he insists on splitting the check. He is a social worker after all and currently unemployed. Some place comfortable. Somewhere with friendly faces. Familiar faces. As evidence of my popularity and to project an image of a man about town. But not too many friendly faces. Wouldn't want the date constantly interrupted. Or the subject of gossip.

Calibration. And recalibration. On the one hand an attempt at highlighting some of my more desirable qualities. The ones that aren't apparent readily. To make up for all my obviously disqualifying flaws. On the other hand, I make little offerings. One at a time. Of unflattering information. Information that doesn't paint me in the best light. A little test. To see if he will run away. A controlled detonation. To check his tolerance for my numerous shortcomings. A white flag. Surrendering the ammunition before he discovers it himself. Like the class clown who laughs at himself before all the other kids can.

It is obvious Adam is younger than I am. Not obvious how much younger. But younger nonetheless. I have the choice to shy away from the topic of age. To demur if it came up. To distract. Instead I bring it up myself. Early on. A little offering, conceded readily and willingly. If the age gap is going to be an issue, I'd rather know now. Before I let him in any further. Before I get my hopes up. I'm prepared to lose him but hoping he'll stay. He stays. Doesn't seem bothered by it. A controlled detonation. I breathe a sigh of relief.

Coming from a position of deficit. Or perceived deficit. I have many protective barriers in place. Each one designed to insulate me from a cruel world. Devised to ward off the hurt. To protect the vulnerable core. The fragile interior. To make living possible. With every piece of unflattering information offered. And received without an adverse reaction. Comes the gradual and incremental, very slow, dismantling of the barriers. For making me feel attractive, I will lower one barrier. For not running away when you found out I was twelve years older, a couple more. The ultimate goal is to be seen. As I am. For who I am. Warts and all. And still be loved. But that's about a million protective layers and just as many years away.

And yet the date is fun. Successful. Despite all the thinking. And overthinking. Calibration. And recalibration. Maybe it is successful because of it. Not in spite of it. There's no way to tell. Nor any way to plan it all perfectly. You know what they say about best-laid plans.

After the last round of drinks, I think I'm saying good night. A dignified departure. Calling it quits while I am ahead. Before we venture into the awkward your-place-or-mine conundrum. Or the way more awkward one-of-us-wants-more, the-other-doesn't predicament. Adam has other ideas though. His methods, suave. His arguments, persuasive. Hard to resist. We end up back at my place. For a glorious, make-out session. Kissing and cuddling. Exploring. Kissing some more.

His lips are pink. Like the inside of a strawberry. Tender like a peach at peak perfection. And just as juicy. The beard tickles, the texture providing an interesting contrast to the softness of the lips. I try to sneak in a peek at his face every so often. Memorizing the curves. Marveling the contours. Up the cheekbone. Across the brow, puckered with pleasure and crunched in concentration. Lashes that won't quit. Eyes shut tight, faint tremors underneath the lidded surface. Slide down the perfect nose. Back to the strawberry lips. Those lips.

A feast fit for a king. After a famine, no less. I've wanted this for so long. And then gave up on it. Convinced I didn't need it. (Mostly because it wasn't happening.) But this taste of physical intimacy. The human touch. Oh my god. I was deluding myself into thinking I was fine without it. The pleasure of it. My hunger for it. It's overwhelming. Earth to Ravi!

My hands wander. Feeling the soft smoothness of his skin. The fine hair on his muscled arms. The ridges and valleys. Crook of the elbow. Veins on his forearms. Engorged. Disappearing into slightly calloused palms. Tricep. Bicep. Peaks and valleys. A little treasure trail where his shirt has come undone. His excitement.

Readily evident. Barely concealed or constrained by the remaining clothes. I go back up. Tracing the outlines of his abs. Skip counting the ribs. Nibbling on the neck. Back to those strawberry lips.

Where our bare skins converge, his feels smooth. Like the surface of a placid pond. Mine covered in goosebumps. A braille map of my body's roiling reactions. Where our bare skins connect, a million little exchanges. Between our individual cells. At every point of connection, a reaction. The byproducts of the reactions aggregate. Grouping themselves by affinity as they flood my brain. Lust. Anxiety. Longing. Desire. Fear.

I leave the scene. Floating out of my body. Watching the intricate origami of our entwined bodies. As if I'm not there. For a brief moment. Until his kisses wake me from my trance. Make me return to reality. To those strawberry lips. I submerge myself in a vortex of fervent kisses. My fingertips tracing the contours of his beautiful face. Touching his taut body. Mesmerized. Spellbound. Yes, heaven is a place on earth. I don't want it to stop. I want to lose myself in the ecstasy of the moment. Forever and ever. But I have my reasons. For stopping when I do.

ADAM

"Ravi?" I call out into the dim room. He's not there. I flail about, pat the bed, looking for him but there's no sign of him. I'm still mostly asleep and I don't want to open my eyes. Where did he go? I didn't even hear him leave the bed this morning. Then I think I can't believe it's been two months since we met. Has it been that long? I'm amazed how quickly the summer is flying by and away. Wait a minute, is that bacon I smell? Mmm bacon. Where's the smell coming from? I squint, trying to figure out the origins of the smell without having to open my eyes completely. This is just how my brain is in the morning, scrambled, like the eggs. Ooh, eggs!

When I open my eyes, I see Ravi holding a tray, a shit-eating grin on his face. Ravi, man! Kid's the real slim shady! He has been planning all kinds of shit for my birthday, in total stealth mode too, with no hints as to what he is planning. I prop myself up, wiping the sleep from my eyes, to see what kind of trouble he's been brewing. That is a giant tray loaded with fresh flowers and all kinds of morning delights. Breakfast in bed, baby! Just kidding, that's just a crumb fest on your comforter. It definitely *isn't* very comfortable and it is convenient only if your lazy ass can't be bothered to make it to the table. We take the tray back to the kitchen where we can enjoy the goodies like civilized human beings.

He's gotten me three kinds of donuts, butterscotch bacon, chai spice, and a vegan miso pistachio, all of them still warm and crazy fragrant. He not only remembered that I love the donuts from this obscure little place at the farmer's market but he also remembered my favorite kind. Butterscotch bacon, in case you are wondering. I mean I *did* say I was flexibly vegan, a'ight? The stuff's like crack, I tell ya. Props to the guy for waking up at the ass crack of dawn to procure these precious beauties before they sell out. That's hella mad dedication, my friend. The breakfast of champions is followed by a leisurely cuddle sesh. Homie knows how I roll.

He could've stopped there and I'd be mighty impressed because I'm already in heaven. But nosireebobberoo, he's got more secret birthday Santa shit up his sleeve. I get dressed and we hop on the T. Destination unknown, but we are heading outbound on the red line. For the love of Curious George, where is he taking me? We get off at South Station, walk past throngs of finance bros and corporate worker bees heading back from lunch, tourists enjoying the Greenway and whatnot. Walk, walk, walk, and we are heading towards the Seaport, methinks, but I hope we aren't. I usually avoid the Seaport, a soulless collection of glass towers and freaking overpriced steakhouses. The water views are nice I guess, if you're into that sort of thing. Let's see where he's taking me.

Heyo, I think I know where we are going! There's a really cool piece by an Icelandic artist at the ICA that I've been meaning to check out. I'm not much of a museum guy but this musical piece is supposed to be the bomb. I must've mentioned this to Ravi because here we are at the ICA.

The guy at the ticket counter asks for an email address and get this, Ravi gives him a Hotmail address. Shut the front door! Who even uses Hotmail anymore? I burst out laughing because what's next? Myspace? A land line? But mi viejito assures me it's not so bad. He uses the Hotmail account for all the spam-type stuff. Yeah right, good thing he's cute, my vintage dinosaur.

Anyway, I was right. We are going to see the immersive piece, *The Visitors*, at the ICA. It is pretty rad. All these dudes, all in different rooms in an old, rambling house, play the same musical piece, while the viewer gets to witness the sum of all the parts coming together. Very cool, man, very cool. We poke around some more around the other exhibits before he leads me to the little dock outside the museum.

From the dock we get on a little passenger ferry with a dozen other folks and head out into the harbor. The harbor is glorious on this summer day, the water all dazzling and the sky all sparkly, not a cloud in sight, a full-on Baskin Robbins style 31 shades of blue as far as the eye can see. The cool breezes offer a wonderful break from the heat and hubbub of the city. We pass sailboats and bigger boats and shit, I feel like I'm budget Bezos here, chilling and taking a leisurely cruise on a Tuesday while the hoi polloi toil for a living. *Lifestyles of the Rich and Famous*, here I come. (Mama had a mad crush on Robin Leach, I think.) Our destination is East Boston aka Eastie, where the ICA has another building. We don't have to do more museum stuff, Ravi explains, much to my relief. He just wanted to get to Eastie the scenic way. And scenic it is, the ferry ride and Eastie both offer some of the best views of the Boston skyline, a modern-day skyscraper Stonehenge, with its glass, brick, and concrete silhouettes in the sun. I've lived in Boston for more than a decade and I'm kicking myself for not having done this before.

Once we get off the ferry in Eastie, Ravi plots an unsteady course, consulting his phone every few blocks to make sure we are heading in the right direction. He seems a little directionally challenged and we may have made a couple of wrong turns and a few loop arounds, but I gotta cut viejito some slack. I am having a wonderful time. I love Eastie but I don't get down here nearly as much as I'd like to. It's easy to forget about it because it's separated from the rest of the city by the harbor, but its relative isolation also works to its advantage. Eastie feels undiscovered, a thriving working-class neighborhood that has (mostly) managed to escape gentrification by the yuppies and guppies, and is still seemingly immune to the great American (real estate) horror story.

I personally have a soft spot for this hood because it's home to so many Colombians (as well as other immigrants from Central and South America) and I can get all sorts of Colombian treats here. I lived in Medellin for a year, traveled around other parts of the country for a bit as well. I know that's not a long time and I hate to go all Christopher Colombus conquistador crazy, claiming illegitimate ownership and all, but dude, I seriously fell in love with Colombia when I lived there. The country and its people captured my soul and seeped into my core. To this day, I'm fanatic about all things Colombian. Sometimes, I even wonder if I was Colombian in a previous life.

As it turns out, our destination is El Paisa, one of the best Colombian restaurants around these parts. My taste buds are already dancing in anticipation. One of Ravi's coworkers from Giovanni's also works here and Ravi's conspired with him to have a mini feast prepared for me. Ooh la la bandeja paisa, mondongo, sancocho… I feel a little bad for Ravi as I dig into all the deliciousness, Colombian cuisine is very carnivore-centric. His friend has made him a little plate with some arepas con queso, plantains, and fries, but it's pretty much carb on carb on carb with a sad-looking salad on the side. He doesn't seem to mind though, or he's putting on a valiantly cheerful front while I go full Miss Piggy on him.

Oh my gato! With every bite, it feels like a part of my soul has been revived and replenished, the warm fuzzies flooding my body and brain. The tastes, the textures, and the aromas trigger so many memories, taking me right back to Medellin. I am a human piñata, filled with pork and happiness and I am not complaining. What a freaking incredible gift Ravi's given me today. It's not just about the time or money or the elaborateness of the plans, I mean it's all of that but it's also about the way he thought of each gesture and gift. I can't stop fucking smiling. And every time I look up at him, Ravi's smiling too.

So much happiness and yet... there's a niggling feeling creeping around the edges of my elation. It's evident that Ravi is developing some strong feelings for me. Look, I like him. I like him a lot but I'm afraid we may not be looking for the same things. I'm a hedonist at heart, meant to be alive in the era of beatniks and free love, not this bullshit one of Snapchat filters and selfie sticks. So, while passion and the physical intimacy of this thing with Ravi is giving me life, I also know in my heart that it is temporary. I don't believe in monogamy or long term relationships, both of which are heteronormative vestiges of a socially restrictive society. The queer community can and should break the mold. We don't need a slightly modified version of picket-fence powered domestic bliss. My ideal relationship would be with someone who cares even less than I do about being in a relationship. I'm happy to go along on this adventure with Ravi as long as it is fun, but for me most romantic relationships have an expiration date.

But for now I push those thoughts aside and tuck in some

more of this delicious chow. Carpe diem motherfuckers!

RAVI

He had other plans for his birthday. His actual birthday. A family celebration. In Vermont. He didn't offer too many details. I didn't ask. So we planned to celebrate his birthday earlier in the week. On a Tuesday. He was mine for the day. Actually, only until 8 PM. He had to pick up his mother that night. From the airport.

Judith Weinstein. Judy. Mama Weinstein. Or simply Mama, to Adam and his brothers. She looms large over Adam's world. Her presence is pervasive. A maternal barometer. Arbiter of right and wrong. Moral compass. Fiercely loved. Much adored. Object of unflinching loyalty. And admiration. She's quite the firecracker, Adam says. Opinionated. Very Southern. Proper. But not prim. Warm. Loving. Fiercely protective of Adam and his brothers. Mama bear. Not to be messed with.

Adam's very close to his mother. Talks to her often, almost every day. Talks about her often, always fondly. She raised Adam and his brothers as a single parent. Her marriage to Adam's father was rough. Adam's mentioned adultery. Abuse. Abandonment. He remembers the rocky stretch from his early childhood. His younger siblings were mostly spared. The parents separated when he was five. Then came the divorce. A messy affair. The father has tried to mend fences on a few occasions. Too little, too late, Adam says. He also doesn't trust the dad's motives. Or their sincerity. Nor the continuity or durability of these motives.

Mama Weinstein did such an incredible job. Raising the boys. Letting them feel neither the absence nor the need for a father figure. Adam feels that any contact with the father. Even a curiosity-fueled attempt at connecting. Reconnecting. Would be a betrayal. An insult to Mama. The dad remains a non-entity. A persona non grata. Frozen out in a no man's land between Judy Weinstein's ample love for her sons. And her sons' absolute adoration of their mother.

It's tempting to draw inferences from Adam's ruminations. About his childhood. The state of his parents' marriage. His (non-)relationship with his father. Draw connections to Adam's contemporary views on relationships. He has alluded to them once or twice. Obliquely. Casually. That relationships based on a traditional facsimile. Characterized by long term commitment. Monogamy. These are passé. It'd be easy to draw a line from his childhood experiences to his current views. But I will leave that to a better armchair analyst than myself. Or at least a more objective one.

I want to ask him. If his views on relationships are absolute. Or abstract. I want to believe it's the latter. Because I like him. I like him a lot. I don't want to spook him, though. Plus it's too soon for *that* conversation. It has barely been two months. Or so I tell myself. Because I'm afraid of what he will say. Terrified. Because I like him. I like him a lot. I would have liked to meet Mama Weinstein. It'd be a sign. That this thing with Adam is serious. It has legs. Except the possibility of our meeting was never broached. I didn't ask. Adam didn't offer. It is probably too soon. Right?

I am thinking about all this on the T ride back from Eastie. The birthday extravaganza I planned was successful. Wildly successful, if I say so myself. We go to my place. Exhausted from the heat. The hectic schedule and the hoopla. The heaps of food we've consumed. There's a little bit of time before he has to leave for the airport. He proposes a nap. I agree even though I am not a big napper. I want to prolong our time together. Hold on to him for as long as I can. His impending departure fills me with a vague sense of dread. Not just today. Always. An emptiness that is then filled with doubts. Paranoia and premonitions of a premature parting of ways. Coming soon, doom and gloom. I know this is irrational. I don't share these thoughts with him. Or the ones from earlier.

The nap. We lie down next to each other. A body-width apart. It is too hot. And I don't believe in air conditioning. The table fan whirs along. Barely making a dent in the oppressive heat. But providing the correct amount of ambient noise. Just before he falls asleep, he puts his hand on my thigh. Just above the knee. Leaves it there while he sleeps. It is so unexpected. Especially in this heat. But his hand stays there. For the entirety of the nap. His hand. On my thigh. Just above the knee.

That little gesture. It takes my breath away. His touch is magic. A soothing balm. A salve for my spirits. Microscopic molecules of magic emanate from his palm. Where it rests on my thigh. Just about the knee. They multiply. And then multiply some more. The army of multiple magical molecules marches up and down. Through the veins. Down arteries. Climbing bones. Crossing muscle and sinew. Enveloping me with calm and contentment. It may not seem like much at first glance. But it means the world to me. I don't know if he sensed my distress at his impending departure, after such a memorable day together, or if he did it without any grand plan to mollify my distress. Regardless. His touch. The hand on my thigh. Just above the knee. It is magic. I remain there. Next to him. Motionless. Lapping up the magic. While he naps, snoring ever so slightly. My heart filled with gratitude. For this simple gesture. Which turns out to be clandestine magic.

My friends ask me why I like Adam. Like him so much. I ask myself. Too. We are so different. On a wide spectrum of subjects, from Sartre to sartorial. His views on social structures, for example, make me feel impossibly old fashioned. As if I am June Cleaver. To his Hannah Horvath. We tend to agree on politics but our approaches are different. He is more plunder and pillage the prosperous and propertied. I am a pragmatic progressive. Divergent sock lengths and styles may seem shallow as a measure of standard deviation. But they are a metaphor. I bring them up as a symbol and a symptom of a generational divide. You can assign an age bracket with some degree of certainty to the wearer of each type. Adam wears crew socks. White and unapologetically athletic. Mine are the no-show kind. Tan, gray, or black, but always invisible.

There are commonalities. Too. Of course. Intersecting interests. Overlapping areas of appreciation. We are both avid runners. And beach bums. Bouldering aficionados. And book worms. Linguaphiles. And lovers of all things Latin American. Fans of philosophy and poetry. And philosopher poets. It is easy to list. Areas of common interest. On one side. Discrepancies and divergent ones on the other. Weigh one side of the list. Then the other. Use them like tea leaves to predict the future. But neither of them matter in the end. The differences dissipate. Disappear even, when you dig deep enough. To reveal the core. The value system. The way someone interacts with the world around them.

His demeanor and deportment are mature. Wise beyond his twenty-nine years. He carries himself confidently. Like someone comfortable in their own skin. How does someone so young walk through life with such enviable ease? The ease and comfort translate to authenticity. He communicates with clarity. With emotional fluency. And a complete lack of artifice. No parsing of words necessary. Nor reading between the lines. What you hear (and see) is what you get.

The clarity extends to his opinions. And there are many. Strong ones, some of them landing between rigid and stubborn. They are a youthful quirk that will probably soften with age and time. Or not. He still manages to redeem himself even when he is most opinionated. For he isn't intolerant. He has the zeal of a new convert. Without the propensity to persecute or prosecute the apostate. His confidence isn't cocky. He is inherently kind. Compassionate. Considerate. He is magnanimous with shortcomings. And failings and failures of others. I love that about him.

Twitch. Mumble. Moan. I thought he might wake up. But the slight snoring resumes. His hand doesn't move. From my leg. Where he placed it. Just above the knee. I give up on sleep. Watch his hand instead. Fingernails. Painted black. Deep pools of onyx. The fingers. Long and slender. The color of peaches and cream. A smattering of fine hair. On the back of the hand. Golden. Glittering. Rippling and dancing when the fan hits the right spot in its rotational axis.

I feel calm. Spellbound by the sleeping siren. And his magical touch. If it's true that your life flashes before your eyes. Before death. I would like this to be one of those scenes. Because I am floating in a sea of serenity. Stretching from eternity to infinity.

ADAM

t takes me a while to find the place. It's hidden behind a fake display in a fake bodega and requires a secret handshake, your left kidney, right nut, and an interpretive dance routine to be granted entry. The price of admission for yours truly may have included an extra organ because the doorguy with a non-ironic pornstache probably confused me for a panhandler. I'm meeting Ravi and his friends at this wine bar. Excuse me, it's a *natural* wine bar. No unnatural wines for us! He is already inside, nestled up on a velvet couch, waiting for me and his friends to arrive. He's always punctual, to a fault, and I'm fabulously late all the time. At least I made it here before his friends.

I need a Rosetta stone to make sense of the wine list. What in Lady Gaga's name is orange wine? The only thing I recognize on the menu are the countries where these fabulously natural wines were made. I joke with Ravi that I'm going to pick something from a place I least associated with wine-making. Should I pick the Moldovan vintage with aromas of terror and tyranny or the Azerbaijani one with notes of crushed roses and repression? He laughs gamely, and then helps me pick something I would like. A sophisticated palate and an appreciation for subtleties of wine are like syphilis, you either have it or you don't. I couldn't tell apart a pinot grigio from a pinot noir. My preferred style is cheap, boozy, and comes with a pretty label.

When I'm with Ravi and his friends, I feel like a tourist traveling in a foreign land where I am neither fluent in the language nor familiar with the local customs and traditions. It's the land of condos and mortgages, fancy dinners, craft cocktails, adulting, and privilege. I'm being a little hyperbolic, I know. He works two jobs, one as a public school teacher and the other waiting tables, and he lives with roommates who help him pay the mortgage. It's hardly Occupy Wall Street material but it's very different from how I live and from the world I seek to inhabit. My world is simpler, potlucks and bartering, hand-me-downs, traveling rough, it's not as materialistic or capitalistic. Don't get me wrong, I am enjoying myself tremendously. His friends are kind like him, generous and welcoming of me, but it's a temporary detour, an enjoyable, voyeuristic peek into an exotic world. In the long run, I can't see this being my life and world, with or without Ravi.

I'm mulling this over as I sip on my rosé, trying and failing to detect the salt-kissed apricots the menu notes promised, when his friends arrive. They are a lovely couple, sweet as can be, and I immediately bond with them over our inability to comprehend the menu and its Greek rosés and Latin whatever idiosyncrasies. He is an electrician, gregarious but considerate enough to allow everyone their fair share of speaking time and attention. She is funny, with a sense of humor drier than the driest Hungarian white on the menu. See what I did there? She works at the post office. Of course, I feel a little regretful about my earlier musings, where I painted Ravi and his world all sorts of shades of bourgeois. I have to calm down my inner-AOC sometimes but we all know it's more bark than bite, I like to exaggerate for effect.

I shouldn't be surprised because every single friend of Ravi's that I have met is invariably nice. These two are certainly not the exception. They are gracious, interesting, humble, and just all-around lovely. They take great efforts to supply me with adequate background when the chatter meanders into their shared history and stories featuring people I might not know. It's evident they adore Ravi and I do too, but it has become harder and harder to ignore signs that it is time I have a conversation with Ravi.

I love him, I do, but love comes in a variety pack and he and I aren't jonesing for the same flavor, ya know? It is still early on and perhaps I am being a presumptuous peacock prick in thinking Ravi is more into me than he actually is, or so goes my rationalization. A part of me feels a little defensive about the idea that I need to be more careful with Ravi, and that I can't just have a fun, no strings attached summer romance. Summer fling, don't mean a thing… Right? (*Grease* is another one of Mama's favorites.) I mean why is it only *my* responsibility to have the conversation? He hasn't brought it up either. Isn't it safe to assume that we *both* aren't serious if we haven't had a conversation about being exclusive or about what we are looking for?

Mira, I am tempted to put off the conversation for as long as I can. This has been the best summer ever. I haven't worked since the old program shut down, aside from a couple of weeks worth of temp jobs to supplement my severance-unemployment combo. It's the longest I've gone without gainful employment since I reached the legal age of consent. Warm weather, beach trips, hiking, camping, visiting old friends, eating good food, and then this thing with Ravi is like the fucking cherry on top of an already ridiculously extravagant summer sundae. He's an amazing person, heart in the right place, brain sharp as a tack, and fucking sexy as all hell. I call him my sexy beast, which he claims makes him blush, although it's undetectable on account of him being generously blessed with melanin. That tight little body, the hairy chest, and a smile that lights up the room, it's enough to drive me crazy every time I see him. Total boner-maker, if ya know what I mean, although that's most likely not his favorite frame of reference. He doesn't even know that he's beautiful, which blows me away, and makes him that much more special. And then there's the way he looks at me. I don't know if I have the words to describe this look but it's like I am the only person in the room, in the city, in the world, the only person that matters. You have to have ice in your veins not to succumb to that sort of attention and flattery. Every so often I even wonder if I could change my mind about relationships, if I should give it a shot with Ravi but I know that that's not for me. Deep down I know. I would hate to be the person that hurts him.

He's been fine playing along with me at my pace, never asking for more time or attention from me than what I offer, nary a murmur of disappointment or complaint yet. But I keep thinking he's putting up a brave front, afraid to let his true feelings show in order to be more agreeable and attractive to me, to hold on to me. Outwardly it is all openness and candor but I don't think I bloody know him, not in any real sense. Have you ever held a bird in your hand, tiny and fragile, scared of being harmed in some manner or fashion, the heart beating a mile a minute? That's what it feels like, sometimes with Ravi.

I want to be able to help him, to have him not be afraid, to encourage him to be himself and let me in but I'm not sure I have the time, the patience, or the willingness to do so. I did caring for a living and I'm good at it. I like doing it too but I can't do it in my personal life as well, not all the time. I want something easy and pleasure-filled in my personal life, casual, low maintenance, and completely drama-free. This is why I don't do fucking relationships.

Honestly, I went into this thing with Ravi expecting and wanting a one night stand, or a few nights of fucking and frolicking, nothing more. Somewhere along the way I was having too much fun to jump off the party train, or to warn him. Maybe it's easier to ignore the red flags because acknowledging them would potentially mean having to end things prematurely, and forgo the remainder of my debaucherously impulsive summer.

He has invited me to join him for a part or all of the week he's in P-town. I am tempted to go, at least for a part of it. I mean it's hard to turn down any opportunity to spend time on the Cape. There are few places more precious than Cape Cod in the summertime. I am, however, wary of committing to the trip because it makes what we are doing seem more serious, more relationship-like, this whole going on vacation with him and his friends. I tell him I can't go because I have other plans. His eyes betray a slight trace of disappointment but he quickly dons his usual aw-shucks eternal sunshine of the spotless mind veneer.

RAVI

The Atacama Desert is one of the driest places on the planet. It consists of vast stretches of desolately beautiful landscapes, completely inhospitable due to lack of moisture. And yet on rare occasions, rainfall produces a phenomenon locally known as desierto florido, or flowering desert. Seeds and bulbs. Dormant for years and decades. Come to life in response to this unexpected and unpredictable bounty. The desert is carpeted with spectacularly colorful flowers. Psychedelically ornate. Flamboyant. Kaleidoscopic.

These last few months with Adam, I've been floating. Intoxicated from a long-awaited, long-overdue romance. My previously black-and-white existence, presented in technicolor now. Human touch. Affection. Intimacy. Evolutionary theory posits that the purpose of a baby attaching itself to only a small number of adults is to ensure it knows who to turn to for help. Too many adults and it can get confusing. Perhaps the evolutionary benefits of attachment to a small number of individuals (or one) aren't just for infants.

Hold. Hug. Caress. Touch is transformative. My heart is a recent witness to its power. And a beneficiary of its benevolence. It is the scene of riotous revelry of unprecedented proportions. Attachment and affection nurture and nourish, in me, a sense of belonging. Someone to call mine. An anchor. Not to weigh me down. But to tether me to a place I can call home. For home signifies safety. An absence of threats.

And yet, every desierto florido must acknowledge the specter of a return of the previously perennial drought. I thought it would happen when Adam found out how old I was. Too old. When I texted him too much. Too needy. I thought it would happen when I couldn't get an erection. Like the night of our first date. Too impotent. I thought it would happen when I couldn't get an erection the next time. And the next one. And the time after that. Too damaged. A lost cause.

Dick. Penis. Johnson. It is a symbol of virility and power. Or the lack thereof. The phallus holds an extraordinary amount of space in the aggregate male psyche. A Venus flytrap for insecurities. Size. Shape. Prowess. My inability to achieve an erection singularly negates all other redeeming qualities I may possess. A limp dick is not exactly a magnet for lovers of the heterosexual or homosexual kind. My only hope is to be with someone long enough to let familiarity and comfort soothe and erase the debilitating anxiety. The sense of foreboding that arises around sex. A collection of jittery nerves that have become more fretful with age. More stubborn in their persistent presence. Recurring regularly. Persistently.

These last few months with Adam. A general sense of happiness. Contentment. And no erection. Not even close. Nor does one seem imminent. My penis is dormant. Stubbornly resistant to stimuli. To prayers and pleas. To caresses and coaxing. I'm surprised Adam hasn't abandoned ship.

"Your sexuality is much more than your dick or an erection," he has told me. On more than one occasion.

Adam's attempts to comfort me temporarily allay my fears of abandonment but they don't make me feel any more worthy of love. Or less of a lost cause. Instead I think I've landed a unicorn. Someone willing to overlook such a fundamental flaw. A saint. A unicorn saint. My happiness and contentment are a gift made possible by his magnanimousness, not by my fundamentally flawed self. I'm filled with gratitude. For having landed a unicorn. For having found a saint. A unicorn saint.

Gratitude. For every moment of intimacy. Each moment, one more than I expected. One more than I think I can have. Or deserve. If I yearn for more, I keep it to myself. Not wanting to tempt fate into revoking my good fortune due to excessive greed. My demands on Adam's time and affections, measured and purposely casual. *No big deal if you can't make it. I'm not disappointed if you don't have time. No problem. No worries. Whenever you want. When you have time.* Patience. Gratitude.

The pinnacle thus far of this tentative truce between my doubt-filled self and the weak-kneed butterfly is the spectacular night at Herring Cove. Two weeks ago. Adam had politely declined my invitation to join me and some friends for our weeklong sojourn on the Cape. He changed his mind, though. Agreed to join me. Us. For a couple of days. I was ecstatic. Euphoric. The anticipation building. Growing. Anxiously awaiting the day of his arrival. Heart, aflutter. The day of his arrival conveniently coincided with the annual beach bonfire. One night, every year, about midway through our weeklong Cape Cod vacation, my friends and I planned a bonfire on the beach.

My dearest friends. Adam. I. We set up shop at Herring Cove. Stacking wood. Spreading blankets. Lugging in coolers with beverages and food. Just in time for the sun to begin its graceful descent. Diving into the bay. Splashing everything and everyone in shades of orange, red, and copper. The beach around us emptied gradually as the daytime beachgoers exited stage left. This

bonfire on the beach was an exclusive privilege. Only a handful of permits were issued each day. Those who remained were blessed with a spectacular sunset. Breathtaking. Rothko would be pleased.

The last of the pinky hues yielded to the blues. The inky sky enveloped us. Dwarfed us. The fire created a warm circle, coloring my nearest and dearest in the most flattering light. A few feet away from its perimeter. A blue-black darkness. Punctuated with a million stars. A celestial grammarian's nightmare. Or her pièce de résistance. I'd witnessed this scene a dozen times. Slightly varied versions over years past. This was my first time sharing it with a non-platonic someone.

Adam and I. We basked in the cheerful camaraderie of friends. All of us bewitched by the magical atmosphere. All our worldly concerns seemingly erased. Adam and I, at one point we walked outside the circle of crimson and gold. Into the blue-black darkness. To marvel at the magnificence of the starlit universe. Here, the sound of gentle waves. There, muffled sounds of merriment and mirth. We kissed. Wrapped in a blanket of stars. I wasn't sure what the future held for us. But in that moment, I felt serenity. Joy. And gratitude.

CAMBRIDGE

I know what my heart is like
Since your love died:
It is like a hollow ledge
Holding a little pool
Left there by the tide,
A little tepid pool,
Drying inward from the edge.

–*Ebb*, Edna St. Vincent Millay

DAHLIAS

am in a small waiting room. Three chairs. A water cooler. Sound machine. Four doors. Identical. One leads to the restroom. The other three have nameplates on them. A harried-looking young man comes in. I can hear the music blaring from his headphones. He plops down on one of the chairs. I'm not sure of the protocol. Do I say hello? Smile? I decide to take my cue from him. Avoid eye contact. Focus on my phone. Maybe fraternizing with other patients is frowned upon.

One of the three doors with the nameplates opens. A man emerges. He is my height and dressed in a tweed coat. Plaid shirt. Corduroy pants. Mid-fifties if I had to guess.

"Hi, Ravi?" He asks.

"Yes, I'm Ravi. Hello, you must be Michael."

We shake hands. I grab my bag. He ushers me into the office.

"Did you find the office easily? The main entrance can be a little tricky."

"Yes, I know the area pretty well. I used to live in Cambridge. Just around the corner. In fact. Before I moved across the river to Boston."

The walls are darker in his office. A deep brown. With undertones of burgundy. There are two sofas. An armchair. A desk against the far wall. A framed O'Keeffe print. Spare. Soothing. A vase on the side table. Filled with half a dozen dahlias. Gorgeous.

"Have a seat wherever you'd like." I scan my options. Worry

that I might be taking his preferred seat even though he says all of them are fair game. I pick the gray sofa. With a view of the dahlias. I sit down. Fidget with the throw pillows. Trying to look poised. Nonchalant.

"Welcome, Ravi. Am I saying your name correctly?"

I nod. I'm used to my name being pronounced in a dozen different ways. At least. His pronunciation is close. Close enough to the original.

"I have some paperwork for you to fill out. All standard forms but take as long as you need to read them. When you are done, sign on the dotted line on each of the three forms and then we can get started."

I don't read them. I never read the fine print. Ever. Comes from an abundance of trust. Or a propensity towards being bored quickly. "Here you go," I handed the signed copies back.

"Great. Now that we have the formalities out of the way, let's get started. Have you been in therapy before?"

"I have. A few times. The last stint was about ten years ago."

"Tell me a little bit about what brings you here? When we spoke on the phone, you mentioned a recent breakup."

"I am here because of a recent breakup. Yes. But I also realized I should never have stopped going to therapy. There's a lot I need to work on. A lot that I should have been working on this entire time."

"It's never too late to pick up where you left off, right?" He smiles. The corners of his eyes. The forehead. His nose. All crinkle when he smiles. He smiles with his entire face. It's endearing. Puts you at ease. I nod, in agreement. "Can you tell me more about the breakup or anything else that you think is relevant?"

Here we go. Deep breath.

"I know this is going to sound ridiculous. I feel ridiculous even saying it to you. We only dated for about three months. Give or take. I feel like it was too short a 'relationship' for me to be so horribly upset about it ending." Michael picks up his notebook. I look over at the dahlias before I continue. "But I was wrecked when Adam and I broke up. I had no idea I could experience this much pain. Physical pain. Emotional pain. I lost fifteen pounds. Fifteen pounds! In one week."

The dahlias are a deep shade of pink. Saturated.

"After the breakup I couldn't breathe. I couldn't be alone. At home. Or anywhere. I was too scared of silence and my own thoughts. I feel a little better now but I'm still scared.."

"I am sorry it was so painful. I do have to ask you if you are or have been concerned about your safety at any point." Michael looks at me. His face is neutral. The eyes are kind.

"I'm not worried about my safety. Even during the worst of it, I did not consider harming myself. No. I'm not worried."

"I'm glad to hear that. For the record, I don't think it is ridiculous to feel upset about a breakup, regardless of the duration of the relationship. Do *you* feel like the pain and anguish were disproportionate?"

"I've asked myself the same question. Considered whether my reaction was overblown. Whether my grief was genuine. I liked Adam. A lot. But if it were only about the end of my relationship with Adam. If my lens were very narrow. I might be inclined to think my reaction was over the top. I might even accuse myself of being melodramatic."

I stop to collect my thoughts.

"But I don't think it was over the top. Or overwrought. Not when I consider it in the broader context. Let me try to explain what I mean. I had not dated in a long time before I met Adam. We are talking a decade. Or longer. Sure, there were a few casual hookups. Here and there. But when I say few, I do mean *very* few. Think Saudi Arabia, not Sitges. So this thing with Adam felt groundbreaking. Shocking. Amazing. Thrilling. I was happy. So very happy. I was on top of the world."

I feel a lump in my throat.

"Sorry. Let me take one step back. Just before I met Adam, I had finally made peace with the idea that dating, love, relationships, these things were not going to happen for me. I was happy then. Happier than I had been in a long time. And convinced I didn't need any of those things to make me happy." I check to see if I've lost Michael, but he seems fine.

"Of course, I met Adam as soon as I stopped looking for someone." I chuckle, involuntarily, at how clichéd that sounds.

"Anyway, I went from being happy. To meeting Adam. Who made me deliriously happy. To sinking into a deep abyss of despair when we broke up. From the Mount Everest of euphoria to the Mariana trench of misery. All within the span of a few months. Sorry for all the geographic metaphors."

"It must have been very painful, Ravi. Sounds like quite the emotional roller coaster." Michael pauses before continuing. "You mentioned that you had given up on the idea of love before you met Adam and that you were happy once you made that decision. Why did the idea of giving up on love make you happy?"

"The idea that I was happy then. And I truly believed it at the time. I know now that it was false. I was the perpetrator. The beneficiary. And the victim of this fraud. Dating Adam, however briefly, made me realize how much I craved. Enjoyed. Needed the physical and emotional intimacy. It's frightening to me that I can lie that easily. To myself. And believe it."

"Ravi, the human brain is incredible. It invents elaborate ways to cope with information and emotions that we deem unpleasant."

Michael pauses again.

"Ravi, what seems like deception or fraud can be a protective gesture. Regardless of whether it is a lie or a coping mechanism, I think it is important to explore why it is needed in the first place. The happiness, albeit temporarily, that you felt upon giving up on the idea of love and relationships tells me that the pursuit of these was challenging, perhaps. What do you think?"

"You are right. I have spent most of the past two decades chasing love. Or at the least the possibility of it. I was lonely. I *am* lonely. And I thought that meeting someone was the solution. Except I wasn't very successful. My track record is terrible. Even before Adam, I hadn't dated anyone for much longer than the three months I was with Adam. I am forty years old. That's not a record that inspires confidence. Giving up seemed like the better option when I was starting to feel like the love child of Jeffrey Dahmer and Saddam Hussein. On the dating and romance front, that is."

"That's a frightening image: the love child of Jeffrey Dahmer and Saddam Hussein," Michael laughs. A belly laugh before he continues. "And I would like to pursue this further but unfortunately, our time is up. When we spoke on the phone, I explained to you that I like to use the first session to give both of us a chance to get a sense for how we work together. *I* would like to continue working with you some more and if you agree, we can make an appointment for the next session but you don't have to answer me right this minute."

"Actually, I know I would like to work with you and I'm very excited to see what I can learn in the process."

"Great, should we say next week then?"

Treatment Notes

Week 2: Ravi is very articulate in how he describes the breakup and he has obviously put in a lot of thought into this. There are two angles that potentially warrant further exploration. He's made several references to flaws that disqualify him from having a romantic relationship. I have also observed that he can talk about his feelings very intelligently, but almost like they are happening to someone else. My hypothesis is that this cerebral processing of emotions serves as a mechanism for dissociation. That the intellectual dissection sometimes prevents him from connecting with the rest of his body, allowing him to escape truly feeling emotions that are 'bad'. As a coping mechanism this is great in times of extreme distress, but it can also disconnect him from certain emotions and from processing these in a healthy manner.

Week 4: It is very clear that there is an exceptional intelligence and thoughtfulness underlying Ravi's statements. I believe (building on the dissociation theory) that he has trained his brain to function as a buffer or a circuit breaker that prevents his emotional circuitry from being overwhelmed. The intellectual processing filters and funnels emotions by parsing them into composed or rehearsed descriptions of the emotions that are, in reality, disconnected from the underlying emotions. My assessment is that while language is used to disconnect from the pain of associated emotions, I don't get the sense that the underlying emotions are misrepresented.

Week 5: Ravi agrees with the theory of dissociation. His instinct when something is painful, is to feel it as little and as briefly as he can. "I file it away somewhere deep inside me. It does come out sooner or later, but as insomnia, anxiety, alcohol abuse, and other behaviors. I have developed an arsenal full of deflection tactics that allow me to continue doing this. Often without realizing it."

COSMOS

The daisy-like flowers in golden yellow, pink, and magenta look stunning in the white vase. Against the burgundy-brown walls. I sit down in my usual seat with a view of the flowers.

"I love these flowers."

"Thank you. I don't think most of my patients notice them but I like having fresh flowers in the office."

"How are you doing, Ravi?"

I don't hear the question. Or ignore it. Eminently enthralled by the flowers. I'm feeling distracted. All sorts of thoughts. Ideas. Half-baked. Fogging up my sleep-deprived brain.

"Are they cosmos?"

"Yes, they are. I'm very impressed that you can identify them."

We are silent. Both of us. For a few minutes.

"What are you thinking?"

"I'm struggling. To be honest. I keep thinking that I made the wrong decision. In breaking up with Adam. That is."

"The last time you were here, you said that you were the one that ended it with Adam. I was a little surprised because based on everything we've talked about, it seemed like you really liked him. What made you decide to end things with Adam?"

I sigh. Silently. I've repeated some version of this story. A million times. To friends. Coworkers. Bartenders. Strangers. Anyone who will listen. I can tell this story. Sleep-deprived. Or well-rest-ed.

"Things were going well with Adam. We had just spent an amazing few days on the Cape. After we returned, he mentioned wanting to talk. I had a sinking feeling about this conversation. You know it's trouble when someone says *we need to talk*. But I was hoping to be proven wrong. When we did talk. Eventually. He told me that he was happy with the way things were going between us. For the time being. But he didn't see himself in a long term relationship with me. Or anyone else. Ever. He also mentioned that he didn't believe in monogamy. He was worried that I expected more from him than he was willing to offer and that he didn't want to hurt me."

"And did you want more or expect something different?"

"I did. And I didn't. The monogamy thing. I am not a prude. I don't really care what anyone else does. Personally, though, I would prefer to be in a monogamous relationship. I want to be with someone because I love that person. In sickness and in health. For richer or poorer. You get the drift. I did, however, feel the need to compromise on that front. I had been having trouble having an erection the entire time I was with Adam. I thought that since I wasn't able to fulfill my part. Participate fully. In our physical relationship. Monogamy was the sacrifice I would have to make in order for Adam to have the sort of sexual experiences he wanted and deserved."

"Was that a hard call to make? I want to be clear that I don't place any value judgment on monogamy or the lack thereof. I am more interested in how you feel about it. If we took erectile dysfunction off the table, how would you feel about being in an open relationship?"

"If it wasn't for erectile dysfunction, a non-monogamous relationship would be off the table. For me. It wasn't very easy for me to tell him that I was fine with an open relationship. Fuck it. It wasn't easy at all. It was downright devastating for me to say that to him. But I didn't feel like I had the luxury. Or the right to demand otherwise."

I look at the patterns on the carpet. They dissolve.

"Sorry. Excuse my language."

"Don't worry about language. It is a non-issue. I want to talk more about ED but let's circle back to that in a bit. How did you feel about what Adam said about not wanting a long-term relationship?"

"I was upset. Very upset. I am a realist. I do not expect some long term commitment after a few months of dating. In fact, were he to have made or asked for such a commitment, I would have been skeptical. Yet, his declaration that this would never be an option for us. The absolute finality of it. That was very hard for me to hear. It felt like a little part of me died there and then. He could tell I was upset and he tried to backpedal a little. He said he cared about me. He wasn't trying to end anything. He told me he was happy to continue as we had been. Casually. Indefinitely. Until it stopped being fun for either one of us."

"I can see why you were upset about it. Very upset, as you put it. Is that why you decided to end it?"

"Yes, but I didn't end it right then. I was so afraid of it all ending. Him. Us. The idea of us. All of it. I was so distraught I agreed to continue. Casually. Indefinitely. Non-monogamously. Caved in on everything to have some more time with him. I thought that him caring about me was enough. I held on to that idea. Like a life raft."

"I can tell it's still painful for you to talk about it. Are you okay to continue?"

For some reason, I start thinking about the cosmos I bought

from the farmer's market. For Adam's birthday. If only I could rewind time. Go back to that day.

I look up to see Michael patiently waiting for my response.

"Sorry. Yes, I'm fine continuing. I stayed over at Adam's place that night. After our conversation. Trying to placate my heavy heart by holding him. Holding him so tight. The next morning, I snuck in a few extra cuddles and a kiss, before I left. I didn't know that would be the last time I was with Adam. Or I would have stayed in bed longer. Held on to him some more. Stretched it out. For as long as I could." I relive that feeling of regret. If only, I think. If only. "That day and the next. I waited for the melancholy to dissipate. For the consolation of having Adam for a little while longer to lessen the despair I felt. Or at least defer it. But the sadness was stubbornly persistent. I cried on my walk home from Adam's. Then sporadically throughout the next few days."

The cosmos are dancing.

For a second, I feel like they are mocking me.

For a second.

"I had agreed to carry on with Adam. Casually. Indefinitely. But if it hurt so much already I couldn't imagine how much more it would hurt down the line. Two weeks later. Two months. Two years later. It didn't matter how long. Chances were that I'd be in a worse position. I crafted an email describing how I felt. But I didn't send it. Left it in the purgatory that is my Drafts folder. Slept on it to make sure I wasn't making an impulsive decision." I check to see if Michael is following my convoluted retelling. He seems to be unfazed so I soldier on.

"A few more days of gloom. Abject misery. Not one sign of anything changing. I hit *send*. Explaining to Adam that if we continued casually, I would be going in with some hope, however faint, that he will feel differently about me. That with enough time, his feelings would change. To be more favorably inclined towards me. Towards us. That faint little hope would stay in me, and persist despite my best attempts to let it go. If our last conversation had caused so much tumult in me, I could only imagine that next time it'd be worse. I wrote all this in an email because I needed to be able to convey my thoughts. Without choking up. Or meandering into tangents. Or changing my mind because this was so hard. I have a copy of my email. And his response. Do you want to read it?"

"I think it's more useful for me to hear you talk about it than reading the email but I'm happy to do it if you want me to."

"No, it's okay. Just wanted to offer it in case it was useful. I carry a printed copy of the email in my backpack. I read it now and then, trying to make sense of where everything went off the rails." I look at Michael. "That's it. In a nutshell. Now you know the whole story."

"Ok, now that I have heard your explanation of why you ended things with Adam, I am curious as to why you are thinking that you may have made a mistake?"

"I had strong feelings for Adam but that is easy. When it's new. Exciting. Before the routines and rituals become stale. It had only been a couple of months. All beach trips and bonfires. Maybe as time passed the euphoria would have been tempered into something more realistic. I have such amazing memories. Of things we did. The times we spent together. And I'm upset that I gave up. I gave up because I was scared of getting hurt. But I got hurt anyway."

"I see what you mean, Ravi. But you were thinking you might get hurt even more."

"Nothing in life comes with guarantees. Right? I mean we, Adam and I, could be madly in love. Totally committed to each other. And one of us gets hit by a bus. If there are no guarantees, why was Adam's saying that 'this wouldn't be anything long term' such a deal-breaker for me? I find myself wondering why I couldn't continue enjoying what we had. For as long as I could. It is entirely possible the sheen would have worn off. In a few months. That I would be just as amenable to breaking things off as Adam."

I fall quiet. My eyes on the floor. Examining the patterns. In the Persian rug. Tick. Tick. Tick. I can hear the clock on the burgundy-brown wall.

"What made you stop just then? You were talking about the possibility that you could be as amenable to breaking things off as Adam."

"I understand the idea of the sheen wearing off. Theoretically. But the idea that *I* would lose interest in Adam. I have a hard time going there. Every time I think about it, I feel a lump in my throat." I pause. Again.

"Why do you think that might be the case?"

Lump. Throat. Knot. Chest. Breathe. Breathe.

"I don't know, Michael. I'm having a hard time imagining a time when I would not be in love with him. I know I was the one who just suggested it could happen. I get it. In theory. But I don't know why I'm having so much trouble with the idea."

"Do you think that saying it out loud would make it come true? Or that considering it would mean you were giving up hope of getting back together?"

"Maybe. Maybe a little bit of both."

The carpet is a little threadbare where legs of the sofa and those of its occupants rest. The blues and reds are slightly faded where sunlight hits.

Treatment Notes

Week 8: Ravi said he had been thinking about it for the last few weeks, since we talked about it in one of the sessions. He explained why he thinks he was resistant to the idea of him losing interest in Adam over time. He is afraid that if he acknowledges the possibility, it undermines the idea of it being a great love. And if his love affair with Adam wasn't special, then his pain and distress weren't any different from "run-of-the-mill pain." He was worried that he'd wake up one day to realize that he was acting like a hysterical teenager. We talked about the idea of acceptable and proportionate emotional responses, how there wasn't a standard scale for these and that he didn't have to justify his reaction, not to me or anyone else.

Week 10: Ravi described his problems with ED. He is able to have erections when he is masturbating but has had trouble getting and/or maintaining them in the presence of a partner. He has always had some anxiety around sex but it has gotten worse over time. ED has been a source of stigma and shame for him. He hasn't talked about it with anyone aside from his primary care doctor, at least not until he started dating Adam. I get the sense that the shame surrounding ED has caused him to feel isolated from his usual support network and compounded his anxiety around dating. He has tried pharmaceutical remedies but they haven't been particularly helpful.

Week 11: Ravi is struggling with the idea that he ended things prematurely with Adam. We discussed the pros and cons of this decision. He is considering getting back in touch with Adam but he doesn't think it is a good idea.

AMARYLLIS

"I did something a few days ago that I am not proud of. I got drunk. Quite drunk. And I called Adam."

"You had been considering it for a while so I'm not completely surprised that you attempted to contact Adam. How did it go?"

"He was nice. Very polite. Listened to me for a while, I think. Then suggested we talk some more the next day. I woke up horribly hungover. I had almost forgotten the conversation. Then I remembered the call. I was mortified because I called him. Drunk. Mortified because I don't really remember exactly what I said to him. I remember the gist of the conversation, yes, but there are some fuzzy parts. Other parts that I don't remember at all. I hate not remembering. I hate that feeling of not knowing what I said or did. I don't like not being in control. Of myself."

"I've been meaning to talk to you about alcohol so let's circle back to that after we talk about your conversation with Adam. Have you heard from Adam since then?"

"He called to check in the next day. We spoke for a while. He's sorry that this has been such a difficult time for me. He feels pretty confused as to what I want. He thought we had agreed to date casually. Then he got my email breaking up with him. He was upset by the abruptness of things ending but he understood why I did it. Then the phone call. The drunken phone call. Months later. He wasn't sure what to make of it. We are planning to meet for a coffee. Soon."

"How do you feel about seeing him again? About reconnecting?"

"I am in two minds. He was so nice to me. From what I remember of the drunk phone call. And then again when he checked in on me the next day. It made me miss him. Even more. There is a part of me that was encouraged by his reaction. A part that can't help wondering. If he still cares about me. If he would want to get back together. On the same terms. As I had agreed to last time."

I clasp, then unclasp my hands. I crack my knuckles.

"On the other hand, Michael, if he doesn't feel similarly I'm most likely setting up myself for another round of disappointment. I probably should tamp down my excitement. But I can't help it. I'm an optimist at heart."

"Would you have called Adam when you did, if you hadn't been drinking? Have you considered canceling or postponing your coffee plans?"

"I probably would have called him. Not when I did but at some point. And yes. I've thought about canceling. Or postponing. But I also really want to see him."

"Let's talk a little bit about alcohol. You've mentioned before that you use alcohol as a way to avoid feeling emotions, as a way to deal with loneliness, and that at times you wish you would drink less. You also mentioned today that you didn't remember portions of your conversation with Adam. Does it happen often, the not remembering part?"

"Not very often. No. It doesn't happen very often."

"Are you concerned about your drinking? Can you give me a rough idea of how often you drink and how much?"

I feel like I am with my doctor. For my annual physical. And I am tempted to minimize both the amount and the frequency. As

I normally do with my doctor. I'm silent for a moment. Focusing on the amaryllis blooms.

"I don't want to answer the question. But I am glad you are asking me this. My instinct is to understate the amount. Fudge the frequency of my alcohol consumption." I hesitate. "I'm a gay man. Working in the restaurant industry. That's double jeopardy. Both are prone to and notorious for their excesses. I will, however, try to answer your question honestly. I drink almost every day. Usually a few beers and a shot. Or a couple of glasses of wine. Sometimes more. Much more."

"Let's start with medical guidelines, an adult male can have two units of alcohol per day. Four or more is considered binge drinking. I certainly understand that 'normal' is relative for many people, and that heavy drinking is especially prevalent in the LGBTQ community and in the service industry, but that's why I wanted to use the guidelines as a reference point. I don't want to nag you or make you feel the need to hide anything from me. Use the guidelines as a reference and if this is something you want to monitor periodically, I'm happy to do so."

"It is something that I want to keep an eye on but there are few things that make me feel a little better about my drinking. I do not drink at home. Or alone. Never. For me it's completely a social thing. Being out and around people makes me feel less lonely. I like the camaraderie and the sense of community. Especially these days when being alone just reminds me of Adam. Sometimes the sadness feels overpowering and I'm afraid to be alone."

"What do you think would happen if you were alone and felt that sadness?"

I'm not sure I want to know what would happen. Michael is patient while I search for an answer. Every possibility feels dark.

Ominous.

"I'm afraid that if I feel all the sorrow and grief trapped in me, I'd lose control. Like I was sinking in emotional quicksand and incapable of escaping. Flailing and failing. There'd be no coming back."

"That's a powerful image. I have noticed that today you've twice described instances where the lack of control has been an issue for you. In the case of the phone call to Adam, you weren't proud of it. Here it's something that you fear. Do you see the parallels?"

I think about this before I reply.

"I do."

The reds and pinks in the amaryllis match the colors in the rug.

"What do you imagine would happen if you lost control? Let's take the example of the phone call to Adam. I believe your exact words were that you hated not knowing what you might have said or done. What do you think you could have said or done that night that you would regret?"

The flowers have become an abstract blur. Because I've been staring at them for so long.

"I don't know..." I'm at a loss for words. I sigh. I exhale. Audibly. "Maybe I would confess that I was in love with him. Maybe I would beg him to take me back."

"Is that the worst thing you can imagine saying or doing?"

"It may not seem like a big thing. To you. But it takes a lot of courage for me to be vulnerable. I don't want to be hurt. Again."

"I get it, Ravi. I am asking you these questions to make sure I understand where you are coming from. I don't want to assume anything. Let's talk about the second instance where you alluded to a loss of control. Have you been alone somewhere and felt grief as overpowering as what you described earlier?"

Tick. Tick. Tick. The silence is swallowed up by the ticking of the clock. Tears threaten to make the abstract amaryllis even more blurry. A pastel Pollock painting in the making.

"I've felt grief. Overwhelming grief. A couple of times. At least. Once when my grandfather passed away. I was very close to him. Closer than I am to either of my parents. And then more recently. With the breakup with Adam. But I wasn't alone. I made sure to have someone with me."

"We are taught that some feelings are 'good'. Others are 'bad'. We are taught to avoid feeling the *bad* feelings. We find ways, alcohol being one, to avoid feeling those feelings. The problem with that is that the bad feelings don't go away. Right?"

I nod. I get it.

"Imagine a child who is afraid of the dark. You can keep the lights on all night but the fear of darkness doesn't go away. Now if someone were to hold the child's hand and explore the darkness together, the child might learn that there isn't a monster hiding under the bed. If you embrace your feelings, good and bad, dance with them. You may find out that you are stronger than your fears led you to believe."

Treatment Notes

Week 13: Ravi mentioned that he had been thinking a lot about what we discussed in the last session. He believes that all of the things he has been doing to avoid feeling lonely, such as drinking too much and going out all the time, work for him but only temporarily. He describes being so afraid of being lonely that most times he doesn't even allow himself to think about it, let alone experience it. He wants to try facing his fear of being alone.

Week 14: Ravi reported that he met with Adam for coffee. Their interaction was easy and effortless. Ravi didn't broach the idea of getting back together. Seeing Adam again seems to make him happier and more upset at the same time.

Week 15: Adam has been trying to help Ravi. Their renewed closeness makes Ravi feel more hopeful, especially when they see each other in person or are communicating frequently, but he describes the withdrawal symptoms as being harsh. We did a little exercise to explore the idea of working with feelings instead of suppressing them. I had Ravi close his eyes and silently go to a place or time where he felt lonely. I asked him to describe what loneliness felt like. I have transcribed the relevant portion verbatim from the recording of the session because I felt that this was a significant breakthrough.
"That was very hard for me. Initially, I felt like I kept running into a wall. A physical barrier preventing me from feeling lonely, from exploring that place of loneliness. The strength of resistance, it was fierce. And surprising. But I persisted. Softly exploring the edges of it. Asking to be let in. This is going to sound bizarre but when that resistance weakened, I felt like I had entered a dark,

cavernous place, uninhabited for decades. Think abandoned stone castle. Moss-covered walls. Cobwebs. Eerie silence. Familiar from a long time ago. Foreign now. It felt so real that I honestly can't tell you if it was an actual place I visited. Deep inside my body. Or if I am resorting to describing a physical manifestation of an abstract emotional state. One that I lack the ability to describe adequately otherwise. Either way I was able to walk through this space. I had a hand to hold. It was my own hand, guiding a younger, much younger me around this abandoned, lonely ruin. I was glad for the company. For the protection. It's not a happy place but it's not as scary as I had imagined. I hope that I can do it again. And again. Until this hostile place feels more hospitable. Or at least less sinister."

Week 16: Discussion revolved around feelings of inadequacy. Ravi initiated the conversation with a comment about his lack of success with dating and relationships. He is intelligent and thoughtful, and on a rational level understands that his sexuality and his ability to give and receive pleasure are not wholly determined by an erection or the lack thereof. But he has a difficult time believing that it's not a disqualifying factor when it comes to gay relationships. He stated that there may be a tiny segment of the community enlightened enough to look past it, people like Adam, but he is not convinced he will find such a person again. He also thinks that Adam didn't want to be with him because he wasn't a viable sexual partner.

PAPERWHITES

"How are you today, Ravi?"

"I'm fine. Thank you. Unusually for me, I'm not quite sure where to start."

"That's okay. Maybe we can continue where we left off last session? You were describing what made you feel like you were not good enough or suitable for dating someone. Is this something you started feeling recently? Because of Adam?"

Straight for the jugular. Good ol' Michael. He doesn't waste a second beating around the bush. How do I answer this?

"It's multifaceted. This feeling of inadequacy." I pause. I want to make sure I use the right words. "Not being good enough. I feel like I've experienced it in some form or the other my entire life. It just happens to shift shape. Morphs into something different every so often. The erectile dysfunction part. That's the big one right now."

"You said 'inadequacy' is something you've felt in different forms all your life. Can you give me some examples? For instance, what is your earliest memory of this feeling?"

"I have plenty of examples for you, Michael. This is something I have thought about. On and off. For a couple of decades. I even explored some of this during my last stint in therapy. You ready?"

Michael nods. Notepad and pen in hand. The recording device already in motion.

"Very early on it was a feeling of being different. Of not fitting in. I have a very distinct memory. I must have been two. Or three years old. I asked my mom to get me something called chaniya choli."

Michael looks a bit puzzled.

"It's an Indian outfit. Typically worn by girls. By women," I explain before continuing. "To her credit, my mother did get one for me. But when the time came to wear it, I refused to wear it. Even then I knew, somehow, that it wasn't okay for me to wear it. It wasn't something a boy was supposed to do." It's an old memory. Still packs a wallop. Emotionally. "I believe this was the beginning of believing I wasn't not good enough. Because I was not normal. Not like everyone else." A feeling of moroseness descends on me.

"It's surprising how quickly and insidiously social norms and mores are imprinted in our brain. Did your parents or other family members make you feel like you didn't fit in?"

I think about this question. My answer feels triggering. Deep breath, I tell myself. I count to three. I breathe again. I look at the wall behind Michael. For some reason I'm sitting on the other sofa today. Facing the O'Keeffe print. One of her vaguely vulgar looking ones. Michael is waiting for my response. Deep breath, I remind myself. I try to steady my voice.

"When I was in second grade. Some kids in my class told me I was adopted. I didn't even know what that meant. But the way they snickered and sneered. Taunting me. I knew it wasn't something good."

"Was it true?" Michael looks surprised. "How did they know?"

"It was true." This part never gets easier. "Let me start with a little bit of background, Michael. There is a very dogmatic rhythm to life in India. One gets married. At an appropriate age. Usually very young, by western standards. Then one has children. There is a lot of stigma attached to a couple's inability to produce an offspring. The brunt of this stigma is always, always borne by the woman."

I check to see Michael's reaction. His face doesn't betray any.

"My parents had difficulty conceiving. I found out all this later. Much later. My mother was subjected to much emotional abuse. By her in-laws. And as if that wasn't bad enough. There was a shadow campaign of shame. Social shaming. Whispers wherever she went. 'Banjar' is the word used to describe a child-less woman. It means barren. When the same word is used to describe land, it means an unproductive wasteland."

I stare at the rug. Look for familiar patterns. The wear and tear.

"Presumably the gossip didn't stop when my parents adopt-ed me. My classmates heard about me being adopted. From their gossiping parents. They broke the news to me before my parents could. Although I'm not sure my parents would have told me. Ever."

"Wow. The cruelty of children, whether intentional or not, rarely ceases to surprise me. I expect it, sadly, from the adults." For once, Michael is silent. "I am so sorry that you had to hear the news like this and at such a young age."

I don't look at Michael. I can bear a lot. But I need to spurn his offerings of sympathy. Of pity and kindness. Accepting them would mean acknowledging the enormity of the emotional as-sault thirty-something years ago. But still fresh, in my body and mind.

"I never talk about this. Neither do my parents."

"Can I ask you why *you* avoid the subject? Why do you think your parents avoid talking about it?"

"I think that for my parents, it brings back memories of all the abuse and ostracism they faced prior to adopting me. Acknowledging my history also seems to threaten their claim over me."

"Ravi, I don't want to interrupt you but I was struck by some of the language you used. You said that they seemed threatened. Why do you think it threatened them? You also used the word 'claim'. I'm curious what you meant by that."

I take a deep breath and think about Michael's questions.

"Maybe I haven't completely sorted my own feelings around this and focused mostly on my parents' feelings. If I had to guess… And, I'm usually much more thoughtful about what I say… I think that I was trying to say that my parents needed to believe I was theirs… I guess in an ownership sort of way… to quiet shame they felt. If they didn't believe I was theirs then all of those shameful taunts would still be true. But also, I think and this might have been after my sister's birth, they needed to prove they didn't treat me any differently from her." I pause to collect my thoughts. "She is their biological child, the miracle baby— they didn't want to appear to favor one of us more than the other. So they embargoed the topic. As if it would go away if we didn't mention it. They would be so visibly distressed if the topic ever surfaced. I quickly realized that I should avoid it. I sacrificed my curiosity about my origins. To absolve my parents of their pain."

Michael is quiet for a moment. Eyes closed.

"Sounds like you made a very big sacrifice to spare your parents. Forgive me if I sound obtuse or insensitive, I can surmise the reasons but I need to ask you why this made you feel inadequate?"

Tick. Tick. Tick. The clock sounds oppressively loud in the intervening silence.

"My biological parent. Or parents." I bite the inside of my cheek. "They gave me away, Michael. I don't know." I bite my cheek harder. I taste blood. "I was so unlovable they gave me away." I don't know if I can hold it together. "I'm sorry…" I couldn't complete the sentence.

The tears. They won't stop. I try to contain my tears. But my body heaves. Convulses from the efforts at containment. The sobs are like falling dominos. One following the other. Carrying with them grief and sorrow that is buried deep within me. When I calm down. Finally. I feel sheepish.

"I'm sorry. I know it's irrational. They could have given me up for a million reasons. Poverty. An unplanned pregnancy, conceived out of wedlock. Death. Disease. I don't know the reason why. I don't know if I ever will. But somewhere deep inside me. Resides this idea. Unshakeable. That they gave me up because I wasn't good enough."

Tick. Breath. Tick. Tick. Tick. Breath. Tick. Breath. Tick. Tick. Tick.

"You have nothing to apologize for, Ravi. Absolutely nothing. I can't imagine how painful it must have been, to carry that with you all these years. Do you need to take a break? Would you like a glass of water?"

"No, I'm okay, Michael. Thank you. I'm a little numb. Dazed. But I feel a sense of relief… Actually, do you mind if I use the restroom?"

When I return, I sit down on the other sofa. The gray one. I can see the paperwhites swaying ever so slightly in the draft from the heating ducts.

◆

"So, our last session was quite intense. We tapped into something that was obviously very difficult. I just want to check in and see how you are doing?"

"I walked out of here completely drained. Once the shock wore off, I felt lighter. Like I had shed a ton of weight. But also numb."

"I imagine there were some strong emotions that surfaced because of our conversation and I do think there is a lot there to explore but I want to do it at your pace. Do you want to continue where we left off?"

"I'm not sure I am ready to go back there. Not just yet. Maybe at some point in the future. Is that okay?"

"Of course. You let me know when you are ready." Michael pulls out his notebook. "What do you want to talk about?"

"Adam. My favorite topic. The object of my obsession." If only that was a joke, I think but don't say out loud. "I've been meeting up with Adam. Not a lot. But pretty regularly. We meet for coffee. Or a drink, sometimes."

"And how's that going?"

"I like seeing him. I have missed him. It feels like old times. Almost. I love that he still cares about me. But we are just friends. I hate sitting across from him. Not being able to touch him. Kiss him. The other day we got a drink. The bar was crowded. We were forced to sit very close to each other. Every time our legs touched, or his arm brushed against me, I froze. I felt like an addict. Desperate for the next fix. For a little more contact. For the contact to last a little longer."

"Have you told him about how you feel? Explained your ambivalence about breaking things off?"

"I haven't. No. He knows I had a very difficult time with the breakup. He's been very sweet. Checking in with me. Making sure I'm doing okay. It's nice to see that he still cares about me. But I haven't told him that I think about us getting back together."

"Is having a platonic friendship fine with you? Why do you think you haven't broached a topic that has been on your mind for a while now?"

"Well, Adam's been lovely and supportive but it's pretty clear that he's being there for me as a *friend*. He doesn't intend to give it another shot, us being more than friends. I care for him. A lot. If all he can offer is friendship, I'd want that. I want him in my life. The idea of losing him. Makes me physically ill."

I am silent for a while. Michael doesn't push me.

"But I am starting to think this is a bad idea."

"How so?"

"The timing isn't quite right. Not now."

I look at the paperwhites. Hoping to find some way to say what I want to say without feeling it.

"Every interaction with him, ultimately brings with it a reminder of the loss. My heart still feels broken. And I need time and distance for it to heal."

"As a therapist, I can't tell you what to do but I do think that you may be right in your assessment. From everything you've said about Adam, it's clear that he is a good person. Do you think there may be a part of him that feels guilty about hurting you and that he feels better about himself by helping you? By being there for you and checking in periodically?"

"He is a good guy. And it is entirely possible that some of this—or all of it—may be an attempt to assuage his guilt."

"I'm not saying that Adam is doing it consciously but he may not realize that the harm he is perpetuating by his continued presence is potentially greater than any assistance he may be providing. You may end up being in each other's lives for many, many years but right now it seems like you are picking at a wound before it has had a chance to heal."

"I agree with you, but I can't just break off contact. Abruptly. Once again. No. I can't. Especially after he's been so kind and gracious."

"So, what are you proposing instead?"

"I think that we need to continue being friends. For the time being. But I will taper off the texts. Gradually. The frequency of contact. Over time. And forgo in-person contact. Slowly. It'll be painful. It already is. I feel it. But I owe it to him."

"I think it's admirable that you are considering Adam's feelings, just like you have been doing with your parents, but you don't always have to do it at the expense of *your* wellbeing."

"Noted."

I changed the topic. I know Michael is right. I just don't think I can break off contact with Adam so abruptly. We talk about work and other life happenings instead. For a while.

"I see that our time is up. This is a little unorthodox but I know that you always notice and appreciate the flowers in the office. I have a few extra paperwhite bulbs you can have, if you'd like them."

"Thank you, I'd love to try my hand at growing them. I've been thinking about getting some since I saw them in your office a couple of weeks ago."

Treatment Notes

Session 20: Ravi is planning on trying online dating as a part of a multipronged plan to move on from Adam. We also discussed why this would also be an important step in gaining control over the narrative of him not being good enough to date.

Session 22: Ravi reports that his attempts at tapering off contact with Adam have been successful but that he feels a sense of guilt about purposely ignoring some of Adam's overtures or delaying his responses to them.

Session 24: Ravi had a rough week. He is feeling pretty upset about the possibility that Adam might be seeing someone else. He knows at a rational level that he and Adam are not going to get back together, but he confesses to feeling hopeful sometimes when Adam is being affectionate or attentive. We tried somatic therapy again to address and process feelings of grief. I am transcribing a part of Ravi's response verbatim because I think it is once again an important breakthrough.
"There is a sharpness and a vibrancy to grief that is still fresh. If it was a color, it would be a shade of red. Blood. Or purple. Bruises. Blood and bruises. Bruises and blood. I know from experience that the grief will fade in due course. Until it fades though, it's alive. Angry. Adamant about extracting its pound of flesh."

ORCHIDS

"So, you seem unusually quiet. What's on your mind?"

"Nothing really. But. I'm having second thoughts about signing up for online dating."

"Is it that bad?"

"Worse than you can imagine. I thought we had moved past the whole 'no fats, femmes, or Asians' bullshit. Sorry, excuse my language."

"You know you don't have to mind your language. Wow, it's that bad?"

"When I came out—became comfortable with the idea of being gay—I was excited. To live freely. To love freely. And by this point I was in the U.S. But the excitement was short-lived. I found that I didn't fit in. I didn't look like the blond-haired, blue-eyed boy next door. I wasn't like the muscle-bound hunks. Shirtless at the drop of a hat. Dancing on the dance floor at Buzz. I didn't look like the miraculously hairless Bel Ami stars. I didn't see people that looked like me. In the local gay newspaper. Or in *Out*. Or the *Advocate*. The gay black and brown men, I saw, inhabited the margins. Fetish material. So I spent the vast majority of my twenties, and quite a bit of my thirties, thinking and feeling that I was single because I looked the way I did. I feel like I'm back. In the same leaky boat."

"I am very sorry, Ravi. I am aware of racism in our community but I don't have any firsthand experience with it as a white man. What I can hope is that this feels like a safe space where you feel heard and that your experiences aren't diminished or dismissed. I hope it isn't difficult for you to talk to me about this."

"Thank you, Michael. I appreciate your candor. I feel *very* comfortable talking to you about it." A thought occurs to me. "You know how we talked about feelings of inadequacy? Of not being good enough? This is yet another example."

"I can see that. I have had many clients, especially people of color, who have described similar experiences while navigating the dating scene in Boston."

"It would be easy to blame the feelings of inadequacy on looking different. Not fitting in. In Boston. On the overwhelming whiteness of the gay scene here. It would be easy. But the seeds for self-doubt were planted long before then."

Those are some gorgeous orchids. They are practically glowing in the late afternoon light. It feels easier to focus on the flowers when we poke around sensitive spots.

"Can you elaborate? Long before coming out or before coming to the U.S.?"

"Both. It started way before I came here. Before I came out. I remember this one instance quite clearly. This was in India. Somewhere in the mid-eighties. I'm guessing the time frame based on the novelty of the shop I'm about to mention. It was a new store. Shiny. Lots of fun clothing options. I remember wanting an orange polo and being told that I was too dark to wear such a bright color. You know who said this to me? I don't remember which one now, but it was one of my parents."

Michael closes his eyes for a moment. Lips pursed. Before responding.

"I know that racism and colorism are pervasive the world

over. But I am still shocked to hear about how blatant this was, and in a country where many if not a majority of the people are not fair-skinned. Are your parents very light-skinned?"

"Light-skinned. And quite open about how that is a factor. A prominent factor. In accounting for their attractiveness." This time, even Michael looks disturbed. He makes no effort to conceal it. "You seem shocked, Michael, but that is just the tip of the iceberg. I have bleached my face. I've waxed my face. Because the fine hair on my face apparently made me look too dark. My waxed face. Temporarily hairless. Looked cleaner, I was told. I have used skin-lightening creams. I've used depilatories to rid my arms and legs of excessive hair. Granted I did all of these things willingly. I might have even asked for some of these treatments. But I was a child."

This office needs more flowers. More distractions. I look around the room to buy some time.

"I must have internalized enough messages about my appearance to have wanted to undertake these corrective actions. These drastic corrective actions."

I made the mistake. Of looking at Michael. Curious to see his reaction.

"Your reaction, Michael. The look of horror on your face. I needed to see that. I needed it. So that I can start acknowledging to myself that this wasn't normal. That it is not okay." I hesitate. My hands are shaking. I'm unsure if I want to pursue this subject but I feel like I need to do it because if I don't do it now, I don't know if I will find the courage again. I take a deep breath. "My stories feel so obviously jarring to you, Michael. But I've normalized these experiences. By making excuses for the perpetrators. Including my parents. Especially my parents. They didn't know any better, I thought. They were a reflection of the society around them, I said. I normalized my experiences. By ignoring the micro- and macro-aggressions. Pretending they weren't happening. Pretending they didn't hurt."

"The normalizing of these experiences can be an essential survival skill, Ravi. It allows you to function in a hostile environment."

"Yes, I agree that it allows you to function but it extracts such a heavy toll in return. The hurtful messages. The slurs. The attacks. The half truths. The microaggressions. The aggressions. They permeate your soul. Your psyche. Your entire being. Gaining residence within you. While simultaneously eating you from within. A classic parasite-host situation. Perhaps I have been crushed into submission by their invisible weight."

"I am so sorry, Ravi. That is a lot to carry on your shoulders."

"It's fine. I have gotten used to it. Those orchids are beautiful, by the way."

"I've noticed that you shut down or change topics any time I bring up the magnitude of something adverse you have had to deal with."

"I'm sorry. It's an old habit."

"That's okay. Why do you think you do it?"

Tick. Tick. Tick. Goes my trusty old friend, the clock.

"Every time I follow this train of thought I encounter doubt. I start to wonder if I'm being too melodramatic. Self-indulgent. Self-centered. I made it sound like my parents were monsters. They aren't." I look at the clock but no relief is in sight. "They really do love me. A lot. They tried their best. *Did* their best. For my sister and me. There are plenty of people with actually terrible childhoods. With actual problems."

"I'm glad that my reaction conveyed how horrible many of the messages you received were, as a child and otherwise. It doesn't matter if the messaging was subtle or blatant, if it was intentional or not. These messages were hurtful and you suffered harm as a result of absorbing these messages."

Michael stops to check if this is sinking in before continuing.

"Ravi, you know that it is possible for someone to be a good person, a loving person, and still perpetrate harm, right? Your parents, for example, could have nothing but good intentions in their hearts, and they can still manage to do harm. In the same way, you can love them back but you don't have to invalidate your feelings to do so. And there will always be people more and less fortunate than you. It doesn't make your feelings and your hurts more or less real."

Tick. Tick. Tick.

"I feel like I have this deep well of sorrow inside me. My heartaches and my heartbreaks. My sorrows and my sadness. They seep into this well. Periodically the well overflows because its capacity is finite and the accumulation of hurts is extensive. The crying fit. A few weeks ago. It was a breakthrough for me. I was able to be vulnerable. In front of someone. It may not seem like it but it's a high compliment, Michael. You have managed to create, even if it's briefly, a space where I feel safe. Safe enough to break down. Safe enough to fall apart."

"Isn't it amazing how long orchids last as cut flowers? These are the same ones as last week, correct?"

"Yes, they are pretty spectacular. How are you, Ravi?"

"I'm feeling a little down lately. No appetite. Insomnia…"

"Anything in particular weighing on your mind?"

"Adam. Things with Adam felt so promising. I allowed myself hope. Not the false hope of an ideal human being and lover engineered by my imagination and residing solely within its confines. This was hope sparked by an actual human. Alive and breathing. Kind. Compassionate. Beautiful. Someone who was interested in me."

"Unfortunately, reality and fantasy both come with constraints, don't they? How are things with Adam? Are you still trying to wind down the amount and frequency of contact with him?"

"I feel bad. He texts me to check in. I don't respond. At least not immediately. I wait for a day. Or two. He invites me to join him and his friends for some social event or another. I make excuses. Telling him I can't attend. I'm mourning the end of Adam and me. But I am really mourning the death of hope."

"Sounds dark. Care to explain what you mean by the death of hope?"

"I'm mourning my past, my present, and my future. I'm most likely at the halfway point of my life, at peak strength, and I am lonely. I am alone. When I look back I see a life littered with dregs of talent untapped. Potential unexplored. And unfulfilled dreams. When I look ahead I see a downward slope to old age. Diminishing vitality and physical capabilities. More loneliness." I look around the room. Breathe, I tell myself. "When I was young, I had dreams and ambitions. I believed in my talent and my potential. It's hard not to take stock of life now and see how much those dreams and ambitions have been circumscribed. By time. By reality. And by neglect."

There's that lump in my throat. Again. Breathe, I remind myself.

I feel like time is running away from me and if I don't change course, what remains of those dreams will perish. I'm afraid I'm running out of lifelines and time. I don't say this to Michael. This is too dark. Unfortunately, sadness has overpowered my natural and adopted defenses.

Michael waits patiently before saying, "Momentous happenings and consequential events, such as breakups, milestone birthdays, deaths, among others, tend to inspire introspection and self evaluation. It's natural to want to stop and take stock, as you described it. We've explored the idea of loneliness before but I'm curious to know what it means for you to *not* be lonely. What does the *opposite* of loneliness look like?"

"That's a very interesting question. Let me think about that for a minute."

The orchids are a very unusual shade of orange. With bits of yellow. And pink. Tick. Tick. Tick. The clock doesn't miss a beat. Keeping my brooding silence company.

"Michael, I don't know if this makes sense but for me, the opposite of loneliness means belonging. Feeling like I have a rightful place in this world. Not feeling like a foreigner here in the U.S., for example. It means acceptance. A queer person feeling safe regardless of their conformity to gender roles and expectations. It means loving. And being loved. There's a poem by Paul Monette that I often think of when I think about love. He says this to his dying partner. Whose side he doesn't leave until the very end.

"...my darling one last graze in the meadow
of you and please let your final dream be
a man not quite your size losing the whole
world but still here combing combing
singing your secret names till the night's gone."

I want that. Not the dying partner, but you know what I mean."

"The poem's beautiful, Ravi. I've read a couple of Paul Monette's books but I didn't know he wrote poetry. I also want to say something about loneliness. It is more prevalent than you think. It is not the exclusive province of people who are single. Some people even posit that loneliness and separation start with birth, when you leave the womb. Loneliness can be an opportunity to discover our own truth. Our genuine essence."

"I hope to get there. Someday. Right now I feel a growing impatience within myself. Because I should be over Adam by now. Because I feel like I have dragged this on for too long. But I am still waiting. For the pain to lessen. I am still hoping. To not catch my breath. When a random thought or a memory crosses my brain. I am looking forward to a night's sleep that isn't haunted by him. For the moment of waking to not be a reminder of the loss of him."

"Be kind to yourself, Ravi. Be patient with yourself. I've said this before but it bears repeating. We are conditioned to believe that certain loves and certain losses are bigger than others, and therefore more deserving of the grief they inspire. For example, a young life lost is considered more tragic than that of an older person. Someone who loses their partner of fifty years is expected to and allowed to grieve more than someone who had a shorter relationship. Yet, we know that the extent of grief not only varies from person to person but it can, even for the same person, manifest differently at different times of their life. Give yourself permission to grieve. Don't feel the need to justify its duration or intensity. It may feel very difficult right now but I think it's important that you feel what you are feeling."

Treatment Notes

Week 29: Ravi didn't show up for his appointment, which is very unusual. I left a message on his voicemail.

LILIES

"Sorry, I no-showed for our session. And for canceling last week's session too. At the last minute. I tried to explain. As best as I could. In my voicemail. But I don't know. If it made any sense."

"Don't even worry about it. I've been following the news around this terrible tragedy and I am very sorry for your loss, Ravi." Michael stops. He seems uncertain, for once.

"How are you holding up?"

"I think I am still in shock. Alternating between despair and disbelief. Agony. Anger." I don't think I have the words to express what I feel. I look at Michael. He doesn't fill in the silence. I'm glad he doesn't fill it with platitudes but I wish he'd say something. So, I don't have to explain. Mimosa pudica. That's the scientific name for the touch-me-not plant. I feel like one. There are waves of emotions. Nausea. Outrage. Panic. In response to all of these stimuli, I've drawn my leaves in. "I've shut down," is all I say.

"That's completely understandable given the events. As we talk about what happened and how you are feeling, please stop me if we are venturing into anything you'd rather not talk about just yet."

I nod.

"All of it feels so inconceivable, Michael. All of it. I can't believe we had a fucking Nazi, white supremacist, KKK rally here. I'm sorry for my language but it's all so unbelievable. This is Boston! It's Massachusetts! It's like a nightmare I can't quit. Except I am awake and it's really happening. I'm horrified. Angry. I'm hanging by a thread, my sanity is stretched so thin."

"Were you there? At the counter-protests?"

"No. I was supposed to be there. Adam had invited me to join him and his friends. I never responded to his text."

I fight back the tears. In vain. The lilies in the vase start swimming in my vision. Of course, the vase is filled with fucking lilies. I always think of funerals when I see lilies.

"I was watching the coverage of the rally. At home. It was surreal watching these vile animals parading around the streets of Boston. With impunity. No shame, no fear. It made me so angry. I turned off the tv. I went to brunch. Fucking brunch. "

The ticking of the clock feels unbearable today. Like it is hounding me to say something. Anything. Tick. Tick. Tick.

"The day after the rally, I was on the T on my way to work. Reading the *Metro*. The front page featured pictures of the rally and of the counter-protests. A small blurb mentioned the counter-protester killed by the man who drove his car into the crowds. The victim was identified as Alex Weinstein. I froze. For an instant. As I do when something reminds me of Adam. But in this case I felt relief. It wasn't him."

I get up from the gray couch. Walk to the window. It looks out at a brick wall. There's an alley. Dumpsters. Recycling bins. Seagulls scavenging for supper.

"I continued reading the paper, flipping through the pages. The blurb from the front page was covered more extensively on page 6. The deceased protester is now identified as Adam Weinstein. The words got blurry in front of my eyes. Drowning and dissolving in the tears that appeared unprompted. It couldn't be true. No, it couldn't."

I return to the sofa. But I avoid looking at Michael. I study the carpet. Instead. Trying to decipher any secret messages the patterns might reveal.

"I didn't believe it. It was just a morbid coincidence. A typo. Maybe the first page was correct. I was paralyzed with fear. Cold sweat. Trickling down my neck. Nausea. I missed my stop. So I got off at the next one. And I ran to the nearest trash can. I threw up. I found a bench. Sat down before my knees buckled in. Trying to breathe. Each breath felt painful. Like I was inhaling icicles. Sharp objects assaulting my lungs. My insides afire."

I'm back at the window. Hoping to escape. From this room. From this story. From my life. From everything.

"I looked for a more reputable source to consult. On my phone. *The Boston Globe*. Adam Weinstein. Identified as the sole victim of the lunatic's rampage. Thirteen others injured. Four of them critical. No photos. No more details on the deceased. There could be another Adam Weinstein. Had to be. It wasn't *my* Adam. It couldn't be."

I sit down on the other sofa. The one facing the O'Keeffe print.

"I texted him. My text went unanswered. I waited. Helpless. I didn't have any way to contact his friends. Or his brothers, whom I had met just once. It probably wasn't Adam. It couldn't be true. No, it couldn't. The *Globe* had messed up. Like the *Metro*. Maybe it was Alex Weinstein. Not Adam. No, not my Adam."

I contemplate walking to the window again. I don't.

"I checked Facebook. Finally. Just in case. His page was over-flowing with tributes. Testimonials. Stories from his short-lived, yet remarkable life. An online memorial brimming with sorrow, disbelief, and anger. Adam was dead. It was him. It was Adam."

I stop. What else can I say?

"I am sorry. I am so sorry, Ravi. There's nothing I can say that's going to make you feel better or explain why this happened. It is such a shame. A tragedy."

I'm angry now. Livid. I want to punch a hole. Punch someone. I want to tear the stupid flowers. Stupid lilies.

Breathe. Breathe. Breathe.

"We live in an era of tragedies. Started with his shocking election. Keeps getting worse. Children ripped away from their parents. Children! Every modicum of decency has vanished. Every racist, misogynist, hate-filled word that a person would have been too ashamed to say out loud, now they are encouraged to shout it. I've been outraged. I've marched. I've protested. I've donated money. I've shut down when it all became too much. Head in the sand. Then another tragedy happens. And another. I can't just shut down. I'm outraged all over. I march. I protest. Yet, nothing prepared me for this moment. It's personal." I look up. Michael's face is calm. He doesn't disguise his concern. The green eyes. Liquid. Filled with compassion. Waiting for me to go on. Querying me silently about my state of being. I want to talk about my anger but it frightens me. I'm worried I will unleash it on Michael. So reckless is the anger. No, I can't talk about the anger. I want to talk about fear. How I feel unsafe here. In Boston. In this country. But I don't have the words. I pivot to grief instead which seems easier to explain. I don't know. I am barely keeping it together.

"The grief comes and goes. In waves. I've been sleeping. A lot. I used to complain about him haunting me in my sleep. But I welcome it now. I dream about him in my sleep. He is happy. In my dreams. His usual vibrant self. And when I wake up, I forget for a few moments. That he's dead. I can breathe then... Until I remember." I look at the lilies again. I wish Michael had chosen different fucking flowers. "The reality of his loss washes over me, assaulting me and leaving me wrecked all over again." Michael passes me a tissue. I didn't even realize I was crying. "I thought this moment of realization was bad when it happened after the breakup. You know, waking up feeling the world was fine and it was a new day, until you remembered you had broken up and that your heart is raw from grief. Turns out that was just the dress rehearsal. For the real pain."

I walk to the window. Return.

"I reached out to his brothers. The few friends that I had met. They are all completely destroyed. Gutted. I feel guilty. For wanting to share their grief. I'm an interloper. After all."

"I don't mean to interrupt you but why do you feel like an interloper?"

"I was a breeze that swept into Adam's world. Briefly. And left. But I wasn't a significant presence in his life. At the most I might have merited a passing mention or showed up in a footnote. I broke up with him." I take another tissue. "I feel so guilty about trying to avoid contact with him before he died. I wish I had talked to him. Taken him up on his offer to meet up. I feel guilty that I wasn't there with him. At the rally. To protect him. I wish I had told him that I loved him. Because I did love him. A lot. My heart is shattered."

"Oh Ravi, I think you'll agree that there's enough grief to go around. You are not usurping anyone's grief. Feel the grief, share it with his friends and family, with your friends, and don't forget to take care of yourself as you try to recover from this senseless tragedy."

I cry silently. Wiping the tears with rapidly disintegrating tissues.

Michael leans forward. Pushes the box of tissues towards me. He waits for a while. For me to recover my composure. Presumably. I signal I'm ready. After what seems like an eternity.

"It is ironic that death releases one party from pain and suffering, from earthly concerns and worries, but for the others, the survivors, it is only the beginning of a complex process of recovery and rebuilding. Ravi, the process and timeline of coping with loss is unique to each individual. The grief will come and go. As you said in waves. It can manifest itself as anger, guilt, disbelief, fear, and as a number of other emotions. I just want you to know that I am here for you as and when you need me."

"Thank you, Michael... There is a vastness to the grief that makes it impossible to see its boundaries. Every so often I think I see the end. The border. Far away. I walk towards it, hopeful, but it turns out to be a mirage. An empty promise. Or an enclave of respite, quickly traversed, and then it's back to the boundless domain of trauma."

Breathe. Breathe. Breathe.

"I know I will reach the end, Michael."

At some point. Maybe.

But I don't say this out loud.

I'll leave behind this scorched patch of land, that is grief. I've done it before. I have survived a few of these patches of incinerated land. Barren. Inhospitable. My very own Empty Quarter. My own personal Rub' al Khali.

I also don't think I will come back to Michael.

Too many memories here.

Too much pain.

But I don't say anything before I leave.

BOSTON

Do you understand what self deprecation means when it comes from someone who already exists in the margin? It's not humility. It's humiliation.

Nanette, Hannah Gadsby

USMAN

am doing timepass with my cup of Bournvita, watching the mynahs gather in the guava tree outside the window. Arre yaar, they look like they are playing langdi, hopping from branch to branch on one leg and at the same time carrying on with their nonstop bird chitter-chatter.

The noise of market day is competing with the rickshaw horns and the roaring of the motorcycles. A loud horn scares the mynahs from the tree so now you can finally hear the koels singing their beautiful songs. The koels are shy, not bindaas like the mynahs, and they stay hidden, singing from behind a purdah of leaves.

The tap turns on and I can hear Ammi's bangles going jingle-jangle as she washes the clothes outside. She too is singing. She loves old Hindi songs, songs that are older than me but she sings them all the time, so I know each and every one of them by heart only.

I am surrounded and comforted by this collection of different-different sounds. These sounds are my friends only, diverting my mind and attention from the pin-drop silence inside me. What a bloody contrast, no?

After Ravi left that day, oh god, I put a curfew on my feelings. All feelings are banned and no funny business, boss. Non-essential activities are strictly prohibited until further notice, full stop. So I go to work and I come home to eat and sleep. I repeat my routine and then do it again. I have stopped painting and I am ignoring all my hobbies and interests. Total curfew only.

Listen yaar, I am very scared of the silence inside me but what to do only? The mental toofan that Ravi had caused almost drowned me and if I start thinking and feeling again, I am afraid all those feelings are going to come back like an angry mob at a riot. So I am the sepoy, the sepoy of silence, making sure the curfew is obeyed. If feelings try to come in and believe me they try all the time, I threaten to give them one tight slap, or rap them on the knuckles with a wooden stick like Father William, my old principal at St. Xavier's Boys' School. I can't take that tension, yaar, kasam se. It's better to stay out of the firing range of feelings by escaping them only.

As it is, escaping and ignoring issues is our national specialty, no? We Indians use masjids and mandirs to escape the miseries of our daily lives. When the gods turn their back on us, we turn to the stars only, consulting with a trusted jyotish or for the trendy types, the daily horoscope in *Navhind Times*. We go to the cinema so we can ignore our pain, poverty, and lack of power. In our movies, a hero and heroine can go from the slums of Mumbai to the snow-covered mountains in Switzerland in two seconds, that too without having to buy a ticket, no problem bhai.

We talk about everyone else's problems, all the neighborhood aunties doing gup-shup over chai and Parle G biscuits. *Have you heard about so and so's daughter, tsk tsk? You should've seen so and so's husband, such a cheatercock.* We talk about everyone else so that we can ignore our own problems, like Ammi with Abba's drinking and me with you know what only. Escaping is a very important strategy for survival in this country.

The problem is that this strategy works on a short-term basis only. The problems don't go away permanently, na? You can pray all you want but you still have to pay the rent and find food to feed all the hungry mouths in your family. You can enjoy the mountains of Switzerland and the cold air conditioning but when you leave the cinema you are going to come back to garma garam India only. Okay sure, some problems go away, like Abba, but the problem with Ravi still hasn't gone away.

Ravi is hiding in some corner of my heart, waiting for a sign of weakness to pounce on me and then parade around, all proud like the Indian cricket team when it beats the Pakistanis. I still stop breathing when I walk by the swimming pool and I see someone who looks even a little bit like him. I see his face in my dreams sometimes. His memory hangs out like a ghost in the almirah, where I have saved his note, the one with his mail ID, neatly folded and hidden under the newspaper Ammi uses to line the shelves.

Sometimes I have nightmares about the note disappearing. It gets lost because of my careless mistake or in some big flood or sometimes because Ammi decided to clean out the almirah. Then I wake up all bothered and angry and sweating like I have malaria or dengue fever!

I have thought about throwing the note in the dustbin so that I am not tempted to get in touch with Ravi.

I have thought about burning the note, like Juhi Dixit burns the love letter in *Mujhe Pyar Karo*, but without the part where she mixes the ashes in milk and drinks the milk.

I have also weighed the idea of sending him a mail but I try my level best to quickly push that stupid idea out of my brain.

"Ajeeb dastan hai yeh, kahan shuru kahan khatam
Yeh manzilein hai kaunsi, na woh samaj sake na hum…"

Ammi is singing another old song, a song about love. *How*

strange love is, with no beginning or end, the destination is unknown, and neither he nor I understand (where we are going). She must have finished washing the clothes and come inside only, because I can smell the onions and curry patta frying in the oil. And there's the whistle from the pressure cooker. Yes, she is in the kitchen only, singing as she cooks dinner.

This is a song I've been hearing since I was a young boy. I didn't even realize I was singing it with Ammi this whole time, until I came to this part.

"Mubarake tumhe ke tum kisi ke noor ho gaye
Kisi ke itne paas ho ke sabse door ho gaye
Kisi ka pyaar leke tum, naya jahan basaoge
Yeh shaam jab bhi ayegi, tum hum ko yaa aaoge"

You know how you can sing the whole song, know all the words by heart, but you have never actually thought about what the words mean only? I am thinking of the meaning of the words for the first time in my life. *Congratulations, you've become someone else's light, so close to them, you've drifted far away from everyone else. You'll take this person's love and create a new world, but I'll remember you whenever an evening like this comes.* It is the idea of Ravi finding love and happiness with someone else that breaks down the curfew.

I can't bear the thought of it only. Jealousy and sadness are like two rivers, swelling from the monsoon rains, and flooding me with feelings. When I had thought about our story, I always stopped before I could imagine any future because I just thought we would be like Laila-Majnu, meant for each other but not allowed to be together in this world. This whole idea that he can be happy with some other person, I don't know why this was so shocking for me. Oof.

I get his note, unfold it, trying to smooth out the creases and I let my fingers run over his beautiful joint handwriting. If only I could bring the writer to life, like Aladdin and his bloody magic lamp. I put the note in my wallet to bring it with me to work tomorrow. I'm going to send a mail to Ravi from the computer at the resort, unless I change my mind again between now and tomorrow.

◆

Dear Ravi,

I hope you are in good health and that life continues to bless you and your family. You may not be remembering me because we met almost two years back. Myself, Usman Khan. We met at Avanti Resort in Goa when you were on your family holiday. Or you may remember me but are angry with me because I am so tardy in my response.

I am very sorry that it has taken me so long to get in touch. You must believe me that I very much regret many of my actions.

Writing this mail is a big risk for me. My family and work do not know about me. If anyone finds out I will be in danger so please don't show this to anyone else, even if you are not happy with me. I am hopeful that you will revert to me as I would like to write a longer mail to explain my reasons.

Sincerely,
Usman Khan

RAVI

Usman's email came as a surprise. Completely out of the blue. His Catholic-school English, nostalgia-inducing. Reminding me of my childhood years spent in a Jesuit school. Learning idioms I had yet to encounter in regular conversation. *Apple of my eye*, anyone? His sentences were oddly formal. The Queen's English. A faint whiff of the Raj. Add a healthy dose of Indian flair. The end result was old-fashioned. Quaint. Yet endearing. Like vinyl records. And analog photography. But I didn't notice any of this. Not the first few times I read the brief message. Surprise. Shock. Disbelief. Those were the primary emotions. Superseding my natural, school-teacher instinct. To parse sentence structures.

The weeks following my vacation in Goa, I had checked my email fanatically. Obsessively. Compulsively. Jumped at phantom pings. Leaped at every actual ping. You've got mail! I even became intimately familiar with the contents of my spam folder. Months into this neurotic routine though, I was defeated. And deflated. My inbox was mostly filled with bills. Email solicitations. Advertisements for bigger boobs and weighted blankets. And forwards from my father.

In the end, I made peace with the idea of not hearing from Usman, but not before I scoured social media and every corner of the Web. For a way to contact him. Just in case he'd lost my information. I checked every permutation and combination of the spelling of his name. Filtered by location. Vocation. Any other detail, actual or plausible. I suffered through selfie after scenic selfie, tagged at the resort, the beach, the town. His online presence, if there was one, was harder to track than that of a mythical creature. Beyond even the reach of my robust cyber-stalking skills.

Then out of nowhere. His email. I happened to be at a bar with my friend, Sean, when I got the email. Sean was outside. Smoking. I was on my phone. As we are wont to do these days. Frequently. Repeatedly. Like opening the refrigerator door for the umpteenth time. Hoping something new and interesting has magically appeared since the last time you checked. So there I was. Double-tapping. Heart. Thumbs up. Heart. Scrolling. Up and down. Swiping. Left and right. And ping. There it was. The email. I speed-read the email. Devouring the words. Too impatient to scan for subtext and subtleties. To read between the lines. Then I read it again. And again.

"I'm going to get myself another beer. Want anything?" Sean asked, rousing me from my reverie.

"No, I'm fine. Thanks. I'll be right back though." I excused myself and stepped out into the brisk night. I just needed a moment to collect my thoughts. To read the email one more time.

When I returned, I told Sean the story. From beginning to the email. I hadn't mentioned Usman to anyone here in Boston. Didn't seem important. Especially after no contact with him. For so long.

"Wow! That's quite the story. Are you going to respond? I mean, I'm assuming you are."

"I am. Maybe not tonight. Tomorrow. I want to sleep on it."

"Makes sense. Well, cheers to you both reconnecting. It's such a cute story. Maybe you'll tell it to your grandchildren."

"Funny guy, Sean. But yes, cheers!" I raised my glass.

I walked home with a smile on my face that night. A big smile. Usman's email made me happy. So very happy. It had been a long time since I'd felt that familiar feeling I used to have. At the merest prospect. And possibility of finding someone. Excitement. Exhilaration. Elation even. And I thought of Adam. (He's never too far from my thoughts.) He would approve. I know he would have been happy for me.

I still needed to think about my response. Carefully. Usman's email had made it clear. How high the stakes were for him. I wanted to make sure I did not mislead him. Or set great expectations. But that could wait. Until tomorrow. Tonight, I planned on enjoying the glimmer of hope and happiness that his unexpected email had set in motion.

◆

Hi Usman,

Let me start by saying that I am very, very happy to hear from you. I am neither angry nor hurt by anything you've done. I understand your concerns even though I haven't lived in India for a long time.

Where I live in the U.S., I can be open about my life. I feel comfortable at work. Safe, with friends. I know it's different there, in India. (And in certain parts of the U.S. as well.) Fortunately, for me, my parents know about me. They are not happy about it. They definitely don't talk about it. But at least I don't have to hide anything from them. Or from my sister. My family also isn't very religious aside from being strictly vegetarian. We are Jain and as far as I know, there isn't a religious teaching in Jainism that explicitly prohibits homosexuality. As far as I know. On all three of these fronts, I know I am very lucky.

I have the luxury and the freedom to do certain things. Things that *are so loaded with danger and consequence for so many people, such as yourself. I had an inkling of what you were dealing with, but your email confirmed my suspicions. It also made it abundantly clear how serious your concerns are. I sincerely hope that I didn't pressure you. Or cause undue distress. It certainly wasn't my intention. Quite the opposite, actually. I will always try to keep you out of harm's way. I am really sorry if I put you, your job, or your relationships in any jeopardy.*

I promise not to share your emails with anyone else. You can be assured of my utmost discretion.

Ravi.

◆

The following day, I got another email. From Usman.

Dear Ravi,

Thank you for reverting to me. You are so kind as to forgive me even though I have let you down very badly by my cowardice and lateness.

Our night on the beach was very special for me. It was the happiest night of my life. When I think of this night and of you, my heart fills with happiness and my sadness goes away. It was too good, first class.

I feel like I must explain why I did not come to see you the second night. I wanted to see you very badly but I was also scared to death because of my family, my religion, and my job. You and I also have different status in life and I did not see how our worlds could mix. These are the reasons I did not come to see you that night and why I had not written to you up till now. I swear it broke my heart and took a lot of control and discipline only. My heart is still paining from my poor decisions.

I am hoping that you are able to forgive me if I have caused you pain or insulted you. If my fortune is good and Allah hears my prayers, we can put any misunderstanding behind us and we shall meet again by hook or by crook.

> *Sincerely yours,*
> *Usman Khan.*

◆

The guilt. The self-flagellation. It was hard to read. I couldn't imagine how tortured Usman must have felt. I fired off a response. I assured him that I did not hold anything against him. I didn't.

I was curious. However. And I asked him. As to what made him change his mind.

After I sent the email, I had second thoughts. I worried that it might be too pushy. That I was being too direct. But it was done. Nothing I could do about it. Now.

◆

Dear Ravi,

Thank you. I am so relieved that you are not upset with me. I may not deserve it but I am very happy to receive your forgiveness.

So you are asking what is it that made me change my mind and write to you after almost two years?

You see, I tried and tried but I could not forget you. I kept on thinking about you even when I tried to bury my feelings and I kept on imagining how amazing it could have been if I had not been scared. Maybe nothing will happen now and my writing to you is a hopeless task. Maybe you are thinking that that night on the beach was a mistake. Maybe you have already made a move to the next chapter of your life.

I have so many doubts and not many answers, but if I don't even ask, how will I get the answers? I do not want to get up in the morning one day when I am old, wondering what would have happened if I had acted differently. I do not want to live a life filled with sadness because I didn't have the courage to act on my feelings.

I would like to see if we can make something of this. That is my hope and prayer, inshaAllah.

Kindly revert at the earliest.

Yours sincerely,
Usman Khan

◆

The allusions to meeting again. To making it work. These felt like red flags. Not the intent behind the sentiments. But the difficulties in actualizing them. I took some time to digest the implications. To envision the possibilities. Before I responded.

◆

Dear Usman,

I hadn't forgotten about you. Or the night on the beach. I waited for you. On the second night. Then for any messages from you after I left Goa. I think we shared a special connection. You are not alone in thinking or wanting something more.

Just like you, I had and have my reservations too. My reservations aren't about religion, social status, or anything like that. Distance. That's my biggest concern. I told you I live in the U.S. In Boston. I've been here for over two decades. More than twenty years! Longer than I've lived in India. I can hardly believe it myself.

It wasn't easy moving here. I was seventeen. I didn't know anyone here. I had never been to the U.S. Neither had my parents. I made the trip alone. I knew I wanted to stay here after I graduated but that wasn't easy either. I almost didn't find a job that could get me a visa. Luckily, I did. Then it took fifteen more years to get a green card. All those years of living with uncertainty. I could have been kicked out at any time. Especially if I lost my job. Some days, some years, I thought I would never get a green card. I did get it. Luckily. But I still feel like a foreigner here. Sometimes.

Sometimes I also feel like a foreigner in India. India represents my origins. A fundamental piece of my identity. My soul. But I became an adult in the U.S. I built a life here. A life of my own choosing. Not my family's nor one dictated by their expectations. That freedom to be who I am, to do what I want. It is very important to me. I often feel like I am stuck between two worlds, in a no man's land, not feeling like I belong to either. Not completely. But If I had to choose, I would pick Boston. Without a doubt. Or hesitation.

I can't really see myself back in India. Not permanently. I visit my family once a year. During winter break or summer vacation, when I am not teaching. Sometimes twice a year. I would love to see you when I am back in India. But is a quick visit enough for you? Is something casual and most likely very slow, fine with you?

Or do you want or need something more substantial? And if that's the case, can an annual visit be sufficient enough to sustain something substantial? I don't know. I do not take this lightly, especially after hearing your concerns. I don't want to lead you on or to hurt you, so I am being honest about my circumstances and availability.

One thing I will say. Neither of us has a crystal ball to peer into the future. We cannot predict what would be. What could be. What will. What won't. But such is life, right? No guarantees. And if there are no guarantees, either way. Nor a clear path forward. How do you feel about getting to know each other?

That would be a good start. A necessary one. We can do this over

emails. We can talk over WhatsApp or message each other. Or a combi-
nation of all of the above. Maybe it isn't enough. Leads us nowhere, and
to nothing. But at least we tried.

Take your time. Think about it. Let me know what you decide when
you are ready. I really am very happy to hear from you.

◆

Ravi

I read the email. Reread it. Revised it. Read it again. Revised
it. Finally, I hit *Send*. All I could do was wait for a response. It
was a gamble. His feelings on black. Mine on red. Outside bets.
The house always wins but that day, I felt like a betting man. A
romantic at heart. Predisposed to believing I could beat the odds.
That we could beat the odds. Usman and I.

USMAN

Dear Ravi,

Thank you for your mail. When I first read it, it made me sad because I was hoping that you would have a solution for our situation, something that would allow us to be together. I guess we cannot fast-forward life to a happy ending just like that. We are not in a Shah Rukh Khan movie, no? I am young and have no experience with this love business, so my heart races ahead fast-fast before reality or common sense can crash the party only. Dil to pagal hai, dil deewana hai! You are cent percent correct, we don't even know each other well. We cannot skip the part where we have to actually get to know each other. I am looking forward to doing the needful so that we get to know more about one another and our lives.

I am jealous of your freedoms. It is very hard for me to imagine a life where I did not have to lie to Ammi and Sharmeen or my friends. I don't know what it would feel like to grow up without your guilty conscience pricking you because your thoughts, feelings, and actions are against the teachings of Allah.

These freedoms are so foreign for me, like a different planet with its own language and customs only. Life ho to aisi! What I wouldn't give to experience such a life and to learn this strange language of love. You are the first person I could admit my feelings to, which is already a huge milestone in my pretty pathetic life.

Sincerely,

Usman Khan

That was very hard to write only. It made me start thinking about my life because it is lonely most of the time. I am like an actor, you know the method acting types? I am always in full costume, living and breathing the role. Only I am not doing it because I'm earning crores of rupees or for some *Filmfare* award. If it slips my mind and I stop acting, I will be caught and I will pay a big price for being exposed as my real self. My role doesn't end in like a few hours, at the end of some weeks or months, or when a new film pushes mine out of the hit list. I must like my role and the costume it comes with because it's a lifetime achievement type role. I don't think this will come as a surprise for Ravi or at least it will remind him of an old chapter in his life, but it is my reality, now and for the future as far as I can see.

I don't want Ravi's pity or help, but if we are to know one another I do not want to lie. This dangerous saanp seedi life is my *normal*. I suppose this reality may feel very harsh and cruel to him but this is the only life I know. I have lots of practice with surviving in this world, whether it is by lying or hiding, or doing both. I have become an expert on avoiding thinking about the subject or burying and doubting my true feelings. What is not normal for me is this concept of trusting other people, confessing my true nature and feelings to other people. That is very new only for me. It is also very scary but as we are sending each other mail after mail, it is becoming easier and we've been writing a lot to each other. Ravi is patient. He is kind. He takes time to explain things when I don't get it the first time. He is always honest with me. He has told me so many things about his life, even if it isn't always good or glamorous-sounding. Slowly-slowly even I am feeling bindas with him. I am also telling him about my life and journey up till this point.

Just two days back I told him how I remembered watching Amitabh Bachchan in all these old pictures, wanting to be like him, powerful and manly, but also wanting him to hold me tight and love me. At first I had thought I was looking for the perfect father, someone kinder than my own Abba, someone who would protect me instead of hitting me. I fooled myself into believing the father figure story for many years but I told Ravi how that bahana started looking very flimsy when I had crushes on boys who were my age or a little bit older. I couldn't very well tell myself this was about finding a better father, no? Yet, I slogged on in trying to suppress my imagination and feelings of longing, and I was mostly successful only.

Ravi replied to my mail. He said how this was quite common only. He also had similar experiences but for him his first crush was his friend's brother only. He told me how this friend's brother used to teach him and his friend swimming and how Ravi enjoyed seeing the guy in his Speedo. Ravi's frankness must be rubbing off on me only. Yesterday, I sent him this email. I even shocked myself by not only remembering this story but then telling Ravi all this! I have never talked about this up till now. What is happening to me?

Dear Ravi,

I can't believe I am telling you this but we have been talking about our childhood and about how we figured out we were different. I've told you stories from my childhood and you've shared your stories also. This one is difficult. I had tried to forget about it and mostly I had managed to do it. But then I started thinking about it and I can't stop now. I am hoping it is ok that I am telling you this.

The first time something actually happened with me was when my age was thirteen complete, fourteen running. I was working at a beach shack after school. I cleaned tables, bringing the dirty dishes to the kitchen to wash and the empty beer bottles to the backside of the building to store for the raddiwala. The customers were mostly foreigners. I stayed out of their way, being very conscious about my English speaking and pronunciation and also because they looked so fancy and big like giants, even the ladies.

Luckily most of the customers paid no attention to me only. I was like the sparrows that quickly pick up the food spilled on the tables and on the floor and then fly away. Not many people noticed me only. Generally speaking, the customers talked to the waiters, only talking to me if they needed something from the kitchen or the bar and the waiters were too busy being chatterboxes.

The few customers who did try to talk to me were mostly nice. They got more friendly after they had some drinks. Some of them would ask me my name and then laugh and laugh when they couldn't say it properly. Some people talked to me because they wanted to talk to a real Indian. I don't know what they thought the waiters were but I suppose the waiters were too busy to chit-chat with the drunk customers. Sometimes the customers would talk to me out of pity, especially the ladies. I was very thin and small and I looked even younger than I was. These types of customers always tried to tell me that I should be playing or doing homework. Sometimes they gave me a little bit of money because they thought that would allow me to stop working. As if the 5 or 10 rupees would be enough and if the waiters saw it, they took the money from me anyways.

One day this older guy came in. He made it a point to talk to me every time he came in. He seemed like the nice, sensible sort, always patient with me when I was shy or stammering when answering his questions in English and I started to feel comfortable with him after 2-3 days. I enjoyed getting all the attention and feeling special. He would secretly bring me Cadbury's chocolates or give me a few rupees when no one was watching, laugh at my poor jokes, ask me about school, my family, my interests, and hobbies. It's amazing what a little attention can mean to someone who is used to living in the shadows only, always afraid of attention but also wanting it.

That week he totally made me feel comfortable around him. I thought I had found a special friend, someone who understood me and liked me. I didn't really have many friends anyways and here was this grown-up man taking me all seriously only. One day he waited until I was finished at work. He asked if we could walk back together. I was happy for the company and to spend time with my new friend. We walked down the beach instead of my normal shortcut to the road. This way was a little bit longer for me but I didn't mind. After the sun set and it started getting dark, he put his arm around my shoulder. You know how in India it is quite common for guys to hold hands or put their arms around a friend's shoulder, na? So I didn't think much and kept on telling him the story about my maths class or something. Then he started touching me, telling me how beautiful I was.

I can remember it like it happened yesterday. I was so, so scared that he had discovered my darkest secrets and that I was in danger. I tried to free myself from the guy but he kept a very firm grip on me, whispering in my ear that he wasn't going to hurt me. I was shaking like a leaf but he held me very tightly. I should have screamed or something but no sound came out when I tried. He took me into the bushes and he started kissing me, his breath was smelling like whisky and groundnuts. He was so much bigger than me and so much stronger that I gave in after some time, surrendering control and allowing him to touch me. He took my hand and made me hold his sex and pleasure him. There was more but I don't want to eat your brain with all the cheap details. The most shameful part of it for me wasn't my helplessness or weakness, it was my own physical excitement. My body had betrayed me with its show of excitement only. When the guy was done he gave me a hundred rupees.

What a bloody bastard, he thought 100 rupees was a good price for my innocence. The money only made me feel more dirty but you know what the sad thing is? I couldn't afford to throw it away because we were so poor.

I never saw him again. I have never told this story to anyone. After that incident, I have been very careful but I have not managed to completely avoid all these lafdas. Five-six times so far I have been with some random guys, all in the dark and with my heart ready to explode from fear. My night on the beach with you was a total surprise only, so innocent in comparison, and for that, I thank you very much only.

I can't believe I am sharing all of this with you. I almost deleted it but I trust you. I know you will not share my secrets with other people. I feel lighter from telling you the story although even now I feel ashamed by my actions. I'm sorry I am burdening you with all this…

I have so much more to tell you but it is time for me to make a move. My night-shift replacement will be here soon. I should log out and go home. Ammi will be waiting for me so that we can eat together.

Khuda hafiz. I will be eagerly awaiting your response.

> *Yours sincerely,*
> *Usman*

PS. I am hoping that all this is ok to share with you and if it is too much, kindly let me know so I can avoid such mistakes in the future. I don't want you to think less of me.

RAVI

sman's words haunted me. They dredged up long-forgotten memories and emotions. Fossilized fears. Trapped in the amber of my childhood. Crystalized shame. From my adolescence. Old memories. New emotions and long-dormant ones. A single tear escaped from its ocular prison. Then a few more. Encouraged by the success of their fellow fugitive. Now a full-fledged deluge as I toured the memories of my sexual awakening. A white-knuckled ride through the rapids of puberty and adolescence. Treacherous desires. Submerged shame. A complete lack of vocabulary to navigate these troubled waters. Uncharted. Unmapped. Class VI.

Homosexual. Gay. Faggot. Queer. Pansy. Poof. These words didn't exist in my lexicon. Neither did an indigenous equivalent. Not in Hindi. Not in Gujarati. My personalized terror didn't have a name in any language. As far as I could tell. Not early on. That discovery came later. Nor did I know another person who suffered from my affliction. The isolation compounded my shame. Misery, party of one.

At some point, I must have gleaned enough information. To put a name to my shame. Although I cannot now tell you where and how I discovered this information. Not exactly. You see, this was pre-Internet. There was no *I'm feeling lucky* button on the Google homepage. I suspect it was from a news program. *The World This Week*. A once a week news extravaganza. That I never missed. I think it was a segment on HIV and AIDS. I think. The anchor explained that the disease was killing homosexual men in great numbers. I remember feeling an instinctive affinity for the beleaguered community as well as a deep curiosity.

The dictionary definition was brief. Unsatisfactory. Not enough information. So, I looked up the term *homosexuality* in a medical encyclopedia, a four-volume set focusing on all things health-related. (The medical set was complimentary with the purchase of the regular encyclopedia set. My parents had picked the two-set combination as a birthday present. The perfect present for their bookworm… ahem, academically-inclined son.) The exact wording of the encyclopedia entry escapes me. But the words *abnormal* and *pathology* rise to the surface from the dark recesses of my memory. I must confess I cannot vouch for the accuracy of the timeline of this self-diagnosis. Nor the sources. Time, the trickster, plays some strange pranks on memory. And on one's perception of reality.

Regardless of the source. Or the accuracy of my memory. I believe the broad details described here are an appropriate estimation. Societal stigma and lack of visible representation, a toxic combination, had already made me prone to believing there was something wrong with me. The definition of homosexuality as a pathology confirmed my hypothesis. And conformed to the contours of my greatest fears. Armed with such a dire diagnosis. Terminal. I resorted to religion. Pray the gay away. Grand bargains with the big guy. Or gal. Or guys and gals. The cast and crew of celestial beings are exempt from crowd control measures in the polytheistic traditions of India. But I'm straying from the subject. Back to praying the gay away. No price was too high. No sacrifice, too big. The cure was invaluable.

Of course, it didn't work. The hormones were coursing

through my system. Ready to devour anything and everything in their sight. Like Mr. Pacman. Except the pickings were slim. And the feeding frenzy. If there was to be one. Must be conducted in stealth mode. Discovery would mean game over. Or worse.

For the country that produced the *Kama Sutra*, we were surprisingly shy. Prudish. Sex and sexuality, even the heterosexual kind, were taboo. Silhouettes and shadows suggested sex in movies. But even then just a hint. A wink. And a nod. Rarely, barely discussed. Behind closed doors only. Lights off, please.

There were underwear ads in magazines and newspapers. (This was the era of tighty whities.) Crotch close-ups. Faces cropped off. Modern-day versions of headless Roman torsos. Clad in white cotton briefs. There were the few shirtless fight scenes in the movies. Rare. Reserved for epics depicting historical heroes. And heroic gods. The Indian equivalent of *Ben-Hur*. The Hindi movies of my youth were not populated with six-pack sporting studs. There was the occasional Hollywood blockbuster. The brief scene with nudity from *Dances with Wolves* is still etched in my brain. Options in real life seemed even fewer. Slim pickings, really.

Yet. For every stigma. Every taboo. That formed a barrier to the quest for sex. Or even the possibility of it. There were greater and opposite forces in search of opportunities for fulfillment. My burgeoning sexuality drew upon innate genetic wisdom. And primal instincts. Both crucial to finding fertile mating grounds and suitable mates. And for learning relevant mating rituals. The mysterious ways of these potent forces led me to Marine Drive. Bombay's three-kilometer-long, C-shaped, seaside promenade.

The promenade is popular. Among locals and tourists alike. Busy all day. And most of the night. There are the walkers. The joggers. The exercise-seekers, most often seen around dawn and dusk. The sightseers. All-day long. The office workers. Crowding the vada-pav wala. During their lunch hour. Foodies and families forming amorphous queues at dinnertime. Crowding around hawkers vending a dizzying array of delicacies. Something to please every palate. Bhel puri. Paani puri. Pav bhaji. Kulfi. The food carts are festooned with multicolored strings of lights and play loud music to attract the customers. Lots of people. Everywhere. A buzzing beehive of frenetic activity.

In shockingly close proximity to this frenzy, lies a hidden world. With a thriving ecosystem of underworld creatures. If you were to clamber down the parapet. Down into the clusters of giant, concrete tetrapods that protect the promenade and the adjoining road from the Arabian Sea. You would enter a semi-private world. A habitat conducive to various and sundry activities requiring privacy. Lovers meet here. Away from prying eyes. In the shadows and relative seclusion, the city's impoverished bathed themselves. Relieve themselves. For those of the homosexual persuasion, these cleansing rituals offer a chance to see men in different stages of undress. Maybe even find a kindred soul, afflicted by the same malady, and ready for more than a furtive glance.

My solo trips to Marine Drive were terrifying. My fear-addled brain calculated impossibly high ratios. For the number of people that I knew in Bombay to the millions of inhabitants of this jam-packed city. This aunty. That cousin. The nosy neighbor. I was petrified of the probability that someone I knew would see me. Scrambling and scurrying down. Out of sight. Into the tetrapods. They might recognize me. Report me to my family. I was also terrified of the cops that paraded through the area intermittently. The ones looking for bribes were easier than the ones keen on inflicting physical harm. On anyone daring to stray from the straight and normal. I was afraid I'd get into trouble with the other inhabitants of this shadowy world. For looking too long. For my interest being too obvious. For being who I was.

I feigned nonchalance. Usually. Pretending to be a casual tourist. Looking for a better view. Of the crashing waves. Cool. Collected. But beneath the flimsy facade of calm composure, a racing heart. Hummingbird heart rate. I would try to stay away. Then abandon attempts at self-control. These trips were the sole source of stimulus. Visual, mostly. That my teenage brain craved. Compelling me to return regardless of the risks.

The fear was real. The predominant emotion. But it was laced with an intoxicating sense of excitement. The hunt for wet fabric. Clingy. Transparent. Revealing. Expectations of exposed skin. Of a towel that slips. The anticipation of spotting a more brazen bather. One who exposes a bare buttock. Better yet. Cock. Balls. Over time, I learned to spot my tribe of kindred spirits. The ones cursed with similar desires and searching for some version of sexual satisfaction. But these pleasure-seekers were few and far between.

The thrills I encountered were mostly of the voyeuristic kind. I recognize now that there was an exploitative element to my journeys. These deep dives into the titillating underbelly of desire. Mea culpa. In essence, my voyeurism was sponsored by penury. Provided by people who did not have the means to afford basic privacy. Exploitation erotica. Poverty Porn.

The line between predator and prey can be blurry though. Permeable. Pliable. My relative wealth provided me with privileges. Yet, many of those privileges were rendered null and void. Offset by my youth. Inexperience. Vulnerability (physical and emotional). And the entitlement awarded to heterosexual men, regardless of socioeconomic stature.

There was this man. Handsome. A bathing beauty. Who caught me staring. For an instant too long. He saw through my camouflage. Of feigned nonchalance. He asked me for money so that I could watch. Openly. My cover was blown. Denying my desires did not seem like a viable option. His proposition was surprising. Seemed like a promising possibility instead of the punishment I was expecting. A reasonable price too, I thought. Fair trade. I handed over the agreed-upon amount. Only to have him punch me. Sucker punch. And empty my wallet as I gasped for air. Then another punch for good measure. I doubled over in pain. Crumpled to the ground. Begging for mercy. Instead, he kicked me in the gut before he walked away. Rough trade.

I lay there for a while. Clutching myself. Praying for the pain to subside. Hoping the man didn't return in the meantime. For a second go at me. The coolness of the cement comforted me until I was able to get up. I climbed up. Over the parapet. Onto the promenade. Gingerly. And I started the long, painful walk home. I didn't have any money to take a taxi. Or the bus.

The street lights had just come on. I inspected my clothes under one. For obvious signs of the assault. Just a bit of dirt. And grime. That I tried to wipe off. I checked my arms. Legs. The parts left exposed by the T-shirt and shorts I was wearing. Some scrapes. No visible bruises. I breathed a sigh of relief. Proceeded to walk home. Slowly. I remember thinking I was so lucky. I was alive. I hadn't broken anything. As far as I could tell. Lucky. The bruises were not visible. Unless I took my shirt off. At least I wouldn't have to tell my parents. Lucky.

I felt lucky. I had avoided the sort of mob violence. Vigilante justice. That I feared. Imagined. And expected upon exposure. Lucky. The man didn't hand me over to the police. Or blackmail me. I did wonder. More than a few times. If death might not have been an easier way out of my miserably precarious existence. But it didn't even occur to me to question whether I deserved the violence. I stayed away from Marine Drive. For a while. Until desire and desperation drew me back. Again. And again.

Now that I'm thinking about it, it wasn't just straight men and cops that I should have been worried about. I was just as vulnerable to the demands of gay men. Older gay men. (Except they were all older than me. I was just thirteen when I made my first trip to the tetrapods.) They knew what they were doing. I didn't. They knew what they wanted. More than I did. They knew what they liked. I didn't. Game. Set. Match.

No wonder then that sex is so fraught with anxiety. For me. To this day.

USMAN

t has been too good being in touch with Ravi again. We talk on the phone or video call when we can, talking nonstop for hours and hours only but it takes a lot of planning due to the time difference, our busy schedules, data tariffs, privacy issues, etc. When the phone or video calls are not possible, we send SMS or mails all the time. We have so much to discuss about na. Sometimes it is about silly subjects like Suppandi and Shikari Shambu comic books or the silly paper boats we used to make in the rainy season or about food that we both love. Same pinch! Both of us love Maggi noodles. But we also talk about serious topics like politics and religion.

I am always surprised by how frank our conversations and correspondences are, there's no beating around the bush, boss. I have informed him of so many private matters about myself and my family. Some of these matters, I hadn't even been able to admit to myself, far be it for me to tell anyone else. There's something about him that makes you want to trust him only. I have full bharosa on him.

At first, I was thinking that he must have had a very easy life because he had money, an educated background, a foreign lifestyle, etc. when he was growing up and afterwards. So it has been very eye-opening listening to his stories and getting to know about his experiences in life. Obviously, poor people have more problems and a harder life but I suppose paisa alone doesn't solve all of life's issues. Ravi is so happy and jolly most of the times, cracking joke after joke and making me laugh until my stomach hurts, but sometimes I feel like there is a shadow of sadness hanging over his head.

For example, we were talking about the elections yesterday only. I wasn't sure how open I should be because you know minorities in India, specially Muslims, have been under a lot of pressure lately. There's the khullam khulla violence like the riots in Gujarat, Delhi, and UP, murders of people suspected of eating or selling beef, abuses by the army in Kashmir, and the list goes on and on only. The psychological attacks are just as dangerous as the physical ones, man. We are called outsiders, foreigners who attacked a Hindu land, thieves and looters who must be pushed back to where we came from. It's almost like centuries of our lives here, our history, our culture, our rightful place here can be conveniently covered up with a coat of saffron paint. They even bloody dropped the Taj Mahal from a government pamphlet on bloody tourism!

Unfortunately, every time we criticize the government they come after us, jailing people and journalists, calling us Pakistan-supporters, traitors, terrorists, and whatnot. We are told we are ungrateful. Our complaints are not considered real because we aren't even real Indians. Even some of my more modern Hindu friends and colleagues think we are simply playing identity politics or worse, "sowing the seeds of communal disharmony". Some of them feel like I am attacking them personally. That is why I was afraid of speaking openly about my political opinions, you see.

I need not have worried because Ravi is just as angry and upset as I am by the crashing of the secular dream and by the spreading of religious nationalism in India. I had no idea he was so interested and knowledgeable about Indian politics! He is surprising me with his amazing qualities all the time, bloody brilliant bugger!

Goa is a little bit better, more tolerant of its religious diversity but even in Goa, I can see changes happening slowly-slowly. Elections are coming and the saffron alliance is looking to make major gains in the state. The opposition parties are weak, corrupt, and completely useless only. What choice do we have? Vote for a Congress party that is hooked on a breathing machine or some regional party that is focusing on very small-small, petty shit. All damn bad choices man, what to do only. I am working with some of the student organizations from my old college, campaigning for my local MLA. She's not perfect but she's the only one capable of holding the seat for the alliance of left and secular parties.

Anyway, here I am going off again making my stories even longer. When I was telling Ravi about my electioneering work, he got a little quiet and I again felt like there was a shadow of sadness on him. I thought maybe I said something wrong or went too far in my cribbing about the Hindu parties. But he said that I was right only in being upset. He was just worried about my safety because something had happened to his very good friend due to politics. He didn't want to go into the story but he made me promise to be very careful. So sweet of him, no? I told him, mother promise I will be careful only.

I have to admit I'm afraid also. All this anti-minority propaganda is spreading like a fast fire and it is receiving a very big and enthusiastic audience across the country. It is a scary time only to be a minority in India right now. I am bloody terrified of what the future looks like and not sure if there is a place for us here anymore, whether we can survive the two-headed serpent of Hindu nationalism and religious hatred.

In some ways, the joke is on me only. The same communities that I am fighting for are also some of the biggest forces in opposing gay rights. The Catholic church and Muslim organizations have been very united in their opposition to the decriminalization of homosexuality, even going as far as joining forces with their usual enemies, the right-wing Hindu organizations. What a bloody unholy alliance of the holy ones, no?

By the way *decriminalization, gay rights, sexual orientation,* and all these damn words and ideas are Ravi's doing. He has introduced me to a whole new language basically. The guy is always dropping knowledge on me, sending me books and DVDs by post, magazine and newspaper articles, interesting forwards by mail, etc. But it is not all serious business with him all the time. A few weeks back he was teaching me about drag and drag queens which was very fun only. If I say something wrong which I am surely doing all the time, he is very patient with me. For example, he explained why he doesn't like it when people say that being gay is a choice. "If you or I had the choice or could change all this, would we be going through all this rubbish? It's not a choice, Usman!" he explained. He has a good point only.

Some of his thinking is very American and quite modern for people like me, but he has also introduced me to some local organizations. I am just now only getting used to thinking about having rights versus all this being something that is shameful and to be hidden. I am not ready to be all open or "come out", as Ravi calls it, to my family, friends, or at my work and I do not see that happening anytime soon. But it is very nice to have someone I can discuss about these subjects. I know that for myself, Ravi has changed my life only. I get up happy every day, my heart is full with songs, and I am not feeling so low or lonely nowadays.

I know that it is very soon and I also know that our situation is not perfect. The thousands of kilometers between us haven't disappeared by some miracle. We are still living very different lives only. But when you start with zero it all has to go up from there, no? I want to be there for Ravi when he is low (or happy) just like he is there for me. He is always listening to me going on and on about this and that. I don't want our relationship to be a one-way road only, you know? Luckily I don't think it is.

He has told me about feeling depressed and alone sometimes. He is very open and frank with me, not hiding or sugar-coating anything. It's nice that he is feeling comfortable opening up to me, not just about the good things but also about the bad things. And the cool thing about him is that he doesn't eat my head with non-stop cribbing or making it seem like he is the only one with problems. People who think their problems are bigger than everyone else's are the worst. Ravi is the opposite only.

RAVI

Tinder. Bumble. Match. It seems we've stopped meeting prospective partners the old-fashioned way: drunk and at a bar. Grindr. Happn. Curtn. Or spelling things fully. Correctly. Can we buy these folks a vowel? Please. But that's my pet peeve. My get-off-my-(virtual)-lawn rant. In these dog days of the digital era, analog old me imagines the sky sometimes. Filled with electronic carrier pigeons. In my mind, they look like the blue bird. From Twitter. There are millions of them. Invisible to the naked eye. Cupid's couriers. Tirelessly darting to and from. Carrying messages of love and desire. From lonely hearts. And broken hearts. Optimistic hearts and realistic ones. Messages suggesting casual congress. And more.

I tried it once. Online dating. I was newly out. Didn't know any other gay people. Didn't know how to meet them. I was way too scared to walk into a gay bar. By myself. I thought online personals could be my entree. Into the mysterious gay world. This was a long time ago. Before digital cameras. Or smartphones. Back when you had to scan a physical photo if you wanted a profile picture. If you didn't scan it right, the picture would be crammed into a corner. Suspended in a sea of null and white.

Generally speaking, I found online dating to be insipid. Lacking nuance and spontaneity. The stilted conversations. The overly scripted messages. Making yourself sound just the right kind of flirty. The perfect shade of witty. All the while trying to pare yourself and your potential partner down into easily identifiable component parts. And categories. Athletic build. Likes to read. Straight-acting. Likes long walks on the beach. At sunset. Match. Check. Check. Match.

Like a slot-machine game. Three or more reels spinning. Whirring. You're hoping to land on the correct combination of matching fruit. The matches were few and far between, though. Or partial and deceptive. He likes reading. Check. I like reading. Match. I like comic books. Dostoevsky in Russian, for him. Partial and deceptive, this matching business.

This one guy, for example, seemed perfect. Vegetarian. Check. Avid reader. Match. Liked long walks on the beach. At sunset. Was interested in languages. Loved world music. (Remember Putumayo?) Check. Match. Check. We emailed each other a lot. For months. Even though I would have preferred meeting up for a coffee or a drink. Instead of endless email exchanges. But he was in Australia. Finishing up school. He was moving to Boston. Soon. So, online correspondence would have to do for the time being. We did meet at some point. He made me a mixed tape. We had no chemistry. None. Zero. Zilch. Nada.

This was all back in the day of dinosaurs. Ancient history. But I've been thinking about it a lot. Recently. Because of Usman and our prolific correspondence. We email each other often. Text message even more frequently. Neither of us is a big fan of old-school phone calls. Video chats are better. But he has to plan those carefully. Private time and space are scarce for him.

I didn't know what we were doing when we reconnected. Come to think of it, I didn't know what I expected when I handed my contact information to Usman on a paper napkin that last day in Goa. So, we've been improvising as we go along. And against all odds, we've managed to create something beautiful. Unexpected. Unlikely. Improbable. A dandelion. Tenaciously defying the tyranny of asphalt. Resilient. Flourishing under less than ideal conditions.

There's an emotional and spiritual intimacy between us. That feels effortless. A shared understanding of things. That feels natural. A lot of it comes from the common culture and experiences. I don't have to translate the lyrics of a Hindi song. Explain that some of the nuances are lost in translation. He doesn't have to justify the outsized importance he places on his family. Our religious, socio-economic experiences may be divergent but there is a commonality underlying these experiences that trumps the differences.

I was thinking about this the other day. It was Diwali. I got messages from friends and family in India. Celebratory greetings and well wishes. Here in Boston, though, there was no acknowledgement of the day. Or its significance. I'm not suggesting this was a snub. A slight. Or an omission by intent. Most of my friends and colleagues probably have only a vague idea of this festival's existence. An exotic event that happened elsewhere. In a land far away. Where tigers and elephants roam free. Even those that might be better acquainted with the festival. And its significance. Probably didn't have it show up on their standard calendars. There are no shelves filled with Diwali paraphernalia to remind the shopper of its imminent arrival. Even in a country that is keen to exploit the commercial potential of every holiday—adapted, adopted, or straight-out appropriated—Diwali is invisible on the retail radar. No earthen lamps. No rangoli kits. No barfis. No laddus. Nothing.

Depending on the whims of the moon, Diwali lands somewhere around Halloween. Or Thanksgiving. There is no space or appetite for Diwali accouterments when there are giant bags of sugar-laden candy to be consumed or doled out. When there are adorable costumes to be procured and donned. Cute ones for babies. And fur babies. Slutty ones for the adults. Of course, there is no space. And definitely no appetite. When there are turkeys to be consumed. With canned cranberries and pecan pies.

This is the experience of minorities the world over. Our celebrations. Customs. Conventions. Ceremonies. Our identities. Our existence. Can feel lost. Can *be* lost in the vast ocean of the dominant culture, languishing in anonymity. Insignificant. We are tiny islands. Clinging on to rites and rituals, foods and festivals. Before they succumb to the vastness of the ocean. Watered down. Muted mimicries of once vibrant traditions.

You don't notice—your lack of representation—until the script is flipped. You show up to a house party. Thrown by a fellow Indian. To find the home filled with others. Who look like you. Snacking on samosas. Chatting over chai and chaat. People who share common bonds and experiences that are foreign to the folks who populate the rest of your life. You don't notice your loneliness. Until you see pictures of communal celebrations. Families. Friends. Food. Pictures that set off pangs of hunger and homesickness deep inside. Familiarity does not breed contempt. Not then. Not in that moment.

Yet it would be wrong to attribute the entirety of ease and comfort that I feel with Usman to a shared national background. Because that would hypothesize that shared communal experiences and history are prerequisites for successful relationships. Because (more importantly) that minimizes Usman's individuality. And uniqueness. Our unique chemistry. Our peculiar connection.

I am older now. Wiser, hopefully. I intend to go along this

journey. For what it's worth. And where it takes me. I've set my-self no goals. No expectations. No paring down of us to checklists or superficial criteria. Affinity for reading. And long walks on the beach. At Sunset. Are neither prerequisites nor predictors of how we match. Or *if* we do.

When I encounter moments of doubt, ponder what it all means (Old habits!), I remind myself of the best-laid plans of mice and men. Then I re-read his latest email.

And I smile as I imagine him. Typing this missive. Pouring a part of himself into these words. Words with meanings and mes-sages far greater than their diminutive font size might indicate.

USMAN

swear Ravi had set something loose deep inside me. I was feeling like someone was untying knots inside me and opening up doors and windows, breaking down walls only. I could breathe and oh man, there was light. I could feel the light and the lightness, a little more every day, a little more the next day, the next month and on and on. I got all senti with these new feelings and emotions and I tried to capture them on my canvas before they became old news.

I was doing the needful during the day, working and doing election work so I started painting at night only. I would get so involved with the painting business that Ammi often had to drag me to the kitchen for dinner only. I didn't even feel the need to eat but she would scold me if I didn't, so I ate fast-fast and ran back to the paintings. I felt so inspired, yaar, that I wouldn't realize the whole night had gone until all the neighborhood roosters started going off like bloody alarm clocks. But it wasn't like I could stop even if I wanted to because my brain did not think of anything else. I was dreaming and daydreaming of paintings the whole time.

Yesterday, Ammi wanted to make biryani so she sent me to the market to buy some mutton. The stall was damn crowded and people were cutting the queue left, right, and center. Bloody idiots. Just before my turn came, this woman started bargaining with the guy for a better cut of meat and a cheaper price. So I was standing there, tap tap tapping my foot impatiently, bloody flies pestering me only. I don't get a lot of paid leave but they'd given us two days' time off because the resort was going so slow. The bloody election and the political tension were keeping tourists away only. Who wanted to deal with all the bandhs and rallies blocking the roads, na? Anyways, I never have leave like this so I wanted to be painting instead of standing in line for bloody mutton. But what to do, na? I couldn't tell Ammi to go herself. So here I was stuck at the market, swatting the flies and waiting for my turn, waiting, waiting, when I felt a hand on my shoulder. I turned around to see my old college teacher, D'Souza Sir.

"Usman Khan! I have not seen you in so many years. How is my favorite student? You must be famous and all, forgetting about your old teacher."

"No, no Sir. Nothing like that. I've been meaning to come to visit but it's hard to get leave from work na."

"Don't worry, I am only pulling your leg. Where are you working these days? More importantly, are you painting, young man?"

"Sir, I'm working at Avanti Resort on Margao Road. And yes I am painting. Actually, I have been painting a lot recently and would like to get your evaluation on them."

"Finish your shopping and I can go with you to see the paintings. There's no time like the present, right?"

"Surely, Sir. I only have one thing to buy if you don't mind waiting."

We walked back together, chit-chatting and catching up with each other on our life stories. I was quite the chatterbox on the outside but inside my excitement and nervousness were growing with every step. I was very proud of my new work and I was excited to show it to D'Souza Sir. He has an excellent eye and I really valued his opinion. But I was also very nervous in case he didn't like the new stuff. It would be a terrible blow, na and I wasn't sure I was capable of handling such a bad review. I was so attached to the work, yaar.

"Sir, please have a seat. Can I bring you some tea?"

"No, no. I just had tea. Don't bother with anything. Let's see what you've been working on."

I put down the canvases, seven in total, holding my breath as I waited for D'Souza Sir to say something but he was mute only. The silence was pin drop and felt unending, as he inspected each canvas, from far and then close up, back and forth, from left to right, as if he was doing a bloody slow-dance routine. Kuch to bol do, Sir! Say something na!

"I can see a change in your style, Usman. You've never shied away from color and that hasn't changed. No, the changes are more subtle and yet completely noticeable. This new work is bloody filled with energy, there is freedom movement, and a velocity to the art. Where I once was seeing cautious strokes and very precise but predictable work, I am now seeing motion and life that can't be contained by borders and boundaries. Your voice feels more confident, it feels more pronounced. It's joyful. "

I was trying to pay attention but I was so nervous for his evaluation that I couldn't very well keep up with all the things he was saying only. That was a lot of information that D'Souza Sir just bombarded me with and all of a sudden only. I could barely make out all the details but generally speaking, I think he liked it. Phew, what a relief only!

"Thank you, Sir. Do you like the new style better than the old one?" I had to confirm because I was still in disbelief only.

"I don't just like it better. I love it! I am super impressed, man. You know I am very kanjoos with praise, making you earn it and today you've earned it, Usman. This sense of gaiety in your work, it's almost like you are in love. Are you hiding a wife or a girlfriend somewhere?"

I laughed nervously, getting all red in the face. "No, no Sir. Nothing like that. No girlfriend or wife in the picture." If only he knew how close he was to the truth, minus the correct sex.

"Fine, I'm sure that for a handsome young chap like you, it's going to happen any day now. In all seriousness though, your new work is damn spectacular. Here's the visiting card of my dear friend, Ruby Kapadia. She runs a gallery showcasing local artists. I want you to get in contact with her. Tell her I sent you and that I insist that she take a look at your work. In fact, I will call her to warn her that you will be reaching out to her."

"Usman, I mean it, don't be shy. Don't let doubt or the lack of confidence hold you back. Ruby is fair and will help you with pricing and all that funny business."

"Thank you, Sir. I couldn't have done this without you."

"What nonsense, mention not! You and only *you* are responsible for the beauty I've seen today." D'Souza Sir went back to look at the paintings closely. "I'm so glad I saw you at the market. I am very proud of you, Usman. Do let me know how you get on with Ruby."

BERLIN

This was love: a string of coincidences that gathered significance and became miracles.

–Half of a Yellow Sun, Chimamanda Ngozi Adichie

USMAN

felt like I was in a dream and I was afraid someone was going to pinch me. Then I would get up and realize all of this was a bloody joke only. It all started with D'Souza Sir's critique. I was so happy I was going to burst into tears but I kept my cool until he left. Then I started jumping up and down as soon as the door shut. Poor Ammi and Sharmeen, I didn't even have the words to explain what happened so I just kept on dancing and laughing and spinning them both round and round. I finally sat down and told them what happened. Ammi, of course, started crying so then Sharmeen and I started teasing her. They were both so happy for me. When I finally calmed down I tried to write down what D'Souza Sir had said, word by word, so I wouldn't forget it.

Obviously, I told Ravi about it as soon as I could get a hold of him. He said he was very, very happy for me and so proud of me. "When are you going to show your work to Ruby?" he asked. I kept avoiding that question only, just as I had been finding all kinds of excuses to not show my work to Kapadia Ma'am. My biggest worry was that she would think I was a fraud. I mean I was just a lowly resort worker who painted in his free time. When I looked at my paintings I was always questioning whether they were good because I only saw things I could do better. I saw all my mistakes only na. When I saw other people's work I doubted myself even more. I had so much more to learn about art and great artists. Plus I'd never even shown my work at a gallery or anything. How could I call myself an artist like that only?

I was damn scared that the whole thing would be a fiasco and a big flop. After all, I didn't know anything about this business only. Even small-small things like what I should wear to go to meet Kapadia Ma'am, I didn't know. Did I need to carry visiting cards or a CV? Should the paintings be framed? If they needed to be framed I didn't have the money to frame them na. All of these questions and my fears were keeping me from calling Kapadia Ma'am. It was also easier to keep pushing back the meeting because then I didn't have to face my fears. I could just keep on painting for myself only and not have to worry about either my work or me being judged. It was fine showing D'Souza Sir because he was my teacher and he already knew me. Showing it to Ruby Kapadia was like taking it to a whole new level na.

Ammi, Sharmeen, and Ravi, all kept on pushing me to get in touch with Kapadia Ma'am. It was no problem to deal with Ammi and Sharmeen because they were family and I could just tell them to stop eating my head. And what did they know about art only? They liked everything I painted, even the ones I hated and ended up painting over. Ravi was harder to throw off because I couldn't very well tell him to buzz off na. But he handled me very delicately and didn't push when I changed the topic. Because of these people, I had become the master of moving away from this topic whenever it came up.

In the end, the decision was taken out of my hands. I got a phone call from Ruby Kapadia. She asked me when she could see my work, joking that she had to see it just to get D'Souza Sir off her back. He had been pestering her this whole time, asking her to ring me if I didn't contact her first.

I had to beg one of the drivers from the resort to help me take the paintings to the gallery on the day of the appointment. We found the address and even from the outside Kapadia Ma'am's gallery looked like a properly posh place, yaar. I entered through these beautiful, antique, Rajasthani carved wooden gates, with two smartly-dressed security guards who opened the doors for me. And then I walked into an all-white world, marble floors, pure white walls, and even the high ceilings were painted in a pearly white color. In the middle of the first white room and in the next room, there were open courtyards planted with roses of different-different colors. The splashing sounds from the courtyard fountains were so beautiful with the soft sitar music that was playing all the time and oof, the smell of the roses, man! Wah wah, kamal hai! Oh and there was a bloody peacock walking around in the courtyard.

There were no windows on the walls so all the natural light came in from the inside courtyards only. But the trees, the sloping roof, and white curtains did a very good job in keeping out the sun so the interiors were shady and quite cool also. It almost felt dark in the rooms if you even walked half a meter away from the middle courtyards but that worked out very nicely because you could put spotlights on the paintings. This way the main focus was on the paintings only. Speaking of the paintings, they were hung on all four sides of the rooms, with three-four feet between one painting and the next one so it was not crowded like a bloody bazaar. Each and every painting was damn amazing.

The third room was like a drawing room with sofas and chairs and a beautiful ceiling light. There was also a bar in this room. After all these public areas was Kapadia Ma'am's office finally. The office was private property and there was no entry unless you were meeting with Kapadia Ma'am. Same white walls here also and an antique-looking desk, behind which was another amazing painting. Wow, this whole place was like a museum only, but I didn't notice a lot of these details on my first visit, only afterwards on my second and third time.

The first time, I was too terrified. I also didn't sleep the night before even though I tried everything from hot milk with haldi to reading to praying with my tasbih, but no sleep only, man. Seeing the fancy gallery had made me even more nervous only. My mouth was so dry and I was afraid I was going to be laughed out of the gallery when I showed my silly, stupid paintings. I should never have agreed to this, I was thinking, but it was too late. Kapadia Ma'am was sitting at her desk asking us to come in. She looked a little bit like Indira Gandhi with her short haircut and white hair.

The driver and I brought in the paintings and she had us put the paintings on the big table in the middle of the office. She shook my hand and made introductions with solid confidence. I was a little bit scared of her, I won't lie. Then the driver left me to go back to the car. So, it was just us two in the room.

"Call me Ruby, Darling! All this Ma'am business makes me feel even older than I am." She laughed at her own joke. She could tell me to call her Ruby but I couldn't disrespect an older person like that na?

Kapadia Ma'am took out her glasses and walked around the table to take a look at the paintings. I didn't realize until then that she was quite tall only and very thin also. She was wearing a purple silk saree with a gold sleeveless blouse and close up actually looked quite young. I was thinking she would look so young if she dyed her hair but I kept quiet only, minding my own business and trying not to show how scared I was. She took her own sweet time with the pieces, giving a running commentary as she checked each one thoroughly.

"Wonderful... I love the brushwork here... Ooh this texture is intriguing... I like the combination and juxtaposition of the colors here... This is very, very unique, Darling..."

She was using some big big words that were going over my head only but I was so happy she didn't torture me with silent treatment while she looked at the paintings, like D'Souza Sir.

When she was finished with all the pieces, she told me, "There's no question this is exceptional work. I'm very happy D'Souza didn't let up with his constant pestering. I need some time to iron out the details but I can picture some pretty grand things for you, Mr. Usman Khan." She then opened the cabinet behind her desk and took out two small fancy glasses. "Cheers! Let's celebrate with some port, darling. It's always five o'clock somewhere, no? You drink, right?"

What a relief, yaar, what a bloody relief! All of the built-up tension left my body and I was tempted to run out of there before she came to her senses only.

One week after that, she had a plan also. First, she was going to have a small party for some important clients and after that private showings. If there were enough pieces left over after the private showings ("Highly doubtful, darling!"), she would organize a solo exhibition for me.

Time was like a damn tortoise, moving so slowly-slowly as we got closer to the date of the party. I did anything and everything to divert my mind. Ammi and Sharmeen weren't allowed to bring up the topic, and Ravi also. When I did think about the party and the showings, which in spite of my level best efforts I could not avoid only, I tried all types of superstitious things to bring me luck. I wore a taweez that Ammi had got from the local khwaja. I started painting only at night because night painting was lucky for me. I stopped using new colors in my work, the old ones were the lucky ones. The day before the party, I even had Ammi make me mutton biryani again. Oof, the damn wait was quite unbearable only.

On the day of the party, I put on my most professional clothes to go to the gallery. The place was bloody crowded. Oh god, I thought Kapadia Ma'am had said a small party! The crowd was made up of different-different kinds of people, young and old and guys and girls, Indians and foreigners but they all looked very rich only. I was watching them from the corner, all of them sipping on wine and fancy drinks, laughing and walking around looking at my paintings, eating the starters being passed around. Oof, I wanted to run away only. I was too damn nervous to eat or drink myself so I just tried to stay in the courtyard, sitting on the bench so that I could avoid talking to people. But then the music stopped all of a sudden and I could hear a clink-clink. Kapadia Ma'am called for me to come to her. She looked like a film star in her blue silk dress and now everyone was looking at both of us.

She introduced me as the guest of honor to the party guests, saying all sorts of nice things and making me sound very important. I was blushing like a beetroot only. I smiled and nodded and said thank you to her and all the other people for coming out to see my work. Short and sweet, hoping they all couldn't hear my voice shaking or see my hands trembling like I was an old man. I tried to hide in the corner again after that but it was bloody impossible. Everyone and their nani wanted to talk to me and there was no escape route. I wish Ravi was there with me.

"There's a method to my madness, darling," Kapadia Ma'am said to me after the party. "No prices when I first unveil the pieces. Money is no object for these collector types anyway. They are all addicted to the idea of collecting art, whether it is by famous artists or someone who they think will become famous. They don't want to miss out on the hottest new thing, right?" She looked at me over her glasses. "What will they brag about at their kitty parties and cocktail parties if they can't say they discovered the newest Hussain or Picasso?"

We were sitting on the sofa, while the bartenders cleared the glasses and the waiters picked up the plates and cleaned the gallery. Ruby Ma'am took off her heels and sipped on a glass of port. I had some tea only.

"They come from all over the country and even from abroad when I throw these bashes. The Gujarals came from Delhi, the Mehras from Mumbai. That guy with the pink tie that I introduced you to, he's a sheikh. Flew in from Dubai." I'm not sure I remembered any of these people. The whole night was such a crazy experience for me.

"For these people, the more buzz there is, the more something feels unattainable or mysterious, the more they clamor for it. And boy are they clamoring for it. I already have requests for a few private showings. That's where the real business happens, darling."

I got myself some more tea and another glass of port for her.

"Don't you worry your handsome self, you are destined for something big. I feel it in my old bones and I damn sure am going to make that happen."

I mostly nodded and listened to her, happy to not have to talk more. Finally, when everything was done, we shut the gallery.

Ruby Ma'am offered me a lift in her car but I lied and said I was waiting for a friend to pick me up. I didn't want to trouble her when it was so late and it would be nice to walk so I could finally think.

There was so much going on in my head, na. I was not sure of what to do with these new new things like praise and flattery and maybe even success. For the thousandth time that night I wished Ravi was there.

RAVI

Usman's excitement was palpable. Bursting through the static on our choppy video call. The smile on his face. His happiness. It's something I'll remember for a very long time. Forever memories. That sort of happiness is contagious, you know.

The private showings of Usman's collection were very successful. A collector purchased six pieces outright. That alone would be huge news but it got better. When this collector came to see the pieces, he brought with him Sanaya Tadiwala. A famous curator, Ruby told Usman later. Ms. Tadiwala had consulted on many previous acquisitions by this collector. He wanted her to weigh in on the new pieces. Usman's pieces. By which he was enamored.

Turns out Sanaya Tadiwala is a very influential person. In the world of contemporary art. In India. And around the world. (I hate sounding ignorant but I must admit I had never heard of her.) According to Google, she had curated exhibits for a number of famous arts events. Including the Venice Biennale and Documenta 14. Ms. Tadiwala was fascinated by Usman's work. Her exact word choice. Fascinated. She approved of the acquisition. Highly. And she convinced the collector to lend the six pieces for exhibition as a part of this year's Berlin Biennale. The exposure would only increase their value. She reasoned.

The Berlin Biennale. I'd heard of it. But I had to research the event to comprehend its true significance. It is huge. Famous. We are talking about the big leagues here! The process of incorporating the new pieces into an event of this caliber would normally take months. Years even. But Ms. Tadiwala happened to be one of the curators for the Berlin Biennale. She had a vision for Usman's pieces. They fit in perfectly with one of the exhibits she was organizing. And she was willing to rush things. Push boundaries. To make it happen. She was so taken with his work.

So. Usman was going to Berlin. He was going to present his pieces. In Berlin. At the Berlin Biennale!

I was so proud of Usman. I had never doubted his talent. I love his work but I was shocked–he was too–at this turn of events. His meteoric rise. And instant success. It felt like I was a spectator. Watching a real-life fairy tale unfurl in front of my eyes. Usman was going to showcase his art on one of the biggest stages for contemporary art in the world. Wow.

Wow. Wow. Wow.

Good things came to good people. My people were big believers of this concept. Karma. Destiny. Fate. All in our wheelhouse. I may not know enough about contemporary art to have predicted his rise but I did know that Usman deserved all the good things heading his way. I believed in his inherent goodness. And decency. I'd be happy to vouch for his superlative character. In any court of law.

Excitement. Jubilation. Euphoria. I told you it's contagious. I was swept up in the powerful currents. Happy for Usman. Giddy. Ecstatic. Carried away in the moment, I offered to meet him in Berlin. An idea that hadn't occurred to him as an option. Or a possibility.

He immediately took me up on my offer. Happier than the happiest he'd proclaimed himself, just a few minutes earlier.

Then came the doubts. The regret. A procession of them. I began to wish I had considered the idea more thoroughly. Before I released it into the world. A trial balloon. Mistaken for the real deal. It wasn't that I didn't want to go to Berlin. It had always been on my list. It wasn't that I didn't want to see Usman. I did. I was worried that I was plowing ahead. Recklessly. While the logistical complications of our situation remained unresolved. We still lived a few continents and two oceans apart. I worried about leading Usman on. Making him believe we could make this work. Could we make this work? Meeting just once or twice a year? I didn't want to give him hope and then break his heart. Because I felt protective of him. Loathe to hurt him.

Then again, maybe the ship had already sailed on this. I hadn't thought about or even tried to date anyone else since Usman and I got in touch again. The frequency of our communication. The quality of it. Pointed to a deeper connection. And perhaps a willingness to ignore. Or work around the clear and present logistical impediments.

Ironically. My ambivalence reminded me of Adam. And his reluctance to pursue anything serious with me. Adam. I didn't think about him very often, not anymore, because it was too painful. But in this instance it reminded me. How it felt to be in Usman's shoes. Not so long ago. Yet, it was different. My reluctance was based on logistics and reality. Not an aversion to the very idea of long-term relationships.

If anything, what I should learn from Adam was that life was unpredictable. Don't overthink. Don't overplan. Carpe diem. I needed to set aside my hesitation. My doubts. To follow my heart. Because life was too short.

Besides, it seemed rude. Callous. To renege on Berlin. Given Usman's unbridled joy and excitement about our meeting. I would deal with any adverse consequences of this decision when and if I crossed that bridge. Restraint and self-control, they were not exactly my strong suits. Particularly around indulgences. I could offer a dozen hangovers and a closet full of impractical purchases as proof of my lack of restraint. And penchant for self-gratification.

Very quickly, I forgot the lingering doubts. And misgivings. I was excited. I was reminded of the anticipation. The thrill. I felt in Goa. Butterflies. There was an instantaneous connection. And chemistry between us. When we first met. The months of conversations and correspondence that had followed more recently hadn't dulled the thrill of our first encounter. The prosaic details of our daily existence had not diminished the longing. If anything it deepened the connection. Giving it a base more substantial than that of purely physical needs and wants.

The doubts dissolved. (Or at least were disguised enough.) To pave the way for anticipation. Eagerness and elation. The prospect of seeing Usman. The idea of the two of us. Alone. Sans impediments such as disapproving family or restrictive social diktats. Free. The possibilities seemed endless. Roses and rainbows. Offer valid for a limited time only. Still. Rainbows and roses.

◆

Delirium and daydreaming. As the trip drew closer. My thoughts were constantly occupied by our impending rendezvous. I imagined it one way. Then another. Berlin as the backdrop for our long-awaited reunion. The (remnants of the) Berlin Wall and Brandenburg Gate. Checkpoint Charlie. Sights to see and places of interest. I looked up restaurants and bars. Design. Dancing. Clubs. I was also completely open to the possibility that we might not leave the hotel room. Much.

USMAN

I didn't have much guidance or support when it came to my studies. Abba, when he wasn't busy getting drunk or abusing and beating us, couldn't be bothered with such things only. And then he just disappeared. Ammi can't even read properly. She never went to school na. By luck or the grace of Allah, I got into an English medium school because of some charity scheme and I was good at studies also. I was the first one in my whole family to go to college. After me, some of my cousin brothers passed out of college but I was the first only. My school teachers were always advising me to go for commerce or science stream because I was bright. They thought I would get a nice government job if I got a degree from college and for a poor boy like me, that was quite a high goal already. Most of the boys from my mohalla were just going to be loafers only.

Choosing arts instead of science or commerce was thought to be a big mistake. They said it was fine for girls because they weren't expected to be supporting the family financially but for guys, it was a big no-no. In my batch in college, there were only a few guys in the arts stream and they were all rich kids who either didn't get admission in commerce or science, or spoiled ones whose families were supporting their *hobby*. I almost followed my school teachers' advice and didn't go into arts myself because I knew I had to support my family, but ultimately I couldn't let go of it. I got good marks in maths and science but I hated studying it, so I knew I would be so damn miserable if I had to study more of that in college also. Drawing and painting were my passion. That was the only subject I truly cared about, na. It may sound like a line from a greetings card but dil ki khushi is important, yaar.

Ammi says I have been very interested in drawing and painting since I was young. She used to bring me broken crayons or old pencil colors that the family she worked for was throwing out. She hid some money from Abba one time and got me a set of Camel poster colors for my birthday present. Even I remember getting this set and painting an old newspaper black and blue. I cut out holes in this newspaper, small-small holes. If I was holding the paper just right, it looked like I was looking at the dark sky with the light shining through the holes and I could imagine I was living in the stars. I was so obsessed only with my sky, holding it close and then far from my face. Ammi was quite mad when I left dark fingerprints all over the house.

Anyway, listen, my school teachers were right in their own way. There isn't a position you apply for after you pass out of college with an arts degree, na? There is no job title that you are qualified for only. My kismat was good and Allah was kind because I got the job at the resort. Maybe I would be getting more pay in some office job if I had done a science degree, but I am happier with my choice. My dreams were simple from the beginning only. I wanted a job where I could support my family and I wanted to paint and I got both of those things. I didn't really think that I could make a living out of painting. The only time I had sold a piece was like for pocket money at our college art fair. Showing my art in a proper gallery and selling those pieces was already pushing me past the small-small dreams I had dared to dream, man.

All this that was happening to me was very shocking only. Kapadia Ma'am and Tadiwala Miss had turned my world upside down. Kapadia Ma'am broke the news gently to me. She told me that six of my paintings sold and that there was a possibility that they could be shown in Berlin. She didn't want to get my hopes up before the details were finalized. A week after that she called me to the gallery so I could pick up a check for the money from the sale. When I went to the gallery, she said, "The paintings are going to be shown in Berlin. Sanaya would love for you to go to Berlin for the opening, if you are interested."

What? I didn't even know what to say and my confusion must have been written all over my face. Ruby Ma'am pushed the check across the desk to me. She told me to open the cover so I could make sure it was right. Like I have any idea of how much I am supposed to get, ha ha very funny. I couldn't believe the amount that was written on the check and in any case, I was not sure if I was even reading the number correctly. I have no practice reading such big-big numbers na.

"You can afford a trip to Berlin and still have a decent amount left over, darling. But I don't think you should spend your money on this trip. It's a shame that they don't provide the artists with funding even though these are multimillion dollar events, all built on the backs of the artists. My advice is to wait and see if we can find you a sponsor or you tell Sanaya you can't make it. She'll just have to show the paintings without you."

Tadiwala Miss did some magic and got the Goethe Institut to sponsor my trip to Berlin. "It was the perfect fit." Taadiwala Miss explained to me. "They are all about promoting international cultural exchange. It took some pushing to get them to work with our tight schedule but I think they are very excited to sponsor you, Usman. So pack your bags and I will see you in Berlin!"

I was going to Berlin.
I was going to Berlin.
Berlin.
Berlin, Germany.

◆

I still couldn't believe how fast-fast my life had changed, man. I'd never been on an aeroplane before. Actually, the only time I had been out of station was for a college trip to Mumbai and now I was traveling to Berlin! I was so happy my heart was bursting only.

I was also very scared, yaar. This was all so new-new for me. Where did one buy tickets for a flight? At the airport like you bought train tickets at the railway station? Or did you have to go through a travel agent? I knew I would need a passport but I had not even thought about the visa. I didn't know if I'd get all the documents ready in time only. Even if I got my passport and visa, I had so many more things I had to worry about na. What did I need to carry with me for such a trip? I didn't know if any of my clothes were good enough for Germany. Aiyo, I was going to look like the village idiot only. And where would I stay? I tried to look for a hotel room but you couldn't book a room there without a credit card only.

Ravi has been so sweet and helpful. He told me not to worry about the hotel and that he was going to book a room for us. He was also coming to pick me up from the airport when I land there. What a relief, na? I couldn't even begin to imagine how much more nervous I would be if he wasn't going to meet me in Berlin. Still I sometimes didn't ask him about certain things because I didn't want him to think of me as an ignorant fool. I also didn't want him to be spending his money all the time because I was worried that he would think I was using him. Luckily, Ruby Ma'am had taken me under her wing like a mother hen. She helped me with all the documents and with the travel arrangements. She even took me shopping and helped me choose a suit. "Yes, the navy one, darling. You look so handsome in that suit." And on top of that, she wouldn't take money for the suit. "It's my treat, darling. I want you looking sharp at the opening." I had no idea what I had done to deserve all the kindness Ravi, Tadiwala Miss, and Ruby Ma'am had shown me, but I will always be in their debt. I was damn lucky, yaar.

As the day of my leaving came closer, it was quite hectic. I kept feeling like I had a thousand things to do and that I was forgetting something really important. Ammi was senti all the time, crying because she was very excited and proud but also very afraid. I'd never been away from her for a whole week and on top of that I was flying to some foreign country. She was worried about everything, from what I would eat to how I would understand the language there. She even turned the whole place upside down to find Abba's old sweaters from when they lived up north, because she was afraid I would freeze.

So to help her feel better, we went to the dargah to get me a taweez to protect me from the evil eye and to keep me safe on my journey. At least she was distracting me from thinking too much about my own worries, and I was happy to have all the distractions so I could stop feeling so scared about the trip only.

RAVI

am waiting for Usman. At the airport. It has been a while since his flight landed. Finally, I see him come out of the gate. Scanning the crowds. Nervously. Like a gazelle. Eyes darting here. There. Here. Until he spots me. The relief is immediately visible. Then comes the joy. Flooding his face. He heads towards me. A small suitcase in tow. Should we hug? Kiss?

I give him a hug. Seems like a safe bet. In case a kiss feels too intimate for him in a public place. He smells ever so faintly of mothballs. A tiny bit out of place. Dressed in a wool sweater on a warm August day. But it feels so good to hold him. He melts into my embrace. Molding himself perfectly to me. I linger for as long as I can. I don't want to let him go.

We step out into the sunshine. It is a glorious day. Usman is quiet. Really quiet. He might be tired. From the anticipation. The excitement. All of the emotions. Brought on by his first trip abroad. And perhaps from the actual flight. I call for an Uber. And hold his hand as we wait. He allows it. Returning my grip with his. Soft but assertive. I think I saw him smile. Out of the corner of my eye. Once. Briefly.

He holds my hand throughout the ride. But his eyes are glued to the window. Taking in the sights and scenes. Mesmerized by the world passing by. Mouth agape as if about to say something but lacking words to say anything. I may be projecting awe and wonder onto him. But I watch him as he watches the world outside. Experiencing the novelty of this new world. Through his eyes. Imagining what this voyage of discovery feels like. For him.

We check in at our hotel. A funky little place. With a design sensibility all its own. He and I are both taken in by the brilliant styling and design. The lobby is particularly stunning. Tropical plants. In every nook and cranny. The lobby and the adjoining lounge decked out in purples and pinks. Formica and felt. Glamorous. Glittering. And gilded. Like the 70s went to space. European design sensibility at its best. Toeing that fine line between being fabulous and forced. Managing just enough restraint to plant itself firmly on the fabulous side. A tiny elevator takes us to the third floor. Pinks and peachy shades on this floor. More muted than the lobby. Quietly elegant.

Our room is small but cozy. Clad in the same pastels. Mostly monochromatic. But texturally diverse. A velvet chair. And linen bedding on the antique bed. Lacquered nightstands. And a matching cabinet with rattan insets. A midcentury mirror. Bronze. Reflecting the light from the two large windows. The light is warm. Filtered through sheer pink curtains, bathing the room in a flattering, rosy tint. When the curtains flutter in the breeze, you catch glimpses of the majestic, old oak tree outside the window.

The visual richness is a good foil. For the awkwardness. A palpable undercurrent. Silently filling the room. Reminds me of those old, black-and-white, Hindi movies. From the 60s. The hero and heroine on their honeymoon. Ostensibly chaste. Eager to consummate their relationship. But fumbling. Shy. Unsure. Awkward. I sit down on the bed. Pat the space next to me. He sits down. Next to me. We kiss for a while. Softly. Gingerly. Then with more urgency. And passion. My hands exploring his lean body. Which remains shrouded in multiple layers. I am about to peel off the sweater. When he breaks it off. Time for a shower, he explains. Unpacking his bag. Putting away neatly its meager contents. Hanging up a suit in the little closet.

I hear the shower turn on. I sit back on the bed. Wondering what will happen next. This is a unique situation that we find ourselves in. Lacks precedent, at least for me. We've been talking for months. Sharing the most intimate thoughts and feelings with each other. The pace of our physical encounters, though, lags behind. Far behind. We haven't been around each other. Alone. Since that night in Goa. Many moons ago. Many worlds away. We've kissed. But I haven't even seen him without a shirt. I have my own apprehensions. And anxieties. Performance-related. I am hoping this will be different from the last time. *That* was with Adam. There hasn't been anyone since. Time for a fresh start. Clean slate. Fingers crossed.

He comes out of the shower. Wrapped in a towel. Beautiful. Glistening. Drops of water where the towel has missed. Shimmering like jewels in the evening light. Amber. Gold. His brown skin smoldering against the white towel. The contrast is striking. Thrilling. Cinematic. The Oscar for best cinematography goes to… I can't help but stare. He is godlike. A work of art.

He comes over to the bed. Takes off the towel. We resume where we left off. I can't keep my hands off him. Exploring every nook. Cranny. Devouring his beauty before he changes his mind. In case he changes his mind. Desperate to discover and celebrate every part of him. To make sure I worship all of it. Miss nothing. It is intoxicating.

Every part of me is reeling from the sensations of him. The pleasure. My head in heaven. Heart going pitter-patter. A mile a minute. A craving deep in my abdomen, a longing so strong it hurts. Toes curled. Tingling. And when I'm not paying attention. Lost in the ecstasy. A much-needed sign. An erection. My erection. Rigid. And at attention.

I could have wept. Of joy. If I had time. If I wasn't so distracted by this man who has set my body on fire. He is sensuous. Sensual. Tender. Then firm. Meeting passion with passion. Fire with fire. Slow. Teasing. Then rough. Playful. A bite. A tug. Followed by kisses. More kisses. Slow again. A symphony of our own creation. Improvised. Unscripted. Incredible.

After the first time. A stunned silence. Bodies entangled. Limbs intertwined. Hard to tell where I begin and he ends. A sated silence. No conversation necessary. Just the reassuring regularity of a heartbeat. His. Or mine. I don't know. It doesn't matter. Usman and I are in our cocoon. Oblivious to the existence of any other world.

Then a second round. Slower still. Both of us taking the time to visit spots we missed last time. And for return trips to the spots we enjoyed. Like the lovely hollow at the base of his throat. Where the clavicles go their separate ways. Delicately prominent. Things of beauty. Then the other hollow. At the bottom of the sternum. From where a line of fine hair points south to the treasures that await. The curve of his hips. The dip of his lower back where the gleaming twilight pools for one brief moment. My golden boy.

His breath on the nape of my neck. A trail of kisses up and down the back. A quick detour to nibble on my earlobe as I squirm, trying to escape the throes of pleasure so intense they border on pain.

He holds me there. Not letting me escape. Torturing me with the tip of his tongue. Cavorting this way. And that. Mapping the constellation of pleasure points on my body. One at a time. Luxuriating in the languid pace of his explorations. Surprising me with detours, just when I am sure where he's heading next. Our breaths are ragged. Struggling to synchronize with the chorus of pleasure of the two bodies hell-bent on pushing each other to another peak. And another. Until we can't anymore.

And just like that we've gone from black-and-white Indian movies—the golden oldies where any suggestion of physical intimacy is conveyed by shadows and silhouettes, and vague vignettes of butterflies and bees buzzing around rose bushes—to *Kapoor & Sons*. And then on to adult content. For mature audiences only. Viewer discretion advised.

USMAN

The flight to Berlin was really-really bumpy. The pilot made an announcement right at the beginning, telling the passengers that there was going to be a lot of turbulence only and that we should keep our seat belts fastened. I was holding on to the seat handles for my life, man, as the aeroplane went up and down, then all fine, and suddenly up and down again without giving a warning. I didn't even get out of my seat to go to the washroom. I was so scared na. I tried to divert my mind but I was imagining the plane crashing into a huge ball of fire and never being able to see Ammi or Sharmeen again. By the time the turbulence was over, I was happy I did not puke and I was starting to regret this whole bloody trip.

I was so relieved when we landed I wanted to kiss the ground only. Oof, I thought the worst part was over. Then I got to the bloody immigration check. The man at the counter looked at my passport and asked me some questions. Then he asked me to step on the side. Three people in uniform came and took me to a private room. The room was small with one table and some chairs, no windows.

"Sit down," said the woman officer. She sat down also, opposite to me. The two guys were standing behind her, watching. She asked me the same thing the guy at the counter asked also.

"Where are you staying, Sir?"

"I'm sorry. My friend has booked the hotel." I didn't know what else to say. "The address is in my Whatsapp. But I don't have connection here. My phone…"

"Why are you traveling to Germany?"

"My paintings. I am showing my paintings."

"How are you paying for this trip?"

"Tadiwala Miss… She liked my paintings. She helped me with the money."

"Who is Tadiwala Miss?"

"She is organizing the exhibition here for my paintings."

"Where are you staying?"

"I told you my friend booked it. His name is Ravi."

"Do you have enough funds to cover this trip? Where did you get the money?"

I explained that Tadiwala Miss had arranged for sponsorships for this trip. We went over the same questions over and over again. I felt like a parrot only. I told them that Ravi had booked the hotel. I had the address in my Whatsapp.

The three of them started talking in their language. I didn't understand what they were discussing only. I just wanted to get out of that tiny room. I was so scared only. What if Ravi got tired of waiting for me and left? What if he thought I wasn't coming?

Then the lady was asking me again how I paid for my trip and who gave me the money. I told them about the paintings and Tadiwala Miss but they weren't understanding me. Maybe my English was bad?

The lady left the room and one of the guys sat down. He asked me the same questions again. His English was a little hard to make out so I tried my level best to answer him. Over and over I had to explain to them what I was doing in Germany, where I was put up, and how I got the money for the trip. I was near tears from repeating the same things again and again and them not believing me. He even asked me if I have any connections with bloody terrorist organizations. So I thought maybe they were confusing me with some terrorist.

Listen, they were mostly polite even if they were looking scary. One of them was even nice but it is really hard when they make you feel like you had done something wrong. You even started doubting your own bloody innocence. Otherwise, why would they stop only me? Did I say something wrong? Break a rule? Is it because of the way I looked? Because of my name and religion? Because I didn't look rich? I was afraid they were going to throw me in the jail only.

When they finally let me go, I was so upset I didn't want to continue with this trip but what choice did I have only? If I some-how managed to change my return flight, I'd be back on a plane, shitting my pants about another bloody bumpy flight. But more importantly, I'd be letting down Ammi, Sharmeen, Ruby Ma'am, Tadiwala Miss, and everyone who is supporting me. This trip wasn't just for me na. I was carrying the expectations of so many people on my shoulders, people I would not be able to look in the eye if I went back now. And then there was Ravi, who I wouldn't get to see. Seeing Ravi was a pretty big motivation for me. So I took a damn deep breath, said some prayers, and tried to move on from this horrible experience.

I found my bag and I walked out of the gates into a huge hall, searching in the crowd for Ravi, very desperately hoping to see his face. I wasn't sure what I would have done if he wasn't there. It would have been too much, man, too much. But I didn't have to worry about it for much longer. He was there only, looking so damn handsome. His long hair was tied in a ponytail and the stylish pink glares made him look like a pukka movie star. He hugged me and I didn't let him go only. I held on to him damn tightly, like a drowning man holding on to a bloody swimming tube. Plus I thought I was going to faint because my legs were like jelly. I didn't tell him about the flight or the immigration people because I was still very upset and I didn't want to burst into tears only. In any case, he couldn't do anything about it now na.

I did not let go of Ravi's hand for the whole car ride to the hotel but I was looking out of the window to divert my mind from all the bad stuff that happened at the airport. This city was quite amazing only. The traffic was moving so fast-fast but no one was honking or cutting lanes. In India, everyone drove like a mad man. I was also quite surprised to see so many cycles, even on the main roads. I mean we only used cycles if we were too poor to afford a bike or a car na. But here even people in proper work clothes were going by cycles.

In some places, there were people walking on the footpath but generally speaking the city looked quite chill, not like the crazy crowded streets of Mumbai or even Anjuna Market. There were no hawkers to be seen or any rubbish on the streets, and no bloody stray dogs or cows. Everything was so clean na. The city was also damn green. Everywhere you looked there were lots and lots of trees. I was starting to think there were more trees here than people.

When we entered the hotel reception area I was shocked. It was so amazing, yaar! It was my first time seeing such a beautiful room. Even in the movies I'd not seen anything like this. The colors were damn bold! I loved the combination of purple with violets and pinks and all the colors looked so awesome with the old mirrors and furniture. The greenery was also adding such a nice touch to the place. It was so cool that someone put all these bright bright colors on the wall and still made it look amazing instead of making it look like a circus. I was clicking so many snaps while Ravi did the check in. So bloody cool only! Wow, I couldn't wait to see what our room looked like.

Our room was very cool also. It was a lot smaller than the rooms at the resort back in Goa but all the furniture and decorations were so smart here. The people who designed it were able to balance all these colors and decorations without making the place look gaudy. What talent, boss! There was a wooden shelf, only about five centimeters broad, that went around the whole room and on the shelf, they'd put different-different pieces of art. I loved this idea because you could move the pieces around and not have to worry about all the nails you hammered in the wall. Every piece of art was quite nice too, some of them were an older style—landscapes and still lifes in carved gold frames—while others were quite modern but the mixture worked. I slowly felt myself coming back to life, so happy and thankful because I had Ravi there with me. Having such a beautiful place to stay was a bonus only. I felt like I had hit the lottery, yaar!

Ravi and I sat down on the bed, next to each other, and then he kissed me. I was ready to go like a racing car but I also was a little bit worried because I was so sweaty and feeling dirty from the traveling. I had even forgotten to take off my sweater when we left the freezing airport. What if I smelled bad? He was in the meantime smelling damn good so I got even more conscious. I stopped kissing him after a few minutes and told him I really needed to take a bath only.

The hot water in the shower was amazing. You didn't even have to turn on the geyser and wait for the hot water! I could have stayed in there for a long time but I finished my shower as fast as I could so that I could go back to Ravi. He was lying down on the bed when I came out of the bathroom, reading a magazine. He was looking so cute only in his shorts and blue shirt and his thick black specs! He quickly dropped the magazine when he realized I was back in the room. Oof the way he looked at me, I forgot all about how tired I was. I forgot about the horrible flight and the bloody immigration people, all of it, because everything I wanted was right there, in front of me. Normally I would have been very shy but I had waited too long for this so I bindaas dropped my towel. He was quiet for a minute, just looking at me, and I was worried that maybe I was too fast but he quickly pulled me on the bed.

Yes, it was my first time with someone in a proper bedroom, with a door and all. Yes-yes, it was my first time where it wasn't in some dirty gully or hiding behind the bushes. Surely it was the first time when I didn't have to worry about the police catching me red-handed or someone seeing me. Yes, it was with someone good-looking and not some old, bald uncle-type with a fat paunch. But even if you took all of those things away, being with Ravi was better than anything I had ever dreamed about. I didn't have enough words to explain how bloody amazing this experience was.

I was so very much in love with this guy that I was ready to give up anything and everything for him. I knew I could get hurt if he didn't feel the same way, or because there were many reasons why this might not work, but at least this time I wasn't going to stop because I was scared of getting hurt. I did it once already and I won't be repeating the same mistake again.

RAVI

Chemistry. Connection. Sparks. Fireworks. Love at first sight. Fairytale romances. *When Harry Met Sally*. *Dilwale Dulhania Le Jayenge*. We love the idea of love. We consume it in vast quantities. In various forms. Hallmark cards. Lifetime movies. Harlequin novels. Hollywood. If I edited this week just right. It too would seem like the perfect love story. Boy meets boy. Circumstances conspire to separate them. They reunite. Fall in love. Differences and difficulties be damned.

If I edited it correctly, this week in Berlin, I'd focus on the sex. Excuse me. The lovemaking. Close up of the faces. Enraptured. Contorted. Ecstatic. Shallow depth of field. To obscure the intimate. Provide an illusion of privacy. Soft filters. Long shots of a moodily lit room. The couple in repose. Backlit. Beautiful. I'd cut out the self-consciousness. The anxiety. The fear that a fickle erection could come or go as it pleases. Leaving it on the cutting room floor.

I'd focus on the opening of Usman's exhibit. The space buzzing with critics. And art lovers. A fashionable crowd. Animated. Dynamic. Spirited. I'd zoom in on Usman's pieces. Each one, brilliant. Magnificent even. Maybe pan out the camera to show Usman. Smiles for miles. Glowing. Belle of the ball. Dapper in his new suit. More handsome than any other man in the room. By miles. A feel-good moment. The poor protagonist conquering life's curveballs. Coming out on top. A Cinderella story. I'd cut out the parts where we pretended to be friends. Platonic. So that Sanaya Tadiwala or the Indian press wouldn't ask any awkward questions about us.

If I edited it right, my version of the *Berlin Stories*, I'd show Polaroids of the couple gallivanting around the city. Selfies at Brandenburg Gate. Goofy smiles on Museum Island. The photos overlaid on vintage-feeling footage of beauteous Berlin. Hearts and thumbs-up emojis peppering the screen to represent the popularity of the selfies and goofy smiles on social media. A nod to the times we live in. I'd skip the parts where the divergence between the two protagonists' upbringing, social, and economic status is evident. Glaring. In a perfect love story, these don't matter. Love is blind. It operates on a separate plane. Above superficial differences and shallow social standards.

This isn't *that* love story. I don't want to share the edited version. Because the unedited one is beautiful. It is grounded in truth and authenticity. Skin and bones. Blood and flesh. It feels real. It has nuance. It is built on a foundation of some very simple ideas. Honesty. Kindness. Sincerity. You can teach many things. You can't teach someone how to be kind. How to be nice. How to be a good person.

It truly has been a wonderful week. It confirmed for me Usman's innate decency. His kindness. What a pleasure it is to spend time with someone so selfless. Giving. Generous with his time and affection. Someone who asks for nothing more than your love and attention in return. Even the simple pleasure of holding hands, walking hand in hand with him, it made me so deliriously happy. Content. Because I felt less alone.

It has been a week of tremendous joy. Discovering Berlin together. But even more so, watching Usman discover a new world.

A world million miles away from Goa. His sense of wonder at the cleanliness of the city. His admiration for the efficient functioning of all things German. His first doner kebab. Mine too, albeit vegetarian. Delicious. (Usman didn't take to the currywurst quite as much.) Our time at various biergartens. His first taste of tapas. At a taberna run by a gregarious Spaniard and his German girlfriend. Usman's incredulity at the freedoms Berlin offered. The nude sunbathers. In the park. In the middle of the city.

I took him to a sauna. A gay sauna. Just so he could see and experience for himself, unfettered access to sex. He refused to leave my side. The entire time. Afraid he'd lose me to someone better looking. (I wasn't looking for anyone else.) The most shocking thing for him wasn't the libertine Berliners. That was shocking. Yes. But it wasn't the most shocking. The most shocking was the woman mopping the floor in the sauna. Oblivious to the naked men around her. The sauna patrons, just as blithely unconcerned.

It has been a spectacular week. Watching the reception to Usman's art. At the opening. Then in three sessions over the course of the week. Q&A. Press availability. Artists' panel. The coverage of his work is unequivocally flattering. The small Indian press contingent going gaga over their unknown countryman who has found fame on the international stage. The only Indian at this year's Berlin Biennale. I have nothing to do with his success. Obviously. But there is a special kind of joy one gets from seeing the success of a loved one. I call it the Transitive Property of Joy.

It has been a week of learning. To live in the moment. Not dwell in the land of hypotheticals. Of what-ifs. And if-onlys. I don't know what will become of us. But I do know that he is very special. I don't know how or what we can make work. But I do know that I should give this a shot. Give us a chance. I can tell he has developed strong feelings for me. That he is upset by our impending parting of ways. I try to comfort him. With the promise of a visit. Soon. He clings to my offer. To avoid feeling distraught. And helpless. I tell him how much I care. I try to show him. I make sure he knows it is only logistics and geography that are keeping us apart.

I am afraid that he thinks there is more than that keeping us apart. I can tell it wears on him. For example, my insistence on paying for both of us. So, I let him buy me breakfast. Sometimes. Or lunch. Using his small stipend. Because I know how intimidating it must be. The prices here. The conversion from euros to rupees. (Ninety rupees to a euro, last time I checked.) I try to reassure him. That it's only geography and logistics that separate us.

The day before we leave. He surprises me with a puzzle. 500 pieces. Of a painting I admired at the museum. And worth a pretty penny. The puzzle is accompanied by a note:

Thank you for everything. I can never pay you back fully for your generosity and support. This is a very, very small token of my love.
Yours truly, Usman

USMAN

t is our last night in Berlin. Ravi and I are damn tired from a nonstop go-go-go, action-filled week, and also a little high from the wine we had with dinner. I quietly and slowly try to shift even closer to Ravi to make my body fit the shape of his sleeping body. He is sleeping like a baby and even snoring a little bit. My arm is under his head like a pillow so I hold him close with my other arm. I can feel his heartbeat, dhak dhak dhak, beating so peacefully against my hand. I am very tired but I can't go to sleep. I only have a few hours left with Ravi and I want to enjoy and store all the little-little details in my head: the weight of his body, the light smell of his deo which reminds me of laung and dalchini, his hairy legs that always give me electric current when they touch me, how he breathes at night, how he sometimes will suddenly hold my hand in his sleep.

I feel like I am back in my college days, revising my syllabus for the final exams except in this case the exam subject is Ravi. I surely didn't take so many notes and revise so much back in college and I am a little bit upset that I wasn't so good about taking notes this whole week. I only remembered to do it just now. The bloody week just flew by only na. What to do? I can cent percent say that this has been the best week of my life. Yes, yes I know I am still young only and that I have lots of years to live but I don't think anything can make me so happy like I have been here this week. InshaAllah, there'll be more happiness and big events in life, but you always remember the first time very fondly, na. In this week, I have taken my first trip abroad, shown my work in a very big name art festival, and I have done it all with Ravi. Listen, I know the trip started quite badly but it has turned out to be so amazing and the response to my paintings has been very good only. But for me, the highlight is Ravi because he is the first person I have ever fallen in love with.

I knew that our time together in Berlin was limited and I came prepared that at the end of the week we would go back to our regular life, far-far away from each other. Still, all the knowing and preparing doesn't make saying goodbye any easier, na. I am quite sad and miserable about our trip coming to an end, and this type of sadness takes over your entire mood only. I am very much in love with Ravi even though I tried to avoid it and chill out for a while. But the heart wants what it wants na, and it doesn't listen to logic or reality. Ravi has conquered and occupied parts of my heart and brain forever and there is no escaping it now, I am sorry to say.

Ravi saw that my mood was off at dinner tonight when I couldn't pretend that our time together wasn't coming to an end. He tried to cheer me up and to chase the dark clouds away only. He'll be back in India in December, he said, for his yearly trip to see his family. He promised to come down to Goa to see me also. So, I will see him again, and quite soon actually, if everything went according to plan, but I fear that this temporary arrangement is not designed for something long-lasting. We can talk on the phone, send mails, meet up once every year, and if that is all I can have, I am willing to do it. I am afraid though that he will meet someone who may or may not be better than me, but is more convenient for him. Oof, I am already jealous of this imaginary character. Who knew I was such a jealous bloody bastard na?

Like I was saying before, I am so in love with him that I am willing to accept all sorts of conditions and compromises and to make the best of what we have. I will deal with the time difference and the distance and all that nonsense but I want one thing in return: I want him to love me like I love him. I want to be his true love also. I don't want to be the side business or some new item that is in fashion for like a few months or a year and then chucked off when it becomes old and boring. Who wants to set roots in soil that can't support the young plant and watch it grow into an old tree, na?

Of course, I haven't told Ravi any of this because I am not sure of what my standing is with him. I don't want to make demands and push him away because I am being so needy. This whole business of love is very hard only. One minute you feel like you are so happy you are in the clouds and the next one you are miserable and crying. It is a bloody balancing act, like playing chess with human beings, and I hope my willingness to sacrifice all my soldiers to save my raja, is not some foolish move that I will come to regret. Only time will tell na. For now, I bring my attention back to the raja sleeping next to me. I close my eyes, testing myself, to see if I can recreate his face mentally, a trick we used in my figure drawing college class.

I start with the wavy hair, long wavy hair going down almost to his shoulders. There are some white hairs here and there but his head is full of beautiful, shiny black hair. Then comes the wide forehead which Ammi always says is a sign of a smart person. His skin is smooth. There are almost no lines on his face and forehead. The nose is sharp, straight, and narrow. The eyebrows are very nicely shaped, bold but not bushy. His eyelashes are so thick and dark that it looks like he is wearing surma. His eyes are like ink pots filled with black ink, reflecting light and holding secrets at the same time. The cheekbones are …

"Are you still awake?" Ravi asks sleepily, breaking my concentration on his mental portrait.

"No-no I am sleeping only," I lie, not wanting him to get up out of worry.

I let go of the portrait in my head and focus on this living, breathing human being sleeping in my arms. He may break my heart and maybe cause me great pain and suffering, but he is also the one that unlocked my heart, allowing me to hope and dream. I will always be thankful to him for that. I just need to remind myself of this every time I feel sad. I slip my arm out from under his head, trying to shake off the pins and needles feeling and then I carefully slip it under him again. He continues sleeping as if nothing has moved only.

"Jaanu, meri jaan, main tere qurbaan..." Another one of Ammi's old songs gets into my head. *My life (my love), I'm willing to sacrifice myself for you...*

BOMBAY

Look at the road. It runs 100 miles in the same direction yet we
can only see a few hundred feet ahead. They call this a trick
of perspective. I wonder, though, if we could glimpse the end,
would we have the energy or courage to travel it?

–*A New New Guide*, Lara Egger

RAVI

The trips back to India feel like torture. A little more torturous each year than the one before. Two long, uncomfortable flights. Crammed in seats that seem to shrink every time. (Or, am I expanding?) Punctuated by a lackluster layover somewhere in Europe. Just long enough to get the blood flowing in my cramped limbs. Then we land in Mumbai. Hooray! Only to realize there is still a bureaucratic gauntlet to run before I can even start dreaming of a bed.

It is my second time back in India as an American citizen. As luck would have it, I breeze through immigration. In record time. My queue is shorter than the one for the Indians. The officer, friendlier. Fast and efficient in his cursory inspection. Waving me by with a genuine, "Welcome to India." Next stop, the baggage carousel. I wait for my bags, which tend to be chronically tardy. Losing any time I gained from the fast passage through immigration. Baggage claim is the great equalizer.

Customs cleared and I make it out of the arrivals gate. The air assaults you. As soon as you exit the automatic doors. Hot. Humid. Hazy. The smell of smoke. Acrid. Eyes burning from the pollution, tired from the lack of sleep. I search for my parents in the sea of humanity that is waiting expectantly. Patiently. For loved ones traveling from near and far. For years I've tried to get my parents to send a driver. Or let my sister pick me up. But they insist on being there. At midnight. At 2 AM. At 4 AM. Depending on the flight. But always a late-night arrival. Some arrival times, more obscene than others. For the first time, today, it is my sister. And her husband. Waving. Trying to get my attention.

"Well, this is a lovely surprise, Sis, Jiju! Mom and Dad ok?"

"They are both feeling a little under the weather but it's nothing serious. Finally, they listened to me and let us pick you up."

In the car, she offers me snacks. Several different kinds. Just like Mom. I refuse them. Just like I did with Mom. I am not usually hungry after making these long trips home. (Home! Amazing I still say home. Even though I haven't lived here in more than twenty years.) Also, I don't like eating in the car.

"I figured you wouldn't eat any of this but Mom was relentless. I felt like I should do it because she's probably feeling terribly guilty for not being here herself."

"Probably. Most likely."

There is a moment when you see some sign of your parents getting older. It is a profound moment when you first note that decline. In physical prowess. Or mental acuity. Because it brings their mortality into the picture. Confirms your adulthood. For most of your life, they've been your caretakers. Guardians. Insisting on looking after you. Well past whatever the legal age is for adulthood. Oftentimes well into middle age, for some of us. The moment when you see that sign. Or a series of signs. It marks a turning point. The point of inflection.

In my twenty-plus years away, with at least one trip back to India every year, my parents have never missed the opportunity to pick me up at the airport. Or to drop me off when I leave. Tonight is the first time they haven't come. I see the sign. The point of inflection. It makes me sad.

I am half listening to my sister. And brother-in-law. Mostly generic small talk. As I mull over the absence of my parents at the airport. I am half watching the city passing by outside the car windows. Still alive. At this late hour. People. Traffic. Auto rickshaws. Buses. Trucks. Posh apartment buildings. Shanty towns and slums. Hawkers. The hubbub of Maximum City. An antidote to my ever-growing fatigue. Half listening. Half watching. When I snap back to attention. Something about Berlin. "What?"

"I'm coming to Mom and Dad's tomorrow. I'm sure we'll rehash a lot of this conversation then. I just wanted to know more about the boy. And Berlin. How was it?"

"You make him sound like he's twelve which thank god, he isn't. Also, his name is Usman."

"Fine! How was your trip to Berlin? How did things go with Usman? Tell me all. You probably won't want to chat about him when the parents are around."

"Berlin was amazing. Usman was amazing. Jiju, has Sis filled you in on the details?"

"I knew from Facebook that you were in Berlin but I don't know who this Usman character is. You know your sister. She doesn't tell me anything."

"Oh what rubbish! Also, you've met him, yaar. He worked at the resort the last time we were in Goa. Remember I told you Ravi had met a cute guy there? You never pay any attention to me only."

"Yeah baba, you did tell me about the guy in Goa but that was such a long time ago. I didn't know they were still in touch."

"Jiju, I had lost touch with him after Goa and almost forgotten about him too. Then he contacted me, completely out of the blue. But he had his reasons. Long story."

"Ok so how did you go from Goa to Berlin? I'm a little confused."

"We started talking. On the phone. Emails. Whatsapp. Slowly at first. But quite a bit eventually over the last few months. We've gotten very close. Anyway, he's an artist. And he was featured in an exhibit at the Berlin Biennale. It's a pretty big deal. When he told me he was going to Berlin, I sort of spontaneously offered to meet him there. Okay, now you are all caught up."

"Wow. That's quite the story, Bro. So, how was it?"

"Berlin is such a cool city. You both should go sometime. I can give you a bunch of recommendations. Food. Sightseeing. Clubs etc."

"Arre yaar, I can look up bloody Berlin on the Net. How did it go with Usman?"

"Haha, good to see you haven't gotten any more patient with age, Sis."

"Honestly, before the trip, I was a little worried. I had no idea what to expect. We knew each other mostly from phone conversations and emails. But we were practically strangers IRL, as the kids say it. Here we were going on a trip together. To a place neither of us knew. But my apprehension was completely unnecessary. The trip was amazing. We got along fabulously. His exhibition was a huge success. We just… we just ended up having a blast. I don't know what will happen to us in the long run. But there's something there. He is special. Very special."

"That's pretty amazing, Bro. I'm so happy for you. Also listen, I've told Mom you want to go back to Goa but she's waiting to finalize the travel arrangements until you get here. You know Mom, she has like the worst FOMO in the world. She just cannot understand why you'd want to go back to the same place when there are so many new-new places to see. She's going to try to talk you into going to Kerala or some fancy place she's heard about from one aunty or the other."

"Sis, you have to help me out here. We have to go to Goa. I promised Usman I would see him when I came to India."

"Yeah, yeah I'll tell mom, Ranbir and I also want to go back to the same spot."

We pass the Sea Link. Beautifully ethereal in its serpentine beauty. The lights tracing a glittering path across the dark sea. We should be in South Bombay soon. Home. I'll sort out the Goa plan tomorrow.

USMAN

ccording to Google, the distance between Goa and Boston is a little more than 13600 kilometers only. When Ravi lands in Mumbai today, he will be approximately 600 kilometers away from Goa. That means he will be nearer to me by 13000 kilometers, but still 600 kilometers too far. I am not sure I liked this bloody maths problem, yaar, but I suppose I should stop cribbing because at least I am one step closer to seeing him again.

Getting back from Berlin has been very difficult for me. It was such an amazing trip na. I got to see and learn so much out there and Ravi was there with me the whole time only. For seven days we did everything together. A whole week of sleeping together, getting up next to him, eating breakfast together, holding hands, talking the whole day, and thousands of other little-little things, and I got so used to having him around only. When you have such amazing, life-changing experiences in the company of someone and all within such a short time only, it makes you connect even more strongly with this person, na? Coming back to my old life felt so boring and lonely, man.

I put on a show only, pretending to be all happy-happy for Ammi and Sharmeen and for my colleagues and neighbors. They were all so happy and excited for me and proud of what I had done, that I felt like I would be robbing them of their happiness by not showing the proper amount of happiness and excitement myself only. Everyone wanted to see the snaps I had clicked there. It was good that I hid the ones with Ravi in my almirah first only. I told the same stories again and again to everyone because they all wanted to know everything about my trip. This was the closest most of them will ever get to going abroad na.

There were so many questions only. *Yes, yes Uncle, it was amazing how clean it was. No aunty, I was only a little bit cold in the night. The days were quite nice only. The traffic was very fast but no one was honking, yaar. Everything was on time, even the trains and buses. There were a lot of people at the exhibition. No Ammi, there were no film stars at the exhibition. Yes, the people were very friendly only. No language problem, most people were speaking and understanding English. The flight was seven hours long. Yes Chacha, I know that is less time than it takes for the Rajdhani Express to go from Goa to Delhi.*

From the money I saved from my stipend, I bought small-small gifts for everyone. I got a bottle of perfume for Sharmeen, Pantene shampoo for the neighbors on one side and Nivea soap for the neighbors on the other side. Ammi, I didn't know what to get only because I didn't know what she would like. Ravi helped me choose a scarf for her but who knows if she will wear it. For the guys at work, I got chocolates. Ammi took the big bags of Milka, Kit Kat, and Bounty and made small packets for them. I got a postcard from the main exhibition for Ruby Ma'am of a painting I thought she would like.

No one told me I had to bring them gifts or if they did it was always jokingly, but I just knew. The neighbors on both sides of us have been like family only, looking after Sharmeen when she was young, when Ammi and I were at work, feeding her after school, making sure she did her homework. When Ammi's sick, they still bring us food. We celebrate Eid with the Nasrulla family and make a Christmas cake for the Thomas family. My colleagues organized a potluck when they found out about my show in Berlin, chipping in for kulfi and phirni to celebrate, along with other homemade snacks they brought in. Most of these people are not rich but they have been so generous and kind to me and my family that I wanted to bring these gifts to thank them for everything they have done.

Of course, I was worried about whether I'd have enough time or money to complete the shopping and it was quite stressful budgeting for enough items so that I didn't leave anyone out. Ravi was a good sport only, helping me find things I could bring back for people. If he was thinking I am buying stupid items, he was kind and classy enough not to rub it in my face. He even offered to help me buy the presents but I didn't want to take his money. I already felt bad because he was spending his money on the hotel and treating me to all these dinners and stuff. He was always telling me not to worry but I worried because I didn't want him to think I was taking advantage of him.

How did I get on this story now? Oh yes, it was hard coming back from Berlin. This whole business of pretending to be happy and repeating all these stories about my journey a thousand times helped me divert my mind off from the heartbreak of leaving Ravi. Plus I had so much work also to make up for all the time off I had requested na. Diverting my mind was all well and good but to be honest, the reason I am able to bear this separation is because Ravi has promised to come and see me when he comes to India in December. That has made the sadness a little less, otherwise the shock of leaving him after such a magical week was too depressing only. He'll be in India for almost three weeks. Most of the time he will be in Mumbai only, but he has promised that he will come to Goa for at least a part of it.

Ravi was telling me that he and his family always take a

small holiday when he comes back to India. His parents and sister would prefer to go to a hill station but Ravi always asks for a beach location. He says it's too bloody cold in America when he goes back so he wants to be in a hot place only. His family goes along with his choice because he's in India for such a short time na. I mean that's how *we* met two years back na, because he and his family came to Avanti Resort.

The only problem according to Ravi is that his mother is very bad at making decisions so sometimes she will suggest one place one day and then the day after she will want to go to a completely different place. Even now she was suggesting five-six different-different beach places for Ravi to choose from. First Ravi said that she wanted their family to go to Lakshadweep or to Bali but then two-three weeks back she said maybe they should go to Kerala.

Ravi has promised to push the family into making a decision a little more quickly this time so that he can give me enough time to plan my work schedule and ask for time off. He is thinking he can get his family to come back to Goa because generally speaking they all like Goa and it is also the closest to Mumbai. But he said that if due to some problem this Goa plan didn't get sorted out, maybe I can come to Mumbai for a few days. I am hoping that he will come to Goa because it will be easier for me, and I will get to see him for more days than if I have to go to Mumbai.

RAVI

"Beta, you're up so early. Did you get any sleep?"

"No Mom, I was tired but the jet lag was so bad I couldn't actually sleep for very long."

"How was your flight? We are very sorry that we couldn't come to pick you up, Ravi. Both your mother and I were under the weather a little bit."

"It's totally fine, Dad. I've been telling you both for ages that you shouldn't come to the airport. What's the point in spending all this time in the car? Plus I'm sure these late nights are tough for both of you. How are you both feeling now?"

"We are fine only. Just some seasonal things. Did your sister bring the snacks I told her to bring? Did you eat anything? What do you want for breakfast?"

"Yeah, Mom. She brought all the snacks even though you both know I don't eat anything ever."

"You never know, beta. The one year I don't bring food with me will be the year you didn't eat on your flight. You'll be starving and I'll feel terrible I didn't bring snacks! But enough about that, what do you want to eat now?"

"I'll have some bhakhri with methi no masalo."

It is a far cry from my usual grab-and-go breakfast in Boston. Granola. Apple. Banana. Or no breakfast. When I'm running late. Which is quite frequently. Of course, Mom has set out seven other items. In addition to the two, I actually requested. God, I've missed savory breakfasts.

We catch up at the breakfast table. About the flight. The weather. Family gossip. Odds and ends. Then Berlin comes up.

"How was Berlin?"

"It was great, Mom. It's a beautiful city. So much history and culture. The arts scene is very lively too."

"Did you get to see the Berlin Wall? There must be a lot of World War history too, no?" Dad asks.

"Yes, Dad. I saw the remnants of the Wall. Pretty amazing to see the relics from that era. I also went to a couple of communist-era apartments that were preserved as museums. We should go sometime. You're so interested in history, I think you would love Berlin."

"Who did you go with? Who was the guy in the photos?" Mom wants to know.

"He's my friend, Mom."

"Acha. What's his name?"

"Usman."

"Usman? That sounds like a Muslim name."

"Yes, Mom. He is Muslim."

"Oh." One word. Two letters. But the *oh* is filled with meaning. And menace. I am approaching treacherous terrain here. The last thing I want is an argument. About their latent and not so latent prejudices. When I was growing up, my parents seemed like paragons of progressive values. At least by Indian standards. But I've noticed a rightward drift over the last decade or two. I've engaged in many a war of words about their growing intolerance. And close-mindedness. I'd rather not have the same fight today. Before my brain can recover from sleep deprivation.

"Is he Indian?" (Translation: I hope at least he's not Pakistani.)

"Yes, Mom. He is Indian."

They seem happy with that answer. Mom and Dad. They are always encouraging me to have Indian friends. *More* Indian friends. Afraid that I am abandoning my culture. And roots. Having Indian friends seems like insurance to my parents. A dam against the torrent of foreign culture. To which I am so susceptible.

If only we had stopped the conversation there. If only.

"Is he from Boston also?"

"No, he's from India."

"Where does he live?"

"He lives in Goa."

"Goa? How do you know each other?"

If only.

"We met when we went to Goa last time. Two years ago."

I can hear the wheels turning. In Mom's head. Calculating combinations. Possible permutations. That would allow me to know this person. Who lived in Goa? Maybe an old school friend who moved there? But the name wasn't familiar.

"When we went to Avanti Resort? We didn't meet anyone there."

I can feel my father clamming up. Hoping Mom doesn't pursue this line of questioning. It is fraught with danger. Landmines every which way. He'd rather ignore it all. Brush it under the carpet. Bury his head in the sand. To talk about breakfast. Or oriental rugs. And ostriches. Or something equally unimportant. Banal banter.

"What does he do in Goa? What was he doing in Berlin?"

I guess we are going there. Dad looks stricken about what is bound to follow. He has pieced together my connection with Usman. Or a close enough approximation of it. The connection that Mom doesn't want to believe. She is desperately hoping she is wrong. Hoping for a more innocuous explanation. Than the one that can not be true.

"Wait, wait, is that why you want to go back to the same place in Goa?"

USMAN

was so excited when I saw Ravi calling but he sounded very low and his sound was a little soft only. I asked him how his flight was and he said something that was hard to make out. I thought it might be the connection, we must have a bad line, or maybe he was tired na. But then he was speaking up and told me what had happened. He landed in Mumbai last night and was having a nice breakfast with his parents. You know just doing gupshup when his mother asked him about his trip to Berlin. She had seen the photos he posted on Facebook and was like who was that character you were hanging out with. Ravi said he didn't lie to her and told her my name and where we had met. His mother never came flat out and asked him what the nature of our relationship was and he didn't say anything to her also but she was very bothered by all this. She wasn't really talking to him the whole day and then came to his room in the evening to tell him she didn't want to go to Goa only.

Oof, I was like a kid who is promised he can have his chocolate only after he finishes his homework. He finishes his homework and he is unwrapping his prize. It is so, so close he can almost smell and taste the chocolate and his mouth is watering only and then suddenly the chocolate is bloody snatched out of his hands. For months and months Ravi and I did our homework, thinking of and planning different-different ways we could spend the maximum time with each other without making my colleagues or his parents suspect anything. In fact, for the last two-three weeks that's all we could talk about because we were getting so excited na.

Ravi had a great idea. He would pretend to go jogging every morning because even if his parents got up early they wouldn't want to go jogging na. That would be too much for uncle and aunty. I was going to meet him on the beach to hang out and then we would walk back together, most of the way anyways. Once we got near to the resort, he would jog back and I would continue walking at my normal speed only. That way we would be entering separately only and no one would think anything shady was going on. I was going to arrange my schedule a little bit differently also. I was going to request more shifts doing supervision of the swimming pool and clubhouse. Plus I was going to take more late shifts so that by the time I got out of work, Ravi's parents would be sleeping only. That way he could come out with me to the beach, like that amazing night a few years back. And one night for sure, he and his sister and jijaji were going to ditch the parents to go out with me to a nightclub. Ravi wanted to introduce me properly to his sister and Jiju. I was of course nervous about meeting them but it's a good sign na that he wants me to meet at least some of his family members. He said his sister was damn excited to meet me this time.

Bloody hell, man, all those weeks and months of planning and it's all bloody gone in a few minutes like a house made of playing cards. I was counting down the hours until I got to see him and now this trip was going to get bloody canceled only. He said he's going to talk to his parents and try to get them to be more understanding but who knows na. He sounded upset and sad and angry. He was trying to keep calm but I could tell he was having trouble staying calm.

"I know this is all last minute. I am so sorry. But please don't give up hope yet. I'm going to talk to them later today, with my sister. We will try to convince them not to cancel the trip. If they don't, I'm done with them. I'll come down by myself. They complain all the time that they don't see me enough. Well, if they want to spend even less time with me, that's their choice. I'm going to see you no matter what happens. I hope you aren't mad at me, Usman."

I was actually quite mad, maybe not at him but at bloody life in general, and I wanted to scream at the top of my voice. Listen, I knew I shouldn't be angry but I couldn't help myself only. I felt so let down na. If Ravi hadn't promised to come down to Goa, I would have been very disappointed not to see him, especially since he was here in India. It would be disappointing but at least I would understand. I mean things were quite complicated for me too when it came to the deal with my family and friends. I knew what it was like to have to hide some things and to pretend to be someone else but he promised me he'd come to see me and it just felt a lot harder to give something up once you had it or thought you would have it.

I felt like I was cheated out of something and I got angry for a few minutes but I wasn't going to tell this to Ravi na. He was already having such a hard time with his family, poor guy, he didn't need me also to pile on and make his life even more miserable. I knew he was not doing this to hurt me and I just had to suck it up and be there for him because that is what you do when you love someone.

So, I put aside the hurt and the anger and told him not to worry about me.

"I am fine, Ravi. Don't worry about me. I totally understand why you may have to cancel your vacation to Goa. Family comes first only. Make sure you take care of your parents. We will meet when we can, inshAllah."

We couldn't talk for very long because he was using his sister's mobile and he had to go downstairs from his parents' flat so that he could talk to me without them listening to our phone conversation. I hung up the call, very heartbroken but helpless to do anything about it only.

"Dil ke armaan ansuon me bah gaye
Hum wafa karke bhi tanha rahe gaye ..."

All of my heart's hopes and desires were swept away in my tears. I was faithful but yet here I am, all alone. As usual there was an old Hindi song that matched my off mood. I guess that was one of the advantages of making so many movies every year na. There was always a song from this movie or that one that matched your mood, specially love songs and sad songs.

Maybe Ravi will talk to his parents and they'd come to see his point of view. I should have a little more bharosa in him and not give up confidence so easily. I wanted to see him obviously but I hoped it didn't come at the cost of creating problems and tension between him and his parents. After all, our culture teaches us to respect and love our parents first no matter what. We might forget it sometimes, but it was very important only.

RAVI

thought this was all behind me. I really did. I had come out to my parents. Not once. Not twice. But three times. Yes. I had come out to my parents three times. Three. Coming out number 1. Happened in college. I had been upset. For days. Moping around. A sad sack. Truely. The boy for whom I had drawn the dolphin tattoo. Arun. He had stopped talking to me. I was heartbroken because I loved him.

I thought I was doing a decent job. Covering my tracks. Pretending I was fine. There was no way to explain the depths of my despair without elaborating on the nature of my attachment to Arun. Not without coming out. I certainly did not plan to come out. Not then. No, I wasn't planning on coming out then.

My mother had picked up on the sadness. Mother's intuition, she said. (Beginner's luck. I thought. Blindly believing in the superiority of my acting skills.) She forced me to tell her what was wrong. My repeated denials and attempts at stonewalling were useless. In the face of her persistence. And the ruthless efficiency of her interrogation tactics. My defenses were vulnerable, weakened as they were by my emotionally fragile state. I broke down in the end. Confessed that I was in love with a boy. That this boy had just broken my heart. My mother started crying. Silent tears. That turned tumultuous. As the meaning and implication of my confession sank in. Tables turned. I ended up comforting her. Assuring her everything will be fine. Instead of the other way around.

She told my father about my confession. Even though I had asked her not to do it. A couple of days later she conveyed to me my father's thoughts. It was a phase. I would grow out of it. She made me promise. To try to forget about all of this nonsense. I was afraid that they would confiscate my passport. Not let me go back to Pittsburgh. To finish college. If I didn't agree. So I did. I promised to try to forget about all of it.

That was coming out number 1.

A few years later. After college. I had moved to Boston from Pittsburgh. I came out to a cousin who was visiting me. He came back and told my mother that she should do something about it. I never asked this cousin. If he meant, do something as in, cure me. Or do something as in, accept and love me for who I am. I hoped it was the latter. But I didn't want to find out. In case it wasn't.

My mother was terribly upset. By my cousin's revelation. And his advice. I, on the other hand, was blissfully unaware of her conversation with my cousin. My mother kept mum. Until later that year. When I went back to India. Walking naively into the lion's den. She called a family meeting. The first one ever. In the history of our family. Mom. Dad. Sis. This inaugural family meeting happened in Goa. Ironically.

At the family meeting, she laid into me. Feeling righteously angry and justified in her outrage. She accused me of betraying my promise. To her. To my father. (Remember I had promised to try to forget about being gay? Under duress, I should add.) I thought I had committed to *trying*. She seemed to have honed into the *promise* part. For all the ensuing years. Between coming out number 1 and family meeting number 1. She had never brought up the subject again. In case I would un-forget. And break my promise. I had never brought it up. Because. Well. She wasn't exactly great about it. That first time around.

So here we were. Ladies, gentlemen, and non-binary beings of the jury. At the scene of coming out number 2: the family meeting. I explained that I had tried. And failed. To change the fundamental nature of my being. I was more prepared to argue my case this time. I talked about biology. Genes and genetics. Nature. Nurture. To no avail. There was no amount of reasoning. Or logic. That was going to convince my parents this was natural. Cute, cuddly, gay penguin couples be damned.

Mom was angry. And there were tears. Dad was his usual taciturn self. Meandering into non-sequitur land when he did speak. Sis tried. To support me. But stood no chance against the determined parental duo and their dubiously definitive opinions. My father, who suffers from chronic impatience, at last put his foot down. After two hours of back and forth. Each side unyielding in their stances. He agreed with my mother. They would never be fine with my lifestyle. Or my choices. But they loved me. And they would do me the favor of not disowning me. We agreed to a detente. An uneasy truce. Because all I wanted to do was to escape that room.

Coming out number 3. Happened a few years after the big family meeting. Dad had been mad at me. Mostly for drifting away. For being aloof. He was afraid he was losing me. Tired of our brief, perfunctory conversations. I agreed with him. That we were drifting apart. But I told him it was inevitable. If our version of *Don't Ask, Don't Tell* persisted. If we only talked about the weather. And food. If we ignored things that really mattered in order to avoid discomfort and difficult subjects. Yes, Dad. I am still gay.

This time he relented. Unwillingly. Mom, too. They admitted defeat. Unhappily. Both accepted that I was gay. There was no ambiguity about my sexuality. Nor any expectation that it would undergo metamorphosis. At any point in time. A huge leap forward. I thought. There's always a catch, though. Always. They made me promise. Not to talk about it with my extended family in India. My parents got to control the flow of information to their friends and relatives. Not ideal. But it seemed like a small price to pay. Since I was in India so little.

That conversation has to be at least a decade old. In hindsight, things didn't change much after that. We still didn't really talk about the gay thing. Neither of my parents have ever asked me if I was dating. Or about a romantic interest. No offers to arrange a match. With some suitable boy. I didn't bring it up either. I was never involved with anyone seriously enough. Or for long enough. To talk about him. To introduce him to my parents. All parties were conveniently able to tip-toe through the pink tulips. Until now.

I can see now that I had been way too optimistic. About the evolution of their mindset. Hoping that time, age, and a rapidly changing world would soften their hearts. Smooth away the jagged edges of their narrow minds. Instead, I have discovered more divisions. And deep-rooted hatreds. Their bigotry comes in so many different flavors. Religion and sexuality may be the prejudices du jour but something tells me there are plenty of others lurking around, waiting to surface at inappropriate times.

◆

"We need to talk. I am so disappointed and hurt that you won't go to Goa. I thought… I thought you both had accepted me for who I was. I thought you had come to terms with the idea that I am gay. Mom, I really like this guy… And I don't know what the problem is. Please don't do this."

"Your father and I accepted that you are who you are. That you won't change. We accepted it because you didn't give us a choice. Be who you are but why do you have to act on it? Even the thought of you with a man makes me sick to my stomach only. I just can't live with that."

"So, you would rather I live alone for the rest of my life. That I never experience love and companionship?"

"You have plenty of love in your life. We love you. Your sister loves you."

"You know it's not the same. You don't think I deserve what you and Dad have? You don't think I deserve happiness and fulfillment?"

"You make me sound like a horrible mother. Like someone who doesn't want her child to be happy. How can you be so cruel, Ravi?"

"You say you care about my happiness. But it's only okay if and when my happiness doesn't offend your delicate sensibilities. You are being so incredibly selfish right now. I know you wouldn't be telling me that I have enough love in my life and that I shouldn't find myself a life partner if we were talking about a woman instead of a man."

"We know what we know. The idea of you with a man is disgusting. And on top of that you find a boy who is a Muslim."

"What is wrong with being Muslim?"

"There is nothing wrong with being a Muslim. But they are different. They have their own culture. Their own ways. And they eat maas-machli. Chee chee, so dirty!"

"Oh my god! You have friends that are Muslim. What about Malik Uncle and Zeeba Aunty? If I wanted to marry Noor, you'd have a problem with it?"

"Malik and Zeeba are good people but our religions are so different. I don't know why we are talking about hypotheticals but it is true, we wouldn't want you to marry their daughter or any Muslim girl."

I am a pretty calm person. Peaceful. Push the right buttons, though. And there's no restraining me. Of course, the most expert button-pushers happen to be the people who know you the best. Your nearest. And dearest.

"I knew you were old-fashioned in many ways but now I see you for the truly disgusting, narrow-minded people that you are." I stormed out of the room. Slammed the door.

Then I came back.

"I'm done with you."

USMAN

Things had gotten quite bad for Ravi, yaar. He called again but now he was calling from his sister's place. He's moved his bags out of his parents' flat and is put up with his sister only. He said he didn't want to go into all the details but that he had a very serious fight with his parents and he wasn't talking to them now. I am hoping that this is a temporary argument only and that he and his parents start speaking again.

Parents and children can fight, they can disagree also, but ultimately it is our duty to take care of and respect our elders na. I know that he is angry with them but you can't stop talking to your parents just like that only. You have to be a good son because that is our culture, na? I didn't say anything to him because he was so heated but I feel like he needs to sort out the issues so that everything can be fine again. As it is, I am feeling very guilty because I feel like I caused problems between his family.

But it is no use talking to him right now because Ravi has made up his mind to come by himself only. He booked his flight and everything. He will be putting up at a different resort because that way I can meet him without having to hide from my colleagues. I wish that his trip was not happening like this because of his fighting with his family but I am so happy to see him, I don't even care. I am in a damn good mood only, whistling away and singing and dancing because I am going to see Ravi after all this drama. As long as I get to see Ravi, I can't really ask for anything more, na?

I started thinking of all the possible ways I could take leave from work while Ravi's here. There are so many people who owe me for covering their shifts. I don't have a wife or children so I am always the guy they come to for getting their shifts covered when their children are sick or something. And I am sure there are others who could really use the extra shifts to cover the Christmas expenses. Maybe I can offer to pick up shifts when the things are slower and the tips get smaller and in return they can take my shifts now when the whole place is booked because of Christmas vacation.

I was still thinking about all of this when I got to work. There was a message waiting for me, from my manager, asking me to come to his office as soon as I got in. That was quite odd but he maybe wanted me to work on some special project or something. So, I walked to his office and knocked on the door.

"Come in. Shut the door behind you."

"Usman, I have received a very disturbing phone call this morning. It's from a guest, a lady who is really angry about your behavior with her son."

I was so confused because I didn't know what he was talking about but then I realized that he might be talking about Ravi's mother. I looked down at my feet, afraid to look at Mohit Sir, in case he could see the fear in my face. I was not even breathing because I was so scared. Mohit Sir was just sitting there quietly, not saying anything for a little while.

"I pulled up the old records to make sure she was a guest here, not some crazy lady from a mental hospital. I have confirmed that we had some guests with that surname and the dates are matching also. They were here some years back. This lady was damn angry and her accusation is quite serious, Usman. Really bloody serious. Do you have anything to say for yourself?"

I could feel his eyes on me, burning holes through me. All I wanted to do was disappear. I wanted to blow up into little-little pieces of dust and be carried away by the wind to a place far-far away from here. My palms were sweating, my heart was beating so fast, and I couldn't even breathe properly.

"Sir, what did this lady accuse me of?" I managed to ask, as the tears were running down my face.

"She thinks you are a person of loose morals and that you tried to take advantage of her son. She said… I don't even know if I can say it. She thinks you are a gay. Is it true you are this disgusting kind of man?"

The tears were not stopping now, and I had become dumb. I tried to say something but no noise was coming out of my mouth only.

"It would be a very serious problem if you had behaved indecently with a lady guest but this is horrible! I can see it all over your face that you are bloody guilty. I had no idea I had hired a filthy chakka." Mohit sir was quiet for a minute so I looked up. He had turned away from me, facing the windows. "I can't have a characterless, low-class person like you working here. Usman, you are fired immediately. You are lucky you didn't get the shit beaten out of you. Get out of my office and don't let your shadow curse my path again."

"Sir, please. Mohit Sir, please let me keep my job. It will never happen again. I will never do this again. I don't know what shaitaan made me do this. Sir, I really need this job to support my family. Sir, I promise."

"You leave this office now or I will call the watchmen to throw you out on your ass. Maybe they'll give you a good beating too.

You want everyone to know what kind of a chakka you are? Get out of my sight before I tell the whole world what a filthy, perverted bastard you are. Get out!"

I left the office because what choice did I have only? I was so shocked I didn't even know what had just happened. My whole life just got ruined in front of my eyes. How would I explain this to Ammi and Sharmeen? Would Mohit Sir tell everyone at work? Would those guys spread this story all over town? How could I show my face to anyone? How would I find a job?

I just started walking aimlessly because I wasn't sure where to go only. I was so damn angry at Ravi's mother but she wasn't lying na. I am terrible. I am filthy. What I had done was haram. I didn't know why I thought I could pull it off. I should have been happy with what I had and not pushed my luck like this. People like me didn't get to have a normal life and live happily ever after like it was a bloody fairy tale. All that stuff was for people who lived in America, people who had lots of money, and people who had connections. I got too greedy and reached for things that I couldn't have.

It was not the first time in my life that I thought about what a relief it would be to just end my life. I suppose when I was younger and more innocent I was more afraid of Allah's anger. "And do not kill yourselves, surely God is most merciful to you." At that time I thought I was already going to hell for being who I was, taking my own life would be like booking a first-class, one-way ticket there. Now, it was not religion that was keeping me from offing myself.

I worried about the people I would be leaving behind. It would kill Ammi and even if it didn't kill her, I would be leaving her and Sharmeen alone to survive in this crazy world. I could leave them all the money from the art I sold but no amount of money could make up for losing your son or your brother na? Even death was a bloody luxury I couldn't afford.

And then there was Ravi to think about na. In spite of everything that had happened I couldn't get him out of my mind only. My heart was still crazy for him and I really, really loved him. I wanted him here so badly, man. I needed him to tell me everything was going to be fine, even if it was a lie. I don't think I can do this by myself. And listen, just so there is no misunderstanding, I don't want his money or anything. I just wanted his mental support to sort out this bloody mess, man.

I thought about calling him to tell him what his mother had done but I was so upset I didn't want to start crying on the phone only. So then I decided not to tell him until he got here tomorrow. He already had so much on his mind and I didn't want to add my troubles on top. Anyways there was nothing he could do to change what had been done na. I just had to be strong until he got here tomorrow. Even that much I didn't know if I could do but I would try my level best. InshaAllah, I would get out of this mess!

RAVI

There is a wave of anger bubbling inside me. Red. Hot. Like magma. Threatening to erupt. Any minute. This stunt that my mother has pulled. Canceling our trip to Goa. It has exposed the deep divides. The chasms. That separate me from my parents. For years I thought I had taken a stance. Drawn a line in the sand. Demanding acceptance. Fighting for it. Coming out. Multiple times. I thought I had made some headway. A tiny bit of progress. That my parents had turned the corner. They were getting better. About the gay thing.

They weren't. They are no better now than they were before. I had convinced myself that they could change. That they would accept me and my sexuality. And if I were lucky, a future partner. I convinced myself that they were becoming more open-minded. Less judgemental. Now I look back and I can't find a single sign of such progress. Not. One. Single. Sign. Was that just wishful thinking on my part? An imaginary world. An alternate reality. Designed to help me feel better about a set of parents who didn't care about my happiness. Or wellbeing. Not outside of their narrow vision of it.

I facilitated this fiction. Condoned their behavior. By not talking about it more openly. About Usman, for example. That first time I met him. About my interest. My infatuation with him. I used the cloak of modesty to mask my fear that they had never accepted me. Not completely. That they would never accept my choice of a partner. I must have suspected that this would be the case. But it was easier to hide behind the fiction that they would accept this person. When the time was right. When the right person came along.

I also facilitated the fiction because I am programmed to seek my parents' approval. To treat them with respect. To love them. To be the dutiful son. *That* is culturally ingrained in me. Any deviation from this role, even the mere thought of abandoning filial duties or culturally prescribed responsibilities, comes laden with guilt. And self-loathing. I can excuse their shoddy behavior by ascribing it to the same cultural norms that I use to condemn the shirking of duties on my part.

This dichotomy is reinforced by every discussion I have about this matter with someone from the subcontinent. It doesn't matter if they were born and raised there. Or if they simply happened to be of South Asian descent, many generations removed from the motherland. Every Desi expresses sympathy for my plight. Followed quickly and unfailingly with a plea for more leniency. More latitude for my parents. Every American friend, by contrast, has found my parents' behavior lacking. Their sympathies residing solely with me.

I find myself trapped yet again. Between two worlds. Two mindsets. Two cultures. One demands complete and utter devotion to one's parents. An unquestioning obligation to serve them and ensure their happiness. The other promises liberty and the pursuit of happiness. The latter sounds tempting. In theory. But it requires a fundamental recalibration of my moral infrastructure. An undertaking of gargantuan proportions with no guarantee of satisfactory results.

There may be other interpretations of my parents' behavior.

Interpretations that are more generous to my parents. But what I hear. Now. Is that my sexuality. My lifestyle. My choices. Are so abhorrent. Revolting. Disgusting. That my parents would wish me a lifetime of loneliness and a life without love over a loving relationship that happened to feature another person of the same sex.

This idea is not unique to my parents. Of course. Nor their own creation. What I mistook as progress. Was really a home-grown version of love the sinner, loathe the sin. I am acceptable. As a human being. A son. As long as I resist my undesirable pro-clivities. Total abstention. Chastity. As penance. And payment for my defective nature. This acceptance, of the sinner, was some-thing for which I was supposed to be grateful. A sign of their immense generosity.

There may be other contributing factors. Of course. But I have to wonder how much of the blame for my chronic singlehood. My issues with intimacy and sex. My inability to have or sustain healthy relationships. How much of that blame can be heaped at the feet of parental disapproval. I have been told. By them. In so many words. That my desires are disgusting. Despicable. Disgraceful. The kind of sex I want and need is dirty. Deplorable. That I am not worthy of love on account of these feelings and fail-ings. That these are statements from people I love. People who claim to love me. Is the cherry on top.

I realize that my fingers are tracing the engraved design on the pendant around my neck. It was the one I had picked out for Usman. At the flea market in Goa. But I never got a chance to give it to him. I had forgotten all about it. Until I found it while packing my bags for India. Tucked into a little side pocket in my suitcase. Wrapped in newspaper. I wore it around my neck. On an old silver chain. So that I would remember to bring it with me. For Usman. I've noticed that when I'm upset. Angry. I reach for the pendant. Subconsciously. Rubbing it for luck. My good luck charm. My grounding rod. It confirms my decision to go to Usman. Towards love and light. Away from the bitterness and darkness.

I decide I'm going down to Goa. By myself. I am going to have a fabulous time on the beach. With Usman. I am going to give myself some time. And space. To think. The current state of affairs is not sustainable. Obviously. The course of action. Unfortunately. Isn't all that clear. I am tempted. And angry enough. To want a clean break. Be done once and for all. With the negativity. And the repression. The hiding. But it is complicated. I don't know if I have the willpower to emancipate myself. I don't know if my parents would survive such a divorce.

I pack the last few items in the duffel bag. Scan the room for anything I may have forgotten. Phone. Wallet. Passport. I am ready to go. I head out the door. To go to the airport. When Sis gets a phone call. From Dad. I don't care what he has to say. Nor do I want to talk to him. So I continue walking. To the elevator. I don't want to be late for the flight.

I wait at the elevator. Impatient for Sis to catch up. She is driving me to the airport. When she comes out of the apartment, I know something is wrong. Her face has suddenly gone pale, all the color having drained out. She is crying. I hope it isn't some more emotional manipulation from my mother. I'm not going to let her blackmail me. Into giving up my trip to Goa.

"What is it, Sis?"

"Mom fell down. They've taken her to Breach Candy Hospital."

"Is it serious?"

"I don't know Ravi. I don't fucking know. Dad thinks it was

a heart attack. He was sobbing, man. Hysterical. I know they've treated you terribly but don't hold out on them right now. You'll regret it if something happens to Mom."

Life. You think it's going one way. Then it goes another way.

We rush over to the hospital. On our way there, I send Usman a message telling him I wasn't coming.

EPILOGUE

The following day, I purchased a ticket for Goa. I send Usman a message to let him know the details.

RM: My flight's about to take off. I land in Goa at 3:30.

I hear back. Almost immediately.

UK: im v excited to c u

UK: wll pick u frm airport.

I smile.

RM: Can't wait to see you, Usman. xoxo

UK: hows yr mothers health?

RM: She's fine. At home.

Mom didn't have a heart attack. It was low blood sugar. She's fine. I think. I stayed with her. Until she was discharged. Told her I needed to do *this*. For myself.

RM: See you soon.

I switch my phone to airplane mode.

www.ingramcontent.com/pod-product-compliance
Lightning Source LLC
Chambersburg PA
CBHW031940010726
47493CB00007B/2016